T0128897

DISCONTENT

Edward Bach

DISCONTENT

DISCONTENT

iUniverse books may be ordered through booksellers or by contacting:

iUniverse
1663 Liberty Drive
Bloomington, IN 47403
www.iuniverse.com
1-800-Authors (1-800-288-4677)

ISBN: 978-1-5320-7349-6 (sc)
ISBN: 978-1-5320-7350-2 (e)

Print information available on the last page.

iUniverse rev. date: 06/07/2019

CONTENTS

DISCONTENT

A sixty-two-year-old man sits partially reclined on the second-floor terrace of his home overlooking the city below, his English-crafted shoes slung comfortably onto a chair turned backward. His shirt is unbuttoned to his chest where moist gray hairs lay flat against it. To his right, and within easy reach of his right hand, sits a bottle of San Pellegrino water. Next to the water rests a cell phone waiting to ring. On his lap and lying open to page sixty-two, the June issue of National Geographic goes unnoticed, the colored photograph of a supernova, known as M-15, is of little interest to the man sitting on his terrace. He has become fixated on something else. Opposite the super nova is a shot from the Hubble telescope where countless galaxies shower across a blacken sky. For a second the man sitting on the veranda stares at the colorful photographs, as if in a trance, his mind temporarily venturing into places it rarely goes, into a world beyond his senses, beyond his reason, into a dimension where rational thought is eclipsed by wonder and time stretches all the way to infinity.

Rather than become blinded by what, to him, are thoughts more difficult than looking into the sun, he quickly turns away. He is a rational man, focused, principled. The day is warm. He does not lick his fingers. Instead he reaches to his right and touches the moisture along the neck of the bottle. His fingers now moist, he turns the page. The pages resist at first, his fingers clinging to the richness of their colors. Soon they give way and the man hears the gentle hiss as the pages peel gently apart. The smell of colored ink wafts softly to his smell, but he shrugs it off as the price one pays to enjoy the richness inside.

It is morning and the day is unseasonably warm. His wife has left for reasons he cannot explain, for a shopping excursion that will prove of little use, for friends that drink and smoke and soil the air with their pretentious chatter, for hands that never touch, for lips that never part, for words that never come. So, he sits alone, as he has done since the children went away to college, their bedrooms having been converted to idle uses and the walls expanded to the point that the entryway echoes every sound in the house.

The man sitting on the terrace is unquestionably rich. The deck below houses the pool, the shallow end designed for grandchildren yet to materialize, the deep end designed for laps he never swims. Ringing the pool is an assortment of tables and chairs and richly colored canvass umbrellas collapsed and shaped into darts pointing to the sky. Across them, and across the expanse of property under his domain, the aqua colored pool, the multi-colored umbrellas, and all the way across the tops of the perfectly manicured trees in the canyon below, is a view of incomparable worth, twenty miles of Orange County dipping into the breadth of the Pacific Ocean. On crystalline mornings, such as this, Santa Catalina appears to the west, to the east, San Gorgonio Peak.

Nothing stirs where the man sits and waits and breaths. He occupies himself with his magazine, but his mind is busy elsewhere, to the phone that does not ring. In the distance, situated somewhere in the canyon too far away to disturb the tranquility of the setting, the pool equipment whirs its machinery and circulates the aqua colored fluid. Nothing stirs except the beating of his heart. The man reaches for the bottle of San Pellegrino water, takes it in his hand and pulls the cool wet surface across his brow. He sighs and looks beside him. He places it back on the table next to the phone that does not ring. Looking down he notices the insides of his legs. Once hairy and taunt, they hang loose and bear. He can feel his penis lying flat against them.

Above his head four crisp fans rotate silently along the entire length of the terrace, their speed determined by a palm-sized remote control sitting just to his left. With the flip of a finger, insects are sent cascading away. Another remote control launches a series of louvered shades to combat the effects of the sun.

All is quiet and good on the terrace where the man sits untroubled and undeterred by the effects of time murmuring through his blood. To him time is eternal, it no longer exists, it is of no consequence for a man of substance, such as he. There is nothing to disturb him, nothing to break the spell, nothing to give angst or pause or set his nerves on edge, nothing, nothing at all, nothing to break the contentment of the moment. Using the palm of his hand, the man wipes a tear from his eye and studies the phone next to him. He settles in his chair and sits motionless waiting by the phone that does not ring.

THE BAT PHONE

*Never exaggerate
the stupidity of those in charge.*

You'll not find my name on the door to my office here at Guarded Life and Casualty, the second largest insurance company in all North America and the third most profitable financial institution on the planet. Nor will you find a door to my office. Fact is, you won't even find an office. What you will find instead is a small metal cube with the numbers C-17 stamped on the front, that's row C, slot 17 and just two cubes short of the end where our lord and master, John Q. Smithy, indulges in the luxury of what looks like, compared to yours truly, a Turkish harem.

My name is Willie Pinkly. I have worked and lived in this wood-simulated, metal-wrapped corrugated corruption for more than seventeen long and torturous years. My contraption is what the company euphemistically refers to as a workstation when, in fact, it is little more than a miniature chamber of horrors.

Consider my cube. It measures 8 feet by 8 feet and has 124 tiles covering the floor. That's big by company's standards. Some poor Bozo's on our floor crowd into spaces smaller than mine, if you can imagine such a thing. Still, what I occupy and what the other Bozo's on my floor crowd their overworked fannies into five days a week pales considerably when compared to that of our glorious floor leader.

All those wannabe's riding the edge of the aisles around me, those pasty-faced, near-sighted suck-ups who come in early and work past dark, they hate my guts. Truly, they hate my guts. They hate my guts because I've got 8X8 and they're only 7X8, even 7X7 if you are a clerk riding the wall at the far end of our floor. Ha! And my killer real estate position near to the big man lounging at the far end of the room, they hate that too. Those cheap-shirted sons-a-bitches would kill for a mere whiff of the perfume that seeps under Smithy's door, the big man's royal jelly that all us overworked and underpaid drones crave more than the cleavage that shows up every Friday when the lunch wagon pulls up to ground zero and Anita flops her sugarcoated tits over the drop-down window.

Why? Why me? Why little Willie Pinkly? Why hate the man who has loyally and faithfully served his lord and master for seventeen long and arduous years?

Because of the way I came sashaying through the front door that first year more than 17 years ago, leapfrogging the entire floor in a superhuman single bound. It was that infamous summersault over 50 people that got them fuming in their J. C. Penny's trousers and their clip-on ties, straight arming everybody in the office, kangarooing my youthful, pimple-free body all the way from aisle F to aisle C. God did they hate me for that. But it was so easy, a single bound and there I was, wham-bam, me, Willie Pinkly, swooping into the office like Superman racing though a storm.

And wouldn't you know it, quick as a wink, I did it again, the very next year, jumped all the way from C-2 to C-16. Then from C-16 to C-17 when Woodman blew his brains out and lucky me got shoved up another notch. God, am I the luckiest son-of-a-bitch in the world, or what?

Yep, that's why they hate me, me, Pinkly, the company wiz-kid from grammar school C, the number-nut from Norwalk High, the bullet-brained maniac who can fart spread sheets faster than the Xerox machine can spit them out. Or could spit them out. Or used to spit them out when I still worked for good old Guarded Life and Casualty.

Still, C-17 was, and still is, two slots short of the big dog himself, John Q., still two to go for Big Willie Stu, still C-17 and no name on the door. Seventeen years and I'm riding in a cube the size of a gas station john. God damned this place.

Fifth floor. Let me tell you a little something about this 5th floor of horrors where I toil and stir and twirl in my chair and make my annual sum. Maybe I've mentioned that we have seventy-six cubes on the 5th floor, mine and seventy-five others, that's counting the big man himself, old John Q. There are enough cubes to reach to the moon and back. A guy can lose himself just going to the can up here. And imagine not just one floor, but twelve floors, twelve friggin floors of nothing but cubes stacked end to end, top to bottom, row upon row, one giant Rubik's cube filled with a jillion more cubes, nothing but cheesy little boxes snapped together like a box full of Tinker Toys, connected and coupled and clicked and falling over the edge so that… Christ almighty, what a place this is… or was.

Was. I say was because one day, this was about a year ago when things had been piling up and I'd been spinning in my chair more than usual, Smithy asked me to come into his royal place to have a chat. So there we were, me and big John himself lounging in his gluttonous glass star chamber when the guy casually mentions something about my two neighbors, particularly the fag Gaylord who sits in cube C-19, and how these neighbors of mine are always talking about me, saying things like how I've become more 'zany' than ever, ha-ha, what a character that Pinkly is, ho-ho-ho, never serious, never know what that shit-face is going to do next, ha-ha. And that's the word he used, 'zany', the word mutating into 'odd', meaning 'crazy', meaning 'fruitcake'. Then about a month later old Smitty calls me into his ranch sized office where his horse grazes peacefully behind his desk and casually mentions something about aisle B, and wouldn't it be great to be on aisle B where Anita, the company slut, trolls up and down her aisle looking for husband number four, and as he says this I get the old 'winkeroo' and an 'Willie my boy' and a 'hardy-har-har', and an 'elbow with another winkeroo'.

Shit, like I don't know what's going on. Like I don't see the handwriting on the wall, all that ha-ha and hardy-har-har crapola. I can see what he is up to, he and the big-boys upstairs. I can read the handwriting on the wall, my seventeen years of sweat and toil and catapulting over the herd the way I did, my million hours of work being sent to the shredding machine rather than being filed away and lost in the enormous vacuum we are so noted for. So, after our second meeting, I went back to my cube and said screw this and quit on the spot. Yep, just gave up the ship, that's what it did. Said adios. Quit working. Not so much said adios as just slowed down a bit, gave up… not quit, just chucked it for a while…flaked out…zoned.

Screw 'em, that's my new motto. Screw the whole bunch. Screw all those overachieving assholes with their pedigrees and fancy degrees, their bloodsucking attitudes, their native cultures, their broken accents. Never in a million years would that miserable lot of prosaic commonality come close to sniffing the crack of someone as good as old Pinkly all these years, me, the company wiz-kid, the guy who has been lighting up the company charts for a million years, ringing the bell, spring-boarding across a thousand drizzling heads, all the way to Coopersville and back. And for what, for Smithy to start talking about aisle B and Anita with the nice tits, not so much talking as suggesting and hinting and dropping clues? Who needs this shit anyway? Try firing my ass and see what happens.

Wiz-kid to company clown? That what all you jerk-heads on the 5th floor think of your old Willie the Hun, that I'm riding side-saddle just because my sideburns look a little gray and I sometimes come to work with my pants unzipped? That what you boys on the 12th floor think of the hot-shot you promised the moon when you anointed him almost seventeen years ago, high-jinx and all, spit-wads, whoopee cushions, squirt-gun antics. Sure, I led that revolt a few years back. And yeah, I got arrested for inciting an employee strike day, but you guys needed a kick in the ass and you got one, didn't you? And that day Darth Vader spoke over the P.A system, had old Grandly shaking in his boots, a real hardy-har-har, that one. Or the work stoppage when you canned that lady janitor? And the computer crash that took down the entire system? Company yo-yo, remember? The guy who spends half his time spinning in his chair, the clown who launches rubber-band propelled paperclips at anyone standing in their cube. Well you ain't seen nothing yet, Smithy, you and all your 12th floor honchos who do nothing all day but practice your putting stroke with the shades pulled down. You know those congratulatory reports Grandly has been kissing your ass for, the ones old Pinkly has been faithfully pumping out for seventeen long years? Well so-long Charlie. You ain't getting' em', Big Boy, cause I'm done, old Pinkly is done... Simpatico?

So, here I sit spinning in my chair doing nothing but counting my revolutions. It's been months now, and the best I can say is: I am up to 22 revolutions without coming to a stop, that's my record. And when I am not spinning in my chair I'm hoping to get Janice and Gaylord in the head with a paperclip, yeah, the two clowns who occupy the two slots ahead of me. I got a novel in the works too. I'm not sure what it's about, but there's plenty of swear words and the main guy is hopping mad at the world. And a chat line. Got this chat line going where me and a few guys downstairs are trying to organize a national spin-off, a sort of a convention of swivel chair psychos, like me. Oh, and Rodriguez, there is Rodriguez, can't forget about my boy, Rodriguez, the English-speaking Mexican the company hired about six months ago to placate the quota patrol a few floors below, a lot of do-nothings who do exactly that, nothing. They hire a few disabled people now and then, hire them to do things they are completely incapable of doing.

Sometimes they'll come around and count the number of minorities we got working on our floor. Last count I think it was twenty-two, twenty-two on our floor alone. God knows how many there are in the whole friggin building, a thousand I'll bet, enough to open a cantina or a Mexican grill downstairs. Right now we got four Mexicans and two Persians and sixteen Nips here on the 5th floor alone, Latin and Asian anyway, I'm not sure what a Persian is and a Nip could be anything that looks Nipish … but that makes twenty two in all… Oh, and the blimp who came to us from someplace in South Africa, or so she claims, graduated from Compton High and talks likes she graduated from Compton High, has her diploma stapled to her forehead in case you missed it, Harvard you'd think by the way she waves the god damned thing around, or Yale, or a birth certificate.

So, I spin and look at this cube I've occupied for most of my life and think of ways to set fire to Smitty and Gaylord, Janice too, ripping her St. John's from her body and setting fire to them as well as Janice herself. Got a file cabinet in this little miniature house of horrors. Haven't opened it since I quit a few months ago. Looks like thunder hit my desk the way I keep it arranged, files, letters, notes, lunch all heaped in a pile so huge that the cleaning people won't touch it anymore. Old Smitty, the guy with the fancy rug, he won't look at me since I quit, me, his number one boy, the guy who set the swivel chair record of 22 consecutive spins without stopping, the same guy who ran good old GLC to the top of the heap, Moody's, Fortune 500, Forbes. But that's all right. He knows. He's just a coin flip away from joining the compost heap like old Moyer did before him.

Two years ago these two football-sized players came elbowing their way into my cube and yanked my kid-sized desk away and replaced it with an exact copy of the old one. Evidently spinning in my chair had worn the tiles so thin that the concrete was showing through and they rearranged my furniture by moving my desk to the other wall. Wow, what an improvement. My chair now spins like a top and spins so silently that Roosevelt, the black guy in C16 next door, can nap without me wakening him.

First thing I did was run down to the hardware story and get me some titanium ball-bearing rollers. I replaced the old ones with the new ones and now my chair spins like a rocket ship. Except revolving so very fast creates this gyro effect that, depending on which way I lean and how tight I tuck my legs beneath me, the gyro effect can send me in any direction I want. I can go all the way to the drinking fountain on one lousy spin. Sometimes I spin right out of my office into Tonya's across from me. Scares the bejesus out of her but I know she likes it because she always laughs when I slow myself by grabbing onto her forbidden territory. She's a big girl, Tonya is, had her third kid recently and looks like she's aiming for more. Smitty got her a company membership to a gym down the street and moved her into an 8X8 like mine. Goes to show, GLC takes care of its people.

Rodriguez and I think there is something suspicious about the floor tiles in our work station. It's mysterious looking, sorta green and slimy when you look at it just right, or if you stare at it long enough, all shinny and slimy and crawling with chemistry. Never noticed it until they moved my desk to the other side. Since then I've made a career of studying those light green, asbestos-loaded tiles under my feet, got this weird propensity where they secrete this grimy, granular shit that oozes along the edge after the night crew comes in and swishes a mop over it. Me and Rodriguez are pretty sure our floor tiles are swarming with something toxic, asbestos, or E-coli. This shit is waiting to hop into our nose. I reported it to Smitty and he said he'd look into it.

Those cubes a row across from me, the ones running along Row D, the ones with one less row of tiles, they're all looking at me like I'm a goner. Those dopes can't believe I spend my days rotating in my office and haven't been fired. Human Resources drained the sewers and sent them up to us 5th floorers, people like Rodriguez and that African hippo who says she's from South Africa when she's really from Compton. Bet she can't even find South Africa on a map. They'll never prove themselves around this place, not in a million years they won't, at least not enough to jump across a few aisles to where I am, me, Pinkly, C-17, the maniac who spins in his chair all day shooting paper bb's at the first person who looks at me funny.

I search my soul for reasons to keep from killing the people around me. I spin in my chair and jostle my brain to keep it functioning the way it should, the way it used to, the way it was when I began my voyage across the floor. I do it to keep my hemorrhoids from leaping from my pants, to keep my moribund sense of balance from running into the woods, from hiding from myself, from me, from old Willie Pinkly, the company D.H., the man always searching for the greatest yield, the highest profit, the sweetest deal. And I do it so our millions of investors can sleep soundly in their sacred glass enclosures, like Smitty, and all those chair-stuffed tycoons working on the 12th floor.

Takes a logarithmic intellect to do what I do every day of the week, scouring the world for the slightest blip in interest rates, the tiniest margin in exchange, the slightest crease in paper-thin margins, and all with the faintest glimmer of hope that someone upstairs will take notice and say, "nice job, Pinkly ", or give a few paltry words scribbled across a jillion columns of numerals, "Atta boy, Willie", or a merry thumbs up in the elevator, which I never got.

Pinkly in C-17 inhales what amounts to a mountain of paperwork most every day of the week. I study it. I consume it. I eat it as if food hadn't touched my lips in years. I analyze the rows of dots, calculate it and shred it. And when I am done digesting and squeezing every morsel from what I have consumed, I blow it out to God knows where, upstairs, my ink and paper excretions landing like a turd on someone's desk, a process, I regret to say, is curiously similar to that of the human digestive system. And sadly, I have done it all my life, or so it seems. And I have done it as if my life had depended on it, no, more as if the company's life had depended on it, barely moving from the slot in the conveyer system of higher yields and better bottom lines, always genuflecting to my place in time, to my dot in space, to my obligation to those above… to my faltering ego.

And there is this too. I am told there are somewhere in the vicinity of 580 cubes in the entire building where I work. I use the words 'in the vicinity' because the total changes most every day of the week, combining and dividing and mutating every time some poor bastard croaks, or makes a move, or takes a dive, which, around here is almost daily, fired, laid off, promoted, demoted, sent to that shrink up in L.A. who is paid a bundle to show just how completely inept you are at your job, or how overqualified you are and how you should be working somewhere where your particular talents are more appreciated. Which is a crock. Most everything that bozo up in L.A. says is a crock. Most everything everybody in this company says is a ploy, an educated devise so the corporate dicks can cheat you out of what is rightfully yours, benefits, not to mention what it does to a guy's psyche to be booted out the door or run up the flag pole or disappear in the night. Like me. Jesus, what a place this is… or was… or used to be when I was living and working at GLC, row C, slot 17.

What happened? Why am I telling you this? Because of what happened the day I walked into my corporate cell and saw that letter leaning against my pencil holder, the one from my big boss up on the top floor, V.P. Investments and Annuities, the big bellied, bulbous bastard who lords over Mr. Smithy and the entire 5th floor. That is why I am telling you this. Because the man upstairs had finally gotten wise to the little game I have been playing for the past few months. He is on to me, or, I mean was on to me. Christ, I'm still living in the past. Anyway, around here, making crank calls to a company Vice President is not something Guarded takes lightly. We have rules you know, spinning or no spinning, you don't follow the rules, those suits up on the 12th floor will make you disappear; that or they'll send you to that Nazi shrink up in L.A. who'll either have you committed or interrogate you 'till he has your gold teeth riding inside in his jacket pocket. Either way you lose, it's so long, Charlie, or in my case, so long, Willie.

But the damn thing was his fault, not mine. The stupid jerk shouldn't have been waiving that phone number around the way he was doing. Okay, okay, so he wasn't waiving it around. He gave it to me though, and what did he expect, that I was going to ignore that little treasure map he put in my hand, just pass it off as one of his little idiosyncrasies? He should have known better than to give something so valuable to the likes of me, the company wing-nut, the guy who never flushes the john, the guy who keeps a rubber snake in his desk, a squirt gun in his pocket, a bean shooter behind his ear. Come on Grandly, you should have known better than to fool around with the people on the 5th floor, we're savages down here, especially being so shit-faced that night that you actually thought you were among friends, me, the Leon Trotsky of the underworld.

What an idiot he is. Bat phone. Called the damned thing a bat phone. Can you believe it? Kept it hidden in his coat pocket, like the Holy Grail was riding around in it. "Nobody's got the number… nobody…shhhh", he whispers, as if we are both in the CIA or something and not just a couple of corporate stooges. "Few close buddies," he slobbers in my ear, "sure, clients… belch…emergencies, sorta thing… can't be too careful… ol buddy… and the ladies… wink-wink." Gave me the number. Jesus, what an idiot.

So, I called him. And I called him. And I called him. And each time I called he'd answer, and I'd hang up. Drove the poor bastard crazy. I'd say something like,

"Batman?"

And he'd say, "Who is this?"

And I'd say, "Robin."

And he'd say, "God damn it, who is this?"

And I'd hang up. And as soon as I hung up my little cube would turn into a lunatic asylum, paper flying every which way, yours truly doubled over laughing like a complete jackass, chair spinning like a top, old Smithy standing in the doorway scowling with his hands on his hips. God, it was funny.

Yeah, he was on to me all right. But what the hell, I'd do it again. And as a matter of fact, I did do it again. I made one last call for old time's sake. Looked at the clock. 9:30 am. One hour and me and Grandly would be nose-to-nose, man-to-man up in that swanky office of his.

So, I dialed the memorized bat-number and waited. Two rings like always. Same familiar voice.

"Hello".

I waited.

"Hello.

I waited.

Finally, just as I knew he was about to hang up, I said, "Batman?" There was a pause, then,

"Hey, come on, who is this?"

And I said, "Robin." It was always same routine. Grandly was such a sap. I couldn't stop laughing.

As I said, Grandly's office was located on the 12th floor, the very top of the GLC tower, didn't get any higher than the 12th floor at Guarded Life and Casualty. To us surfs down on the 5th, the big shots on the 12th were mindless car-farting, ass-holes who spent their days doing nothing but roaming those galactic offices trying to perfect a perfect golf swing. Yep, that's what they did to earn those annual six-figure salaries, sling the old umbrella stick around while giving dictations to a tube of lip-gloss riding a pair of too-tanned legs, a great life for the chosen few living in the clouds high above our heads. Yes, lording over the mob down on the lower floors; that was a biggie for the twelve VP's living up in heaven, keeping a lid on the revolution that kept brewing in the basement. And yes, there was showing deference to Mr. Tribe, the company President, a lot of bowing and genuflecting and ring kissing when he showed his face. But that was only on Mondays when the ring-kissing ceremony in the boardroom took place and Mr. Tribe mounted his reverential throne for his weekly baptism as our master and messiah to all.

The big-boys upstairs. What a core. It was always the same with those guys, showing up around 8:30ish, or so, spending an hour harassing the gum smacking temp sent over by the agency across the street. Then around 10ish, or so, they'd all posse up in a big troop of twelve and synchronize their walk down to the executive coffee room. They'd grab-ass for another half hour or so then it was back to the office for a few phone calls with their feet slung a top of their desk 'till around 11:30 when one of the pack would shove his face in a door and suggest an early lunch, and they'd posse up again, pinstriped coats layered atop of a pair of red suspenders, crowd four abreast into the company elevator, push the express button so as to dodge the riff-raff surging beneath their feet, riff-raff like me, that is, sink to the street level and walk the three blocks to either Richey's or Robert's or Spangola's. There they'd rush a few drinks, toss a dart or two, cajole the tray-toting brunette who was doing all she could to find a bachelor among the bunch, prattle with a table of blonds sitting at the bar, grab a roast beef sandwich or a plate of pot stickers then beat it back to the office so they could get in a quick putting lesson before the 3:00 o'clock gabfest. That is what the 12th floor brass did all day; they screwed around.

In all the years I worked at Guarded Life and Casualty I had only been to the 12th floor twice, once when the company was forced to pay on a south Pacific oil spill and our irate policyholders began a campaign of letters threatening to sue the company for gross incompetence. On that occasion, most everyone in the building sat in on the meeting, including old Pinkly, the company traitor who backed the payout as justly deserved. The other time was about a year ago when I inadvertently stepped off the elevator and found myself standing on the 12th floor. Seeing my mistake, I had to stand frozen like a jackass for a full five minutes waiting for the damn thing to run to the bottom and back.

On my few trips to the executive suites I couldn't help but notice how serious it was in the holy realm. Not a paper airplane anywhere. Not a scream or a spit-wad or a paperclip. No clacking or whacking or whirring or whizzing or whining. No farting either. And certainly no vomiting. And I'll bet wet willies were on the shit-list too. It was as peaceful and serene as the pastoral painting. Those secretaries sat like starched figures glued to a keyboard, typing, filing, talking on the telephone, not amongst themselves as was the norm on a fifth floor, but serious and severe, as though every letter they typed and every call they took was capable of launching a nuclear strike. Weird.

And there I was rebelling and slamming my fist and raising holy hell at the ivory chambers above my head when it struck me how sad it was up there in space, the rigidity, the military discipline, all of that struck me as marbles rolling in a porcelain tub. It was nothing like the new republic operating just a few floors below, the peasant rebellion boiling downstairs. We had a real, honest to goodness Mardi Gras going on down there, objects flying in every direction, people shouting in the phone, across the aisle, at each other, paper strewn like ribbons, undisciplined, uncivilized, primal. We were a culture of miscreants who were incapable of controlling ourselves. Like me getting McCleary in the ear with a paperclip that time, the poor bastard having to spend all day standing in a Medi-quick line while I sat with Smithy trying to explain why he deserved it. Served him right though.

But democracy has always been unable to control itself. Fascism, on the other hand, like what I witnessed up on the 12th floor, tends toward martial order.

It has always been a great amusement of mine to notice the way civilization creeps its way through the hallways of history and into the ballrooms of life, creeping and crawling to the very top, like it has in our twelve-story monstrosity of cubes. From the depths of the mailroom, to the spires of empire, to the place where executives fashion twelve tones of corporate gray, to the place where dictators goosestep to the tune of the company credo, Darwinism is at work at good old GL&C. It is a manicured world at the very top of where I work… or used to work. It's where a nation of robotic motion and synthesized minds spend their days, it's where theology no longer exists, except in the leaden brains of its subjects who man the oars of empire and enrich the pockets of others.

We in our postage stamp chambers survive on theology alone. It is our sweet nectar. It is our food, our drink. It fuels our hearts and souls with hope. We are a culture that feeds on theology, we tormented, joyless, impecunious, underpaid urchins of the underworld. We are the underworld. We live in the killing fields of industry. And yet we desire nothing from our tormented existence other than to be like them, our idols, our gods. We mimic all they do. We love them for what they are.

What fools are we. What bastards are they.

No one at Guarded Life and Casualty ever received a letter from the 12th floor and liked it, not unless you are that company dolt, McCleary, six spaces to my left over on aisle B and one across, a guy who is totally obtuse when it comes to the workings of mankind. Getting a letter from above is like a lightning bolt from heaven and not an invitation to the prom. It can mean only one thing when a letter comes from above… that something bad is about to happen. Good things, like raises in pay and periodic promotions come through the mail, glad tidings parsimoniously doled out by our elderly, 5th floor leader, Smithy.

It is a known fact that everyone on the 5th floor is afraid of everyone on the 12th floor. It's true. And it is an even greater known fact that everyone on the 11th floor is afraid of everyone on the 12th floor. In fact, it is safe to say that the whole building is afraid of the people on the 12th floor.

Like the rest of corporate America, cubical hierarchy, or 'tiered fear' as it is sometimes referred to in certain graduate school textbooks, is well at work at GLC. What I like about the system of 'tiered fear' is the fact that everybody on the first four floors of our office building is afraid of everybody above them, and that includes me, Willie Pinkly on the 5th. But that is not entirely correct, actually it's better than that. It is correct to say that the first five floors of our building fear everybody on the 5th floor, and that is because the basement houses the mailroom and everyone in the mailroom is afraid of everybody in the whole god-damned building. Unless you work in the mailroom, somebody is afraid of you. Even the first-floor people have the mailroom to lord over.

Having someone afraid of you is a great perk at Guarded Life and Casualty, the great staying power for those of us with enough Zamboni to try and move up the corporate stack of cubes. And if you are lucky enough to climb all the way to the highest stack, the glorious 12th floor of Guarded Life and Casualty, you can walk every floor in the building and shake your booty with impunity. You are top dog. You fear no man. Having an office on the glorious 12th floor at GLC means you are the master of the entire universe.

Which isn't entirely true. There are the other eleven VP's to worry about. The VP's all fear one another. It is fair to say that all twelve Vice Presidents on the top floor are afraid of each other, and that is why all the backslapping camaraderie exists in the first place, a sort of executive, butt kissing trade-off to keep them safe from each other, a way to insure not to be frozen out of existence by the other eleven who, most likely, hate their guts. It's a sort of symbiotic, Darwinism at work among the chosen twelve on the 12th floor, a claw-footed get-along, suck-along mentality where a man must cozy up to his rival in one big neighborly conspiracy because, if he didn't, the other eleven would tear the flesh from your bones.

But there is the big cheese too, the man in the moon who fears no man alive, the man with 'President' inscribed on his always-closed, oak-paneled, Gordian, 12-stories-high, door. Everybody is afraid of the President, especially the twelve VP's. If you are standing in front of the elevator ready to ride upstairs and you see his majesty, Mr. Horace Tribe, President, heading your way, you immediately turn and pretend to have either forgotten something, or are really disembarking and not going up.

Everyone at GLC fears Tribe. Tribe is the real master of the universe, not the VP's. He is a man who fears no man. Except the Board of Directors, that is, and of course the mighty Board of Directors fears the mighty stockholders.

It was the night of the last Christmas party that the bat phone donned its pretty head. Grandly was unusually drunk that night, pawing his way like a sailor at sea, the drink in his oversized paw sloshing merrily from side to side, like an old sea-bucket in a storm. As I watched the great sea captain stumble from one person to the next, manhandling left and right and grabbing onto whatever lay in his path, the back of a chair, a desk, a pair of breasts, he spotted someone out of the corner of his eye. He spotted me, his 'one true friend in the whole wide world'. Tonight, I was his bull's eye.

Slogging through a room full of arms and legs, I watched as he slogged to where I sat in one of my blacker moods, alone with my ass crabbed tight to my chair doing everything I could to avoid all human contact, particularly the swashbuckling kind I noticed sashaying in my direction. But here he came anyway, arms and legs splashing like a jellyfish at sea, his limp inebriated body slamming into mine, the way a yacht slams into a dock, slinging his moist limbs around my neck as if I were an old war buddy from Nam, slouching and pushing a huge, bulbous nose against my face so that I had no trouble naming each pizza topping he consumed that evening on the way to the party, going about the business of confiding the holiest of holies in my ear. "Ya know, old buddy, old buddy," he says to me, "old buddy of mine... ol buddy... ol buddy... That little gal you married... what's her name... that peach, that ripe little peach...say, where is she... but... that Maggie ... shit... me and Maggie of mine... 'burp'... not like before... nope... know what I mean... nope... old buddy... how it is... old buddy".

Then, while drooling in my ear, and in great graphic detail, he goes about explaining the many varied and erotic techniques he had learned on his many visits to... ahhh... where was it... Bangkok...? Hong Kong? elaborating on his two or three most favorite bodily positions, describing in grotesque body language all the various contortions required to perform the oriental pleasures he had come to master, his manners so expressive and so energetic that it made me cringe to think that the people around me might misconstrue his naughty positions as some form of mutual attraction, Grandly going on to describe which particular techniques he routinely practiced on his adorable wife, Maggie, describing in graphic detail the nine fluid positions most preferred by our little Asian friends, and the six different rooms he used to practice them in, and the choicest pieces of furniture, and on and on until I could stand it no longer, especially when he told me how little Maggie always liked a little "Cool Whip" on her desert, ha-ha, wink-wink, almost falling onto the coach when he said it.

I could stand no more. I pulled away and that's when he grabbed my arm, almost ripping the sleeve from my seventeen-year-old blue blazer, pleading, "oh, don't go buddy-boy." And then he belched. "Say," he said, his eyes brightening as a new thought popped into his head, "that pretty little wife or yours?" slobbering the words and temporarily losing sight of the fact that he hadn't seen Linda since the Christmas party almost 10 years before when he planted a wet kiss on her mouth and Linda gave up the annual event for good.

And that's when the little black cell phone went off. He reached inside his coat and yanked it out, a portion of his jacket lining coming with it. He mumbled something into the mouthpiece then shook it once or twice before returning it to his ear…upside down, his knuckles hurriedly clicking a series of buttons before hitting the 'off' button so that the conversation came to an abrupt stop. "Shhhh… Don't tell anyone… bat phone," he slurred, secretly slipping the small black object into his jacket as if he were hiding a nude picture of his wife.

By a stroke of good fortune, or was it bad fortune, I had become his confidant, Grandly 's number one man, his number one buddy in the whole wide world. "Nobody's got the number," he slurred and then belched… "ol buddy, buddy." He was still shushing when he suddenly began a search for a piece of paper and a pen. "We's buddies… me and you…old buddy, buddy" almost tumbling into me as he felt for his wallet, clumsily retrieving what turned out to be a 'get one free' yogurt card, scratching the number on the back and slipping it to me with the secrecy of a double agent. "Shhhh…" he said, "and keep an eye on that little hole… " Meaning the department where I worked… "Smithy, oh he's a clever one… call me, we's friends, buddy boy… ears and eyes…ears and eyes… belch… shhh…"

Now I don't mind telling you that having Grandly's bat number was like owning Sutter's Mill, and given the state of mind I was in, I felt as if I had struck the mother lode. And I don't know for certain exactly when the idea struck me, but one day, about a month or two later, as I was twirling in my chair at the speed of light, feeling ebullient and slightly out of control, I picked up my extension and dialed old Grandly's bat number and, not surprisingly, he answered immediately.

"Hello?" the voice said.

I ratcheted my voice down a notch or two and said, mysteriously, "Bat Man?"

"Bat Man?" There was a pause. "Hey, who is this?"

"It's Robin."

"God damn it, who is this?"

And that's when I hung up. And I did it almost daily, did it for five months, and the big lout fell for it every time.

It's my guess that he had probably figured out the identity of that Robin character who kept calling him on his bat phone, and I suspect that is the reason why I was being summoned to the 12th floor for a little meeting with Mr. Chester Grandly.

I have never played the political game in my life, my tendency toward self-devotion and my self-destructive unwillingness to kiss butt, is probably the main reason why I had been promoted only twice in the more than 17 years at Columbia. Never did I get that merit pay increase I was promised when I skydived all the way to C-17, never was I assigned the better investigative job, never given the newest company car, never been invited to the boss's house for dinner. Simply put, I tend to be a jerk, especially the last year or so, notwithstanding the fact that I am the genius of the 5th floor. Linda says (and I love her for saying this) it's because I am smarter than everyone else, or at least I think I am smarter than everyone else. And I wouldn't be honest if I didn't say that there is an element of truth in what she says. After all these years of living in the big-time corporate landscape, I find that it takes a certain degree of poltroonery and great deal of incompetence to get ahead in a world of schmucks, like Grandly, and a lot of other guys living on the 12th floor. To my good fortune, I lack both.

I was in elementary school when my third-grade teacher took my mother aside one rainy day in May and suggested that her 8-year-old son, that's me, was, perhaps, a little slow, perhaps, with an ah-hum in between, that he may be, in fact, ahh-hum, slightly retarded, at least that is what she told my mother. And while telling her this she said it as nicely as she could, hoping that my mother wouldn't bash her skull in. It came as no surprise to me, or to my parents, for that matter, that a teacher would think that I was a little behind; we had all noticed the baroque and peculiar world I lived in, my daily ups and downs, my proclivity for the unnatural, my unwillingness to conform.

But isn't it true that sanity is the highest degree of conformity? Genius nonconformity? Think about it.

Anyway, it was with my parents blessing that I moved back a grade in school. It was hoped that their son, little Willie, the boy who could be so lethargic at times, and so 'inspirational' at others, would find himself in second grade and show a little more enthusiasm toward his work.

But I fell back even further. Didn't matter that I was barely keeping up in class, they passed me into third grade and I kept trekking along until I reached high school. It is there, in my sophomore year of high school that the family doctor got involved in what can only be called my curious and, sometimes, oddball behavior. He did a complete examination, a physical from top to bottom, head to foot, mental, psychological, the whole works, and explained to my two bewildered parents that their adorable but seemingly dimwitted son wasn't retarded at all, fact was, he was unusually bright. My being bi-polar, he told them, might go a long way in explaining the way I was, why I tended to lollygag and daydream my way through school and at the same time play the part of the obnoxious jester. And why I was so often distracted, or so direct, or so… so… peculiar at times.

They were overjoyed to learn that their only son, me, was brighter than they thought, but they also seemed unfazed by the fact that their only son may suffer a serious mental disorder. Yet mental disorders of one sort or another were a family tradition around my house.

Then my senior year of high school came along, and it was discovered that some brainy kid on campus was doing the homework for most of the kids in the physics class. As you may have guessed, the brainy kid was yours truly. Hard not to when you are getting a buck a page and making a bundle doing it. So, a student councilor by the name of Mrs. Charlemagne got involved (yes, same as the 9th century Charlemagne who beat the shit out of Gaul) and decided that I should take the SAT exam to see how smart the brainy kid really was, whether I was indeed smart, or really stupid, or some sort of genius-psychopath. I mean, how else do you explain a kid solving physics problems faster than the other kids can write them down.

So, I took the exam. Scored a 725 on the math and 644 on the verbal for a total of 1369. Not bad, the councilor told my parents, especially for someone as ill prepared as the brainy kid was. Nothing changed though; I was left to my own devises and to do as I pleased, to be a curiosity in life, like my mother.

And here I am riding the rims of life at the ripe old age of 55, no longer a person but a stickman taking the elevator to the 12th floor to be led into the company extermination chamber. With trepidation and a bit of gleeful anticipation I stepped off the elevator for the third time in my life and made my way along the center aisle expecting at any minute to hear gas hissing through a ventilator. But I quickly found the office with the right name on the door and through the opening I could see old Grandly sitting at his big, mahogany desk talking on the phone. The sight reminded me of a sultan ordering up a fan dance. Seeing his 'good-old-army-buddy' standing outside, he gave the 'come-on-in' sign, so I tiptoed past the bi-speckled secretary, who sort of snarled as I squirmed by her desk, swung the door open, and sauntered in.

And so it began, me and old Grandly, me and him, him and me smiling into space, me standing beside his desk like a member of the Swiss Guard. The fat boob didn't move a finger, didn't motion for me to sit down, or mouth hello, or give me the old 'how ya doing' sign, didn't even look me in the eye, or acknowledge the fragrance of the bathroom soap I had just splashed on my face before walking into his office. Nothing. Just sat reclined like a big fat raja giving some idiot on the other line a cock and bull story about his new putting stance, as if he could even see his feet over that size 50 waist his suspenders were holding up. It was if I wasn't even there. It was like all the times when he ignored me in the halls, or on the elevator, or all those times when it became obvious that his royal highness wasn't about to acknowledge a human form so grossly applied as the creature who inhabits cube C-17 on the 5th floor, the short sleeved scrawny mutant with the shirt from Penny's and a lunch stained clip-on tie.

Standing there not knowing what to do with myself, I began to look around his office feigning an interest in certain objects on the walls, focusing in particular on a picture of a ship just behind him, then the other walls where more pictures were hung with executive precision. Next, I looked to the table just beside his desk where a rustic African carving was evidentially on display. An overhead spotlight was directed onto it. African art had always been a sour subject of mine, this one looking as though it was something shaped from tree branch by a child or a member of the handicapped brigade, or quite possibly by Grandly himself, the big slug forging his masterpiece late at night while the little woman slept upstairs, whittling and carving and using nothing but the blunt end of a screwdriver. But then art in general has always inflamed me, especially the tree bark variety riding the top of his table. Music too. The world would be a better place without the esthetic always butting in.

So Grandly kept talking and talking while I kept scanning and scanning. I felt like a tourist on a ride. Grandly was droning… blah… blah…blah, until suddenly I became aware of my hands. They hung limply at my sides. Embarrassed, I shoved them into my pockets and fumbled with the paperclips I kept stored there. Took them out and crossed my arms hoping my hands would somehow disappear.

The droning continued. It went on for what seemed like hours, Grandly chatting into the phone with his Nam buddy standing watch at his side. The standing routine was beginning to get on my nerves and I began to feel dumb and mistreated all the more.

Then a thought struck me. The son-of-a-bitch should have motioned for me to sit down, and he didn't. He liked seeing his old army buddy standing at attention. He enjoyed seeing me defer to his royal majesty while he kept his fat ass lodged in his chair bullshitting into the company telephone. It was all part of being the big dog living in the top cube, Vice President, 12th floor, mahogany door, snooty secretary with an attitude.

What Grandly failed to take into account by making me stand at attention while he prattled into the phone was this: I was not some butt-kissing lackey he was dealing with. Oh no. I was Robin. And Robin was capable of just about anything. Robin was capable of taking his totem-pole stance and shoving it into that comfy looking chair Grandly didn't want Robin sitting in. That's right, Grandly, old man, the chair with the table standing next to it, the one with the handicapped carving riding on top, the one just to your right, you big-lard-ass, the sacred chair reserved for your little corporate chitchats, your out-of-town clients who need that late night pampering you're so good at, your bat-phone mischief, your late weekend romps with the secretarial pool when good ol' Maggie thinks you're playing golf in Palm Springs. That plump upholstered chair just to your right, that's the one I am talking about, ain't for the like of me, right Grandly old boy? Batman's friend, Willie Pinkly, 5th floor, casualty, section 5. Corporate hierarchy don't allow no 5th floor types to sit just anywhere they please. Ain't allowed. No way. There's something called protocol and protocol dictates that I sit in that hard-oak upright chair with the marble-ass seat. The one made by the Amish. Ain't that right, you fat son-of-a-bitch?

So, was I going to surrender to the proper mechanics of corporate protocol? Not on your life I wasn't. Not me. Not Pinkly. I did the opposite. I chose to plop my royal fanny right there in that upholstered chair. Yep. And that's what I did. And when I dove in I did something else. I slouched. Not only did I slouch, but I really slouched, big-time slouched, a few degrees just short of horizontal, slouched. Oh yeah. And that wasn't all, I reclined even deeper, the way fans do at a ballgame when the bleachers are empty, and their team is down by at least ten runs, deep and slouchy and big-time disrespectful. The only thing slouching more than me was the smile on Grandly's face. The son-of-a-bitch wanted to kill me.

Ahh…but I knew he was going to get me. One way or another, Grandly was definitely going to get me back. He finally placed the phone in the receiver and did something I hadn't expected. He raised his finger as if to suggest, "much too busy, old boy, stand by," and he picked up the phone again and rotary dialed another number. Damn. He had done it; he had one upped me again.

Whoever answered the other end got a curt, angry message, and I watched as Grandly stretched it out and stretched it out for at least another five minutes before finally hanging up for a second time. Having gotten the last word, he rolled his chair back and gave a good, corporate plastic smile, "Willie, nice to have you drop by," as if it was my choice to be there, as if his threatening letter gave me any choice. If Grandly could have, he would have reached into that fancy wood-grained humidor behind him and pulled out a big, black cigar, and lit up. Only the company no smoking policy prevented him from doing it.

"Nice of you to ask me, Chet." From the 11th floor to the basement, the word 'Chet' rang through the building. I imagined people running from their cubicles with their hands in the air, shouting... "Ed...dee"... "Ed...dee"... "Ed...dee".... No one called anyone on the 12th floor by their first name. It was heretical to do such a thing. Corporate suicide. Profane. But I had been doing similar things for 17 years and getting away with it for 17 years. I was so good at my job that flying kamikaze didn't matter anymore; I was invincible.

The stunned look on Grandly's face proved that I had scored a hit. I was on fire and he knew it. Did he have anything in return, did he have another salvo ready to launch, something beyond his ability to humiliate and lord over the man melting in his chair like a warm loaf of bread. It was his privilege, his right to sling a sword across my throat and decapitate me right then and there. After all, he was the boss.

"Hmmm..." he said, smiling, "yes... and that sweet wife of yours, how is she getting along, well I hope?" The mention of Linda set my blood boiling. Belts and pulleys could be heard whirring in his head. I imagined Linda's corpulent image flashing before his executive imagination and his perverted, provost mind disrobing her piece by piece, dismantling my little Linda like a set of Legos. "Haven't seen her for... ahhh... her name escapes me for the moment?"

"Robin."

"Robin?" The mention of the name caused Grandly to jerk back in his chair. I had scored another hit. Yes!. He stiffened. "Robin, is it?"

"Like the bird," I told him.

His reaction told me that he was much too cowardly to bring up the bat phone incident. Either that or he was still unsure just who the true Robin was, certainly not my adorable wife. But if he was not going to bring up the bat phone then what the hell was I doing in his royal chamber besides being a royal pain in the ass.

Grandly is younger than me, about ten years younger, college graduate, MBA I am told, joined the company about a year after I did, became my immediate supervisor, then was promoted to floor manager (Smithy's current position) before being promoted to Vice President. I watched as he quickly recovered from the arrow I had plunged into his neck and leaned even further in his chair, plopping his two big feet on the desk so that his Italian, leather, handcrafted shoes waived in my face. "Tell me Willie, ever thought of early retirement, I mean, what are you now, 60… 61?" He knew exactly how old I was; my file was open right on top of his desk.

Never one to back down, especially in a time of crises, like the one I was in, I raised my forty-dollar loafers above my head and dropped them onto his mahogany desk. They landed with a bonk. Grandly knew he is being outplayed. "Fifty-five this week," I told him. "And no, can't afford to retire. Too young. Ten percent a year from 65 gets me to zero." Early retirement before the age of 65 chopped ten percent a year from my pension, meaning that at 55 there would be no retirement available.

"Well, the guys upstairs have been talking and…"

"There's an upstairs?"

"The oversight committee, not really upstairs, it's… oh, you know what I am talking about. Anyway, more to the point… Blah… blah… blah."

Grandly didn't scare me the way he did everyone else at Guarded Life and Casualty. I may have been the only person in the company that wasn't completely terrified of the people above us, and if I ever do get those feelings of fear and intimidation from someone, all I have to do is imagine that same someone straining on the toilet at 6am in the morning and that squatting image sort of evens things out for me. In fact, I do it almost every day. I do it with most everyone of importance; squatting on the john is the great equalizer among men. Bowel movements can be very democratic that way. I can humanize the entire planet if I want, all it takes is to imagine every human being on the planet squatting on the john and they become my equal. Everyone sits eyelevel when it comes to squatting on the john. Even the queen. If I imagine Queen Elizabeth sitting on the bathroom throne she loses all sense of royalty to me. She is no longer the queen; she is just some dame taking a crap. Whether you are the pope or a possum, it doesn't matter; it's pretty much the same throughout the animal kingdom when taking a crap.

Same with gorgeous women. Think Madonna. No, not Madonna, Madonna is a bad example. Think of Julia Roberts. Think of Julia Roberts on the john and she loses every bit of her sex appeal. Right? Or sitting on the pot at six in the morning, straining, as I imagine he does every morning, what with all the tension his job dishes out, he is no longer scary when I conger up an image of old Grandly's eyes bulging a big one.

"They have been reviewing the in-house budget…Blah…blah… blah… and what with the recent developments in…in…"

But that is not the only reason Grandly did not scare me. The dark stains under his oxford-cloth, button-down, $95 a pop, light-blue dress shirt purchased at Sak's was a dead giveaway. All it took was one meeting with Pinkly and the guy was done. He would be popping a Valium the minute I left his office.

"As a matter of fact, I was chatting with Mr. Tribe only yesterday when…"

Racehorses knew. Racehorses can detect superior breeding the way women can detect a lie: by smell, by instinct, by intuition. MBA, fancy office, secretary with the disposition of a post office mug shot, it didn't matter, Grandly knew he was no match for 'wonder-boy'.

And yet there I sat. And the funny thing is he knew that I knew that he knew. Grandly was riding the Peter Principle bareback. He had reached his level of incompetence a long time ago and was doing everything he could to prove the principle a fake. But the sweaty armpits told the story, that and the 6a.m. struggle to move his bowels, and the bottle of Valium in his jacket pocket, and the getting sloshed at the Christmas party every year. He knew.

"You are aware, I presume, of the significant increase in non-payments do to… "Here he stopped. I had picked up the picture of his wife and was inspecting it up close. It was almost touching the end of my nose. "Do you mind Willie, I am trying to discuss something important with you."

"Sure Chet, the guys upstairs have decided to can my ass. Go on."

"Don't be so smug, Willie, no one is canning anybody. They just thought you might wish to consider early retirement, that's all. It's a good program… and…"

"They guys upstairs want me to retire?"

"Well…perhaps. Should you wish to make that choice I am sure we could work out a financial arrangement that would prove suitable for both you and Linda, (as I thought, Grandly never forgot a pretty girl's name) something the two of you could manage on, at least until social security kicks in, then maybe a small adjustment."

"You're serious."

"Very." Once again Grandly pulled forward, this time with a look of feigned sincerity on his face, not that chic corporate pose he practiced in the halls and on the elevator, but dead, flim-flam serious. "Willie," he said, the new look reminiscent of Nixon when he told the world, 'I am not a crook', "there are some rumors going around… no… no… it's more than rumors. People have been saying things, things that concern us a great deal, things about your mental state of mind."

"That right?"

"That's right. Mr. Smithy has recently reported to us that you…"

"Smithy? Jesus Christ, the guys got a week to live and you listen to him?"

"You are referring, I presume, to the fact that John Q. will be retiring in the near future and… Oh… let's cut to the chase, shall we Willie. You wanted that promotion and didn't get it, isn't that right? And consequently, you threatened him. You threatened him so that he feared for his life."

"You're talking about that little bump in the parking garage? He told you about that? Christ, the man works in a root cellar; he's lucky he finds his way to work every day.

"With your car. He says you practically ran him down with your automobile, that you actually laid in wait and that… Willie …" and here he calmed himself and began to ruminate back into his chair. For a minute I thought old Grandly was going to reach out and take my hand. "It's not only that," he said, calmly, "it's what's been going on for a long time now, months, years. People used to enjoy your brand of humor, the gags, the pranks. Now they are terrified of you. Look around, they avoid you like the plague; no one wants to talk to you. Your office has become, how do I put it…"

"No man's land."

"That's right, no man's land. And what's his name, that colleague of yours you shot in the eye a few months back, he has been trying to get relocated for the past year, says coming near your workstation is like committing suicide. Even your work has slowed to the point that we are not even sure you work here anymore. Do you? You work on that novel more than…"

"Hey,

"Don't deny it Willie. I have a copy right here in my desk. Security found the floppy and made a copy.

"Really? Isn't that intellectual theft?"

Here I paused to take notice of the stains once again. They had grown in size and lengthened all the way down to his belt. My guess was that if we went on much longer the stains would soon find his shorts. I remember feeling pity for the man; he was in such agony, not for having to let me go, but because he was afraid of me. He was like the coach who plays his son over the better player, or the minister who reads his lines in church. And that is when it occurred to me that this is the way I always talk to people; I don't listen to what they say, I am too busy measuring the affect I am having on them. Grandly seemed pleased every time I said the word really, especially when it came out sounding like a question. So, I said, "Really?"

And he said, "Really."

I said, "Really?"

And he said, "Really."

I sat and thought of how I had managed to put myself into this position and what my next move would be. "You said should I chose early retirement. What if I don't? You gunna fire me?"

Grandly smiled. "Have you ever heard the name, Dr. Simon?"

Simon's six-thou a month office sat atop Century City Tower No. 2, the latest in a series of mega-structures sprouting from the soil in the Beverly Hills section of West Los Angeles. My appointment was for 4:00 P.M. As I approached the tower, a profusion of concrete ramps jumped in front of me, snaking down into a deep labyrinth of such confusion that I thought of turning back. Gathering myself, I grabbed the first one I came to and descended into it. Luckily it turned out to be the one marked visitor's parking, so I made several laps around the same parked cars until I realized what I was doing and turned, luckily as it turned out, on the blue level where an empty stall quickly jumped in front of me. As I parked, I noticed the clock on the dash. It read 3:33, still plenty of time for my appointment.

Friday afternoon. Naturally, GLC would pick a Friday afternoon to make Willie come all this way, sending me half way around the world knowing every maniac with a car would out headhunting anyone not keeping pace with their rush hour hysteria, the worst possible time to send a lonely soldier like me motoring through Everglades of Beverly Hills.

But that's okay, I'm here, I'm inside. Getting out of the car I feel as though I am standing mid Atlantic, everywhere and anywhere nothing but automobiles crammed door to door. There are no bearings in this swampiness, no east/west, no north/south, nothing, all the same, concrete as far as the eye could see. I decided to head to my right and up-hill a-ways, and wouldn't you know it, dead-end. I found a blue arrow just above my head, so I followed the arrow until I came to another blue arrow and then to a blue arrow with the word elevator printed just below.

Soon I was inside the lobby facing four pairs of platinum doors with an enormous gilded directory, fourteen columns of bigshot attorneys and doctors practicing their various forms of witchcraft and flim-flamers of every sort and size all snuggled up in an array of lush, bohemian suites listed in alphabetic order. I saw enough names to form a small country. Finding Simon's name at the top sent a surge of importance racing through my veins. I slung my shoulders back and entered the crowed elevator. "Top floor, please," I told the lady in front as every eye shifted my way.

Getting off, the first thing that struck me was stuck by how quite it was. The place reminded me of the year Linda and I took the girls to Carlsbad Caverns and the quite so deafening that it hurt your ears. Nothing. Not a sound. Not a murmur. Not even the traffic from below could be heard. What I was experiencing was in complete violation of what I was used to at my good old Guarded Life and Casualty, my monkey filled gymnasium where I spent the past seventeen years of my life inventing ways to cheat our customers out of that which what was rightfully theirs. Where I was standing was the Medici Chapel compared to what I was used to on the 5th floor at home, vending machines selling peanut brittle and Diet Coke, desks pushed end to end, grey metal encloses. No screaming in this ivory tower, no paper airplanes, no Chinese laundry, no insect thumping machines, no sweating bodies clamoring against each other, no shuffling, screaming, devouring. This was a foggy night in Paris. This was nice. This I could get used to.

Somewhere in the distance I could hear the hum of conversation taking place, a boss conversing with a secretary, a client questioning a proposal, a patient awaiting a diagnosis. A lusty smell was in the air, like pockets of money hidden in a vault, buried treasure, pirates booty. Passing through one of Beverly Hills most gold encrusted shrines, embroidered walls, silken floors, I imagined old-money clients sitting in waiting rooms crossing their legs, flipping pages of *Business Week, Psychology Today*. My mind spoke of linen-white smocks and hand-tailored business suits, new-money swindlers punching buttons on cell phones, surfing the web, arranging games of racquetball with old college chums. luncheon dates confirmed, vixens arranged. Through my vexed and venerable imagination, I could see the varied and textured ways wealth was being passed from one generation to the next, new-economy forces carrying traditions of old, a generation of shill-masters doing little with their days but fleecing the pocketbooks of their crestfallen benefactors.

Reaching the end of the hall, I found the name I was looking for etched onto a glass-paneled door, *Dr. Morice Simon, Psychiatrist*. It was then, just seconds before stepping into a room that could easily become the biggest step of my life, I began to have regrets about not bringing my gun. How do you kill a man with nothing but your bare hands? It would have been perfect, small enough to be hidden in a jacket pocket, a 25 caliber my father left me in his will, not a lot of punch cause it's a small gun, small enough for a guy to carry in his jacket pocket. But, damn it all, the thing could easily drill a hole between old Simon's eyes and come out the back of his head cleaner than a whistle.

I stepped inside and noticed a middle-aged woman sitting behind a sliding glass partition. I approached, but as we came face to face the woman behind the partition took no notice of me and turned her back instead. She began applying makeup to a face that was clearly a century past its high school prom.

As I stood watching, the woman was making a career of lifting instrument after instrument from her leopard spotted bag while dobbing at her face. I took pity on what I saw sitting no more than a meter away, a thrice-divorced, middle-aged woman pathetically exercising the daily practice of trying to restore the 50-year old relic glaring back in her mirror.

Finally, Spandex Lady turned in my direction and began rearranging a few strands of brittle hair. She shoved a form and a pen at my belt. Next came a few quick instructions of how to fill out a questionnaire any child could do. She then turned around. I dutifully complied and looked for a place to sit down. While I fiddled and scribbled my answers to what were ridiculously elementary questions, probably given as a way of keeping you busy while Simon sat at his desk arranging his billable hours schedule, I could hear the gal behind the partition zipping a thick, glossy leg over the other producing a hissing sound not unlike someone striking a match.

After scratching in briefest details and answering 'no' to every question but one (was this my first visit to see Dr. Simon) I handed it back. Acting bothered, she snatched the form from my hand and disappeared.

As my head bobbed lethargically toward my shoulder and the magazine on my lap was in the early stages of freefalling to the floor, something told me I was not alone. I looked up. High above in the clouds stood the great man himself, or so I assumed.

"Willie," he said, hovering like a giant sequoia. A large nodular hand came swooping from the sky. The hand took hold of mine and pulled me from my seat. "Nice of you to drive all the way into the city," he said. "Come in, come in." The great man guided me in the direction of the door where the spandex queen had disappeared moments before. I stepped inside and noticed two very manly black leather chairs facing each other. Every wall was saturated with affidavits and certificates of every size, shape and dimension. From the cherry-wood wainscoting, to the heavy textured ceiling, the walls contained nothing but framed and matted testimonials to the man's greatness. Simon was, indeed, the real deal.

He gestured that I sit down. I responded by plopping my fanny into the chair nearest me and as soon as it hit the cushion, a whoosh of air came squeaking out the side. My pledge to say nothing suddenly renewed itself and I vowed that no matter the pain, no matter how sever the torture, no matter how sharp the instrument being driving under my nails, he was getting nothing from the likes of Willie Pinkly, nothing, not a god damned thing.

"Well, how was the drive?" he asked. "Not the best time of day to be coming all the way into the city, is it?"

"Not bad," I said, avoiding what looked like a pair of eyes that hadn't slept in a month. The clock on his desk blinked out the time, 4:07 pm, seven minutes into my allotted hour. All week I had been pulling at my chin trying to imagine what the great Simon looked like. Short I figured, and dark, with a pointed beard and a long, hooked beak, not unlike the image sitting at the end his credenza. My mistake became obvious the minute I looked up and saw the sequoia tree hovering there. The guy was three-hands bigger than I expected, four maybe, somewhere in the vicinity of 6'4"-6'5", tall enough to yank the rim from the backboard. He had long, angular arms and long, bony fingers that appeared hardened and dulled with age. His hair was thick and silvery and combed back into a knot where a rubber band held it in place, the custom, I presumed, for healers of the soul, such as he, he and all the other magna cum somethings who graduated from an elite private university.

There was the required salt and pepper beard, not too different than I had imagined, half-glasses, which he kept glancing over, and the cardigan sweater with the scruffy necktie tucked inside. And I couldn't help but notice the stains on the fingers of his right hand and how his gold ring saddled into it. And there was the incriminating bulge in his sweater that suggested a pack of cigarettes, and the deep, mellow voice resonating from the bottom of a bourbon glass. The man had his secrets.

Mundane matters of no interest passed between us, the weather, my dread of having to drive home so late in the day, which he apologized for. He was polite, courteous, even a bit deferential. But he wasn't kidding me. The son-of-a-bitch would get nothing, no secrets, no information, nothing; he would have to kill me first.

"I understand you play a little golf," Simon said, his lanky frame unraveling from the chair opposite mine, the cushion momentarily clinging to his rear-end before breaking free and taking a breath of air. "Here... take a look," he said. I got up and followed him to a place just beside his desk. Simon flipped a switch and to my amazement the shades behind the desk whirred and slithered apart like water over a dam. There below was Los Angeles spilling into the room; sky, hills, city streets, cars rushing like parading insects, people moving without direction or care, buildings jutting skyward, a helicopter purring across the sky. I felt like a child taking his first glimpse of the ocean.

"Pretty remarkable, isn't it," Simon said, resting his large frame against the glass wall. It was like leaning against the sky.

"Yeah," I told him, fumbling for leverage lest I fall onto the nearest rooftop. Floor to ceiling and seventeen stories was more than I was used to. I thought of Smithy's shitty little porthole and what the old bastard would say if he could see me now. Letting go, I moved back a few paces, and drew a breath.

"Never get tired of looking at the city from up here; busy place, the city. Look there, that's Los Angeles Country Club." I stepped a little closer and saw the green concourse below, tiny golf machines zipping up and down fairways like ants at a picnic. "Million to join," he said. "Not to mention the two thousand monthlies, a tidy sum just to follow a tiny white ball around. Look there, just above," Simon said, pointing to line of cars stacked against a traffic signal, "that's Santa Monica Boulevard. And up there, see it, a little higher, that's Wilshire. You've heard of Wilshire Boulevard, right?"

I shook my head yes, annoyed that Simon was beginning to treat me as a country bumpkin. Wilshire Boulevard. Who hadn't heard of Wilshire Boulevard, I lived in Fullerton, not Indiana.

"Bet you didn't know your Wilshire and our Wilshire are named after the same fella. Guy by the name of Gaylord Wilshire. Real, slick real estate fella back in the days when there was nothing but cactus and tumbleweed everywhere you looked. Con man, I suppose you could say, one of those robber barons you read about and see in the movies, huckster type, inventor, gambler."

"How'd you know I lived in Fullerton?"

"What… Fullerton? Oh… read your file last night. Born and raised, right?"

I glanced at the folder on his desk and said, "fifty-three years."

"One day old Gaylord teamed up with the Amerige boys, paid some Southern Pacific engineer by the name of Fullerton to run a set of rails though a bean field they owned. Put a dump station on it and the next thing you know, a town's springing up."

His familiar way of talking was beginning to annoy me, that phony hickish manner of speaking. "How do you know all this, I mean… Fullerton is thirty miles from here…"

"Oh, I dabble a little at local history; the Wilshire thing among others. Just so happened that when old Gaylord left your little burg he came running up here and started another. 1890 I think it was. A coincidence, I suppose. Now before I get too carried away with how brilliant I am, look up just beyond Wilshire a-ways."

A-ways. Sounded like something out of *Old Yeller*.

"See those buildings? That's my old alma mater, UCLA. Spent ten years of my life learning my trade up there. Best time of my life too." Simon turned and looked at me, "Cal State Fullerton, right?"

"Right, statistics."

"How did you enjoy college?"

"Everything but accounting."

"You didn't like accounting? Me neither. I can barely count my change." The great man paused as if contemplating what to say next. "Sometimes I wonder if I shouldn't have spent my time doing something besides giving advice."

His narrow eyes ran around his perfectly appointed office and he gave out a big, deep sigh, the sigh, like his phony manner, resonating more as an attempt to gain my sympathy than a genuine reflection of some distant remembrance. I hadn't come expecting to be teeing it up with the guy on Saturday, or that we would spend the day shucking corn. No, I wasn't going to be fooled by the great man's trickery, or his phony camaraderie, not Willie Pinkly, I was prepared.

"But this is the business I know; it's what I've done all my life. Suppose it's too late to be starting over now." Simon smiled and the crease in his face made me wonder if the 'starting over' comment was a dig of some kind, or whether he was setting me up for the bad news he'd be transmitting later. "Here, let me show you where I live. Look up there." His finger pointed to a place well beyond the campus of his youth and into the hills above.

"See that? That's Benedict Canyon. All those hills you see surrounding it, that's called Beverly Glen. Right there, just toward the place where the canyon makes a bend... see it?" I nodded. "That's where I live. Lived there for more than twenty years. You've lived in Fullerton your entire life, isn't that right?"

"Like I said, fifty-three years."

"Same woman too, thirty years, isn't it? You must be a happily married man,."

"Suppose so." The man had evidently memorized my entire file.

"I'm remarried ten years now. Was married before but got all caught up in the razzle-dazzle of my profession. Before I knew it, lost it all, everything."

To my great relief, Simon had yet to mention the large corduroy coach riding low along the wall where a jumble of upholstered pillows decorated the ends. The arrangement looked perfect for diving into. "Well Willie," Simon said at last, "what do you say we sit down and get to business. You didn't drive all this way to discuss the landscape or talk ancient history with the likes of me." Once again Dr. Simon guided me across the room to where the two chairs awaited us. I was starting to like the guy and hating myself in the process.

What was the purpose of the little presentation, I wondered? Did every patient coming through those doors get licked in the balls?

Simon gently nestled back in his chair trying his best to play the old chum. "Let's begin with you telling me why you think you're here?" he said.

"But I am here."

"Huh." Simon looked me over. "Yes, how stupid of me, I suppose I phrased that question rather clumsily, didn't I? He was becoming slightly more formal now that the tour was over and the meter was running. "What I mean to say is... Why do you think your employer, the people at Columbia, wanted you to see me? Why do you think you are here?"

"You did it again."

"Did what again?"

"The think thing, why I thought I was here."

"No, no, the reason for your being here... why you came to see me?" The clock was blinking out 4:16 and already Simon's perfect composure was beginning to splinter. For the first time I was enjoying myself.

"Right. Well, looks to me as if you have it all right there in front of you," I told him, "in that little folder you got on your desk." The file had a little yellow tag with my name sticking out the side, the color yellow implying 5th floor, Claims Department, with my name, Edward Pinkly typed in. Just below my name was the name of the company I worked for, or used to work for, Guarded Life & Casualty.

Simon gave the file a little tap. "You are a very interesting fellow, Willie, you know that? You have an excellent work record, as far as I can tell, a promotion or two, bright, promising, one of the "wiz-kids", according to your superiors. And that battery of tests you took when you first entered the firm," he said, glancing at the file on his desk, "they indicate a higher than average level of intelligence, much higher. Tell me, have you ever taken an IQ test?"

"High school." Rank, file and serial number, that was my pledge.

Simon paused and looked at me. "Well?"

"I did all right." Offering up my IQ results would undoubtedly place me in the "underachiever" category, or at the very least, classify me as one of those screwed-up, savant types who find themselves unable to function in the real world.

Simon smiled and gazed into my eyes. "Mr. Grandly is concerned about you, Willie; did you know that? He tells me…"

"Concerned about me? Grandly's the guy who should be sitting here, not me?"

Simon frowned. "Why do you say that?"

"He's the guy with a 'bat phone'."

"Bat phone?"

"You don't know?"

"I'm afraid I don't follow you, what's this 'bat phone' you're talking about." He was lying, of course.

"Forget it," I said.

For the first time Simon look bewildered. He sat puzzled and unsure of which way to proceed.

"According to your superiors at Guarded, there has been a recent change in attitude, Willie." He calculated and rubbed his brow, "changes like those related to me by some of your colleagues at work; they are the cause of some concern. My guess, and this is only a guess having not spent enough time to make a… ah… assess the situation, is that these changes are probably the result of stress… quite possibly some sort of experience or event you are completely unaware of, consciously or subconsciously. The death of a loved one, for example. You may be suffering the effects of trauma and not even realize it. Sometimes we discount what may, if fact, be killing you. Anything can do it." And here he waited thinking that I would jump on his bandwagon. He waited. "Can you think of anything that has changed in the past year or so, anything? And please, don't hold back, I am here to help you. So, anything, anything at all, can you recall anything in the recent past, any episode, any event… let's say something that may have taken place in the past year? Anything? Just bring it out and we'll talk about it."

"Carter gets a paperclip in the ear and I'm yo-yo, that the kind of thing you're looking for?"

Simon stiffened. "Yes, I am aware of the incident. Mr. Carter's complaint hit my desk months ago. And there have been others. I was hoping you would cooperate and not become antagonistic. We can accomplish a lot more if you would try and cooperate. What do you say? Can you do it? Will you work with me?"

I sat sober and calm and said nothing."

"Willie."

"Morty."

"Okay, okay, Willie, have it your way. Just so you know, Mr. Grandly thinks you are bitter because you were overlooked for promotion…" and here he looks over his glasses to make sure I am listening. "And that is why you threatened Mr. Smithy last month, isn't it? Is that indeed what is bothering you? Being sore over losing a promotion? If so we should address that issue and not become mired in all this silliness." He hesitated, waiting for a reply. "Just so you know, Mr. Smithy's complaint is in your file. Would you like me to read it to you?"

"Smithy ought to be strung up and his body drug by a team of horses… just so you know."

Simon picked up my file and rummaged through it until he found what he was looking for. His hands were trembling. He scanned the document and read from it. *If I hadn't looked up when I did,* "and I am quoting Mr. Smithy here," *I don't know, I think he would have run me* down. I... I... I honestly believe the man was trying to kill me.' That was taken from a transcript the day he reported it. And to Mr. Smithy's credit he has resisted reporting the incident to the police.

"Let's cut the crap, okay... Simon?"

"Dr. Simon."

"Mort." Simon frowned at the obvious slight. "This is a set-up and you know it. Coming to see you is nothing more than a fat-assed, fact-gathering crusade to get rid of me. And you're the hired gun. Am I right? Christ almighty, a guy would have to be a complete lunatic not to see what's going on around here, all this 'we're here to help you, Willie'... 'Mr. Grandly is concerned about you, Willie'. You, Grandly... Guardian, the whole bunch... you want to see me out, simple as that. No severance, no retirement, no promotion. Shit, you don't even have to say you're sorry, just push Willie out the door. Bullshit, I'm not saying anything... nothing... zippo. So, how's that grab you, Morty, my man?"

Seemingly unfazed by my diatribe, Simon sat with his arms folded across his chest, a steely grin across his face. Smug bastard.

"Well, well, well, Grandly was right about you, you are belligerent. And you are extremely suspicious and uncooperative. And no Willie, I am not here to gather facts about your employment with Gaurded; I am here for one reason and one reason only, to assist you in your recovery and your full reinstatement with the firm. And we can only do that only if you speak truthfully and willingly about what is on your mind. You need to give up this 'you are out to get me' mentality. Okay? It borders on paranoia. So, please, let's set that aside, okay? I can assure you that nothing you say in this office will be relayed on to your employer or recorded for future use. You will notice that there is no note-taking going on, no hidden recorders, nothing. I will visit with you for a short time then, after a few sessions, send my findings to the company. That's it, nothing more, a brief statement as to your mental state of mind and your capacity to fulfill the requirements of your job."

"Whether or not I'm nuts."

"Oh, come on Willie, you're not nuts, you are too smart for that."

"Then why did I try to kill old Smithy? A guy's got to be nuts if he wants to kill his boss, right?"

With this, the pack of cigarettes in his shirt pocket came perilously close to tumbling onto his desk. He recovered the pack and leaned forward. Calmly, he said, "Did you really intend to kill Mr. Smithy, or did you just want to scare him a little?"

"I wanted to kill him."

"Then why didn't you?"

"Cause, I got scared."

"My guess is that you were angry about being passed over for promotion and you didn't know what to do about it. So, you tried intimidating poor Mr. Smithy. Sort of the way boxers do in a face off." With this Simon sat back in his chair and raised his two knurly hands into a fist. "You've seen them, right? The way those guys stand in the middle of the ring sticking their noses in their opponent's face. Maybe that's all you were doing, sort of like a prank that gets out of hand. Perfectly normal. Especially normal for a man under a lot of stress, as you apparently are. Can happen to anybody, I assure you, even to me. Maybe a little depression has set in, troubles at home, something like that. What do you say Willie, sound familiar?"

"Nope, I wanted to kill the son-of-a-bitch."

Simon tried to look unfazed. "You actually intended to run the man down, to kill Mr. Smithy?"

"Right. And I'll betch ya wish ya had your little recorder about now."

"I find that hard to believe."

"What? Kill Smithy? I'd probably kill a lot of people if I knew I wasn't going to get caught. That's the only reason I didn't run old Smithy down that day, cause everyone in the world would know it was me that did it. My fanny would get tossed in the clink so quick I wouldn't have time to take a shit."

"You are pulling my leg, right? You trying to say you're a serial killer?" Simon chuckled, nervously.

"No… no, it's true. You asked that I be truthful, right? Don't hold back, just say what's on your mind. Well it's the truth. So, start filling out that little report, Morty, 'cause this is the real deal, this is the real Willie Pinkly talking."

"No fantasies, please. Be serious for once. Give me your true feelings, just tell me exactly what you intended the day Mr. Smithy was walking to his car and you went skidding into him."

"Truthfully, Mort?" The grin was gone now. His eyes had narrowed, and his lips were clenched as if he were holding a chickpea between them. "I didn't intend on killing Mr. Smithy that day. No... I am much too cowardly to go around killing people. But that doesn't mean I wouldn't like to, or that I wouldn't kill somebody if I had the guts."

I had his complete attention now and his eyes were riding on my every word.

"If I had the guts... and this is the real honest-to-god deal, Mort, no messing around, I'm telling you the honest-to-god truth here, straight from the heart... I'd do it; I really would. But I wouldn't run over somebody with a stupid car. No way I could do that. No, if I knew I wouldn't get caught, I'd walk into Mr. Smithy's office, close the door, put a gun to his head, and "pow", blow his fucking brains all over the room. I really would. No... Wait. Come to think of it I wouldn't do that either. If I did then I'd have see all that stuff flying out of his head, Smithy's brains going every which-way... holy cow... they'd be all over me, the walls... Christ almighty, people don't think about brains and guts and all that gooey stuff when they plan on shooting somebody so...no... I couldn't do that, not that way I couldn't, I'd get queasy seeing that stuff flying all around. No... now that I think about it I couldn't do it that way either... nope... not with a gun I couldn't."

Simon sat forward with a perplexed look on his face. He had no way of knowing what he was dealing with. Whatever it was, one thing was sure, he was getting his money's worth.

"I think that is just about enough imagination for one day."

"I couldn't club somebody to death either. Or knife somebody. No way I could knife somebody... feeling that thing go squishing into somebody's meat. Ugh. Or into his bone. Jesus, just the thought of hitting a bone in some guy guts gives me the creeps. Nope, I couldn't live with that either."

"Okay Willie, you've had your little fun."

"I could maybe poison somebody. No... No..." Silence. "Blow them up maybe?..."

"Willie."

"Yeah, blow 'em up while they're sitting on the can, I could do that. Oh, yeah, I could do that sitting on the can. Or in their car. I could do that too. And now that I think of it, I might be able to push someone off a bridge, or a building, or set them on fire. Yeah, I could do that; I could definitely set someone on fire. Or poison them. I could easily poison someone so long as I could get away with it. I wouldn't want to get caught though. And I don't want to feel bad about it either."

"Willie?"

"I don't think I could kill a friend though, or a relative, or anyone I really liked, including some celebrities. Imagine killing Anthony Hopkins. Hey, how about Michel Douglas? Well maybe I could kill Michel Douglas. I couldn't kill the President though; I couldn't kill anyone like the President. Or anyone in uniform, our uniform, that is."

"Willie, Willie, Willie."

"Morty, Morty, Morty."

"Come on Willie …"

"Come on Morty."

"I believe our hour is up."

"I suppose if I were to kill someone it would have to be a stranger. I wouldn't feel too bad about killing a stranger. Or maybe a shrink."

Simon was such a schmuck.

What was supposed to be a year's probation followed by early retirement turned out to be a big promotion for slick Willie Pinkly, the numbers guru from good old Norwalk High. I was given an honest-to-god office with four pictured walls, one of which turned out to be a partially clothed Tahitian gal I quickly fell in love with. I had my own copy machine, a drink dispenser and shelving galore to store all my personal shit. Because I was the quickest brain on the entire floor, my new assignment was for every Bozo on the floor to come to me for a complete review of their paperwork before sending it upstairs to be chewed, swallowed and digested by the rest of corporate bureaucracy. What happened after that I didn't know or care.

On that very first morning my fellow employees started showing up around 9am, sometimes one at a time, sometimes in little groups of twos and threes, but they came. By the looks on their faces they weren't too happy about having to deal with crazy Willie Pinkly, not that I cared. They'd prefer me dead rather than look over their work before signing off on it. I'd see them plop their fannies in a chair and glare in my direction while I set to work reviewing their imbecilic scratching's and columns looking for mistakes. If I was lucky enough to find a flaw in their strategy, all the better, I'd beat them over the head with it. My sole purpose in reviewing their bits of crap was to teach them all a lesson, to prove to the entire floor that Pinkly was still Sir Willie Pinkly and still master of the universe.

"This the best you can do, shithead," I'd say. "Our strategy is not to pay out a million bucks just because some poor bastard got his head knocked around a little. Suffering's no loss, it's a mental condition, a weakness of character. Take this load of shit back to your cube and find a way to cut it in half."

My office would really get busy around mid-day, people standing in line, sitting in every chair waiting for me to take a look at their stupid paperwork. Later in the day the office would thin out and I'd have the place all to myself. I'd sit in my old office practicing my spins while counting them on a clicker I bought at a nearby sports shop. Someone would come in and plop their paperwork down and it would take all of three minutes before I'd be creaming them with criticism and personal insults. They'd go away whimpering and promising to report me to J.Q. for my rotten attitude, that I spent all my time spinning in my chair and not working. But I didn't care. I had my own office and I was just as senior as my good friend Smitty was. No one could touch me.

Two weeks following my promotion, Gaylord, my new boss, stuck his head through my door to ask if I had a moment. "Sure," I said. "Anything for you, Gay Boy." Because of all the traffic in and out of my office, my door was always open. In fact, Gay Boy had it removed months ago. He stepped inside followed by Melonie Hardiman, the plump, good-looking gal three cubits down Aisle C from my old office. Melonie was the implied mediator around the office. In her hand she held what looked like a document of some sort. Gay Boy set down as did Melonie. I smiled.

"Willie, Melonie and the others, the entire floor in fact, have some concern about your recent behavior."

"That so."

"Yes. For one thing it appears you've quit working altogether, that you do nothing all day but spin in that chair of yours and work on that novel you keep hidden. They also complain about your attitude. They say it is demoralizing and demeaning and that..."

"And with good reason. Have you taken the time to go over the crap these morons expect me to pass upstairs? They come into my office asking me to sign off on stuff I wouldn't bother sending to the shredder. I can't sign that shit, it's dribble. And yeah, I get a little steamed now and then, who wouldn't?"

Melonie broke in. "See. See that. That's what I'm talking about. He's a lunatic. Sign off, indeed. Everybody who goes in there gets their stuff snatched right from their hand. We can't even use the copy machine anymore because of him. He's crazy. You have to do something to get him out of here, Mr. Gaylord. He scares everybody. The entire floor signed on to get him gone and here he is big as day." She threw a piece of paper on my desk, table actually, table and six chairs.

Gayboy stared at the two of us. He looked at me. "Willie, I made you an appointment for this afternoon with Dr. Simon. He wants to see you in his office at 2PM sharp. I hope you will make plans accordingly. Otherwise I'll have to have someone from personnel come by your office and escort you out of here. I strongly advise that you see Dr. Simon, Willie, otherwise it might put your retirement plan into jeopardy. You don't want that, do you?"

Gaylord's calm demeanor was so annoying that I sat there close to the point of revolution. The dolt had obviously been rehearsing his little speech all morning otherwise I would have had him in a headlock by now. Clean out your desk, escort you from your office. Who does he think he is talking to?

"So, the two of you come waltzing into my office for the sole purpose of firing me. That the idea, Snookems?" looking at Melonie. "This is my office and it's staying my office. The two of you won't last a week without Pinkly cleaning up your messes."

Gaylord broke in. "Willie. This isn't your office. You don't have an office anymore. You work in the mailroom. This is the lunch room, Willie, not your office."

I met Simon at 2 o'clock.

A week later I retired.

That was it. The meeting with Simon was a year ago, my pension deal approved, 70% salary for the next ten then 50% thereafter. Not bad considering. Social security will be kicking out almost $1200 a month after ten. Add the wife's stipend of $350 a month, and we're doing okay. Linda does some kind of counseling down at the church, a weird sort of voodoo stuff which she claims she can cure the sick by touching their feet and chanting some sort of Haitian prayer. Oddly, it seems to work.

Right after I retired they threw a little party over at the Olive Garden restaurant near the office. About 35 people showed up. Smithy was there. And to my surprise and his butterball wife, Maggie, showed up too. She's a nice little gal, about 5-foot-tall, pixie faced, button lips, and round as a billiard ball.

About half way through our dinner Smithy stood up and said a couple of nice things about me, shook my hand, gave me the proverbial gold watch, then asked me to do my birthday trick where I guess the day a person is born by giving me their date of birth. It's no trick. All you do is figure the number of weeks by multiplying 52 by the number of years, add the number of leap year days and the plus or minus remainder will give you the day of the week. That's an oversimplification, but anyone can do it with a little practice. The people in the office who had never seen me do the trick banged their fists on the table, calling me a genius. Even Grandly looked at me with a certain awe.

Then Grandly stood up. He gave a fatherly toast as he stood among the 7 or 8 tables where the humbled masses sat trembling in their stain-resistant chairs, all misty-eyed and reverent as he raised his glass high above his head, telling the multitude of my valuable service to the company and how much they would miss me.

'No one, and I mean no one', he told his cheering fans, 'no one had a crisper eye for the numbers than old Pinkly down in Risk Management. Ten men', he said, 'it would take ten men to replace the likes of my good friend sitting here next to me'. And then he told of my countless shenanigans around the office, getting so chummy and full of camel-colored spirit that he almost blurted out the bat phone escapade, catching himself instead before settling on the 'chowder-head' incident and just who was it that sent that singing telegram to his office on his birthday last year.

And, of course, that had everyone rolling with laughter because everyone knew exactly who it was.

On a roll, Grandly was. He went on and on, asking who the 'crazy-yokel' was who smashed his kisser against the copy machine and sent copies around the office with the message "guess who" on it, again to enormous laughter. And who was it that drove a company car with a bumper sticker that read, "World Peas" admitting that he (Grandly) had no clue what "World Peas" was supposed to mean. He called me zany and a guy who is always good for a laugh. Grandly worked hard to ingratiate himself into the motley mix of 5th floor friends. He was good, really good. And it is fair to say that, all in all, Grandly was a good guy. But still I couldn't help getting in one last lick, after all, how many more chances would I have to stick it to the big boob.

The desert had just arrived, those little brown and white squares of tiramisu the Olive Garden gets about $5 a pop for. The waiter had just sat them in front of us and little Maggie was about ready to swan dive her swollen mug into hers when I leaned across the table and said in a conspiratorial voice loud enough for everyone at the table to hear, I said, "Maggie, would you like the waiter bring some 'Cool Whip' for your dessert?" Maggie, keeping her head in her plate, uttered something into her lap, something that sounded like, "No, no, it's fine just the way it is." Unsure she had made the connection, I glanced at Grandly. From the look on his face I knew I had struck gold. Again, speaking to Maggie, and in a voice so the entire table could hear, I said, "Your husband says you always keep a little Cool Whip in the refrigerator, says you like it on everything, even on your biscuits. The little cannonball almost fell through the floor. I have never seen a face swell so big as when she heard the words 'Cool Whip'. Her two squinty eyes widened like cigarette burns in a nylon blanket. She stammered something that sounded like, "Ah, I am sure I don't know…" looking at her husband who was glaring two bazooka sized eyeballs in my direction. The table was very quiet after that and Maggie spent the rest of the evening staring at the floor.

Well, that chapter in my life is over. I'm in the second year of retirement now, the house has never looked better, it's brighter than it's been in years, the yard's neater, Linda's happy. Like I said, things are going pretty damn good.

My sciatica is killing me though. Trenching in the yard, probably. Or it could be all the wild sex Linda and I have engaged in during the last year or two, ha-ha. Didn't hurt while I was doing it, the trenching, that is. Woke up the next day and it was like lightening shooting down my leg and into my shoe. Can hardly climb in and out of the car.

So here I am at 56 and still haven't figured out what I want to do with my life. Working for GLC was just a way of passing time until I figured out exactly what it is that I am good at. I don't mean to suggest that I am in any way ashamed for having accomplished so little in my 56 years of living, not at all; I've done all right and my wife doesn't complain. Nor am I apologizing for being little more than a number on a street or having worked most of my life in an 8x8 cube. I don't lament transgressions like so many of my middle-aged friends do. I haven't involved myself in nefarious activities like most of the men I know, or have regrets by the thousands, or wish to rush to the nearest bridge and leap into oblivion, nothing like that. It's just that I am a man of passion and, being a man of passion, I have always shown a tendency to push the edges of normalcy, and thus, have spent the better part of my life being buffeted by the expectations and the politics of normalcy. I am a live wire in a rainstorm, a crazy, juiced-up person who shares the mind of his long, deceased, mother, God bless her soul. At times I feel like Alice in Wonderland, "Which way? Which way?" expecting things to be extraordinary when, in fact, extraordinary is ordinary to me. I have been ordinary, and I have been passionless, and I have had regrets. A jagged mind on a straight path, that's my story, a retired stickman who spent half his life working as a risk analyst for a huge insurance company where, I'll bet, no one remembers his name.

And Grandly was right. And Smithy. And Simon too. I had been cracking up. It took years for me to take stock in my life, to think about where I had been and where I was headed and to decide what course to take, kind of like the old Greek saying: to know thyself.

This tendency toward self-destruction has always lingered somewhere in the mental neighborhood of my cerebral cortex, but never to the extent that it had over the last few years. If I had to guess I would say this movement toward self-destruction started about the time the girls moved out. One of the girls got married and the other disappeared when she went away to college and never came back. By leaving, the two girls left Linda and I to our own devises, and that meant having to fill a chasm with a teaspoon of love.

Linda, lucky for her, found a lifeline in that little white building down the street, the one you hear rattling and rolling all the way to heaven every Sunday morning: The First Brethren Church of Christ. She is a spiritual healer of sorts, anointing those who need anointing with magic potions and healing hands.

It was around the age of 50 that my eyes went bad. My knee sorta collapsed so I could no longer take my evening jog and the next thing you know me and Peter Jennings are sharing dinner together. Not long after, the girls in the office began calling me Mister and Sir, two titles I can live without. And that hardly-noticeable little facial tic that I've had for so many years, the cute little mannerism that most ladies find quaint and adorable, it has turned ugly and the twitch has become spastic and uncontrollable so that people turn in disgust. And menopause, that too, the deadly monster that devours a woman's sex life, turning them against their husbands so that they are forced to turn to their own clumsy devices when the mood strikes them. In short, life is crap.

Fact is, I have never been an overachiever. Nor have I been an overly ambitious person. Nor have I been someone well-endowed in the art of social manipulation. When it comes to surviving the slings and arrows of human competition, I have always leaned on the advantages nature bestowed on me at birth, my bull-dozing quickness of mind, and the absence of self-doubt.

As I said, it was about the age of fifty that I started to notice the change. The change came without warning, nature doing what I had always thought impossible, retrieving my special endowments like a fish on a string. I was beginning to come undone, my so-called special advantages in the world were being taken from me. Without my mental prowess to carry me through, my thoughts began to bog like a boot in the mud. Without warning, I became lost in a sea of confusion. I found myself wrestling over mundane and trivial problems. I began contesting with surfs and dregs. Calculations that had once zipped through my mind with the speed of an electron now slowed to the pace of cold gravy. I was lost in a maelstrom of mediocrity, a man without advantage or privilege. Without my special advantage I could no longer function as before, superior, grandiose, master of the universe, knower of all that was knowable, or so I believed.

So, I bailed; blindsided by the fates of nature, I caved, gave up, wimped out. My esoteric failures become a reason for torment, a 5th floor Robespierre was I, a Judas to my trade. And because of it, I covered my failures by becoming an even greater prankster than before, driving poor Smithy crazy and Grandly to drink. Not that I really did, but, for God's sake, I gave it a good try. For God's sake. For God's sake.

And that is where you think this is leading, don't you, that all my many years of mischief-making and all that mental and physical abnormality was really nothing more than a cry for help, me, the pitiful, 50ish recently unemployed man searching for a transcendent, otherworldly path to follow, that all I had to do was give myself permission to surrender to some new, more powerful form of justice and move away from the mortal reasoning I had always done before. To find a new path, a new road, a road to Damascus, the way Paul did. And that, dear reader, would ultimately take me to Jesus Christ. And if you believe that crap, then dear reader, you haven't been paying attention.

I am not one to walk into the quicksand of faith the way most people do, not the kind of person to be drug into the tar-pit of mass hysteria where people throw their hearts and minds into the abyss of thoughtlessness. I have no plan to follow Linda onto the steps of our Lord, to splay my prostrate arms and legs across its steps, to throw my merciless body onto the compost heap of faith. 'Trust me', they say, 'trust in the Lord'. But what if one is possessed of a heart that cannot be trusted, as is the case with me. My heart leads me to unspeakable wrongs, away from civility and common sense, away from health and happiness to something far different than that, to what I call the bonfire of self-destruction. Am I to ignore William Blake for Lady Gaga, run from Paul Sagan to the arms of Mr. Rogers? Swap a fairy tale mind for self-reflection, for critical reasoning, for intellect? And do it for the simple pleasure of a peaceful mind and a good night's sleep?

I learned at an early age that, cruelly, life is stacked against us. Sadly, each of us is born with the gift of our own mortality, a part of an existential food-chain that been around for millions of years. Like me, you probably learned by the age of ten that we are destined to die, maybe even to burn in hell, should that happen to be your persuasion, and that each of us has our own hourglass and that hourglass has been turned on its end and the sands of time will continue to run until we are no more, gone, zippo. So given this fuse against our head, given the knowledge of our impending departure from the planet, how is it possible to play the game with any joy, with the daring and the zest to make our pitiful dot in time meaningful and proud, to fight the good fight, to take patriotism seriously, to take God seriously, fatherhood seriously, all our meaningful moments seriously when the consequences of our existence is so god-damned irrelevant, so readily transparent, so temporary as to make the whole thing, not only meaningless, but absurd?

My missing daughter called last week. Seems Linda and I have a grandchild. She wants to stay with us until she can find a job. There is no husband. Now that I am unemployed, we eat a lot of peanut butter and watch a lot of TV, and how we are able support two more people in this Christ infected bungalow we live in is a question we'll have to deal with when she gets here. For now, I am content to know that she loves me, something she told me when Linda handed me the phone and Mona wailed out the words, "Daddy, I'm sorry," her voice trembling. "I love you so much." And I never felt better.

We are what we are, and we want what we want, even when what we want might kill us. Like war. Like religion. Like race and culture and language and real estate. We kill for our loved ones though. And as terrible as all that killing is, somehow, I get it. And as much as I'd like to believe there's a truth beyond this illusion, we call life, I've come to believe that there's no truth beyond our pitiful few years of life. Because, between reality on the one hand and the point where the brain strikes its sword against reality, there is a middle ground, a place where Willie Pinkly rests his head and goes to sleep every night. To exist is all there is, to find *contentment* in this exotic and fanciful brain is my mission in life, to blend two ends of the rainbow together and make one, one continuous glowing gift of nature that I can wonder about and analyze and contemplate until I am no more. And yet, knowing what I know, I continue to submerge myself in all its majesty. I get it, I really, really get it.

WALLY

*The boys in this story
are not morons,
they are simply young.*

Monday, 1958, five jackasses crammed in a car. A water-logged surfboard rides butt-first on top. Trackcrap is driving. I sit next to Trackcrap. Trackcrap always drives because he is the only one who doesn't smoke or drink. Behind me sits Goats and Wally and Fanch, all riding shoulder to shoulder. Wally is the youngest. It's July. It's hot as hell. It's overcast and muggy. I'm in my idiot-colored Jams, the one's I swiped from a department store I can't remember the name of, Akron I think, cheap place in the crummy part of town that sells all kinds of shit to kids with cash. I remember trying the jams on and slipping my Levi's over them and walking out. Simple as that. Shopping 1958.

Got a cooler in the trunk stuffed with Ripple wine. Fanch's sister's boyfriend bought for us. Comes in clear bottles and looks a lot like Hawaiian Punch. We threw in a couple Cokes for Trackcrap. Wally too. Kid's only fifteen. The rest of us are eighteen. I think.

Trackcrap is this super-duper track guy who just ran the second fastest high school, 800-meter time in the U.S. He'll go to Oregon State one day and become a huge track star where he will miss the Olympic team by a nose when he dove for the tape and stumbled over his feet and went skidding across the finish-line, fourth. Dumb shit. All he had to do is keep his stride and he was a shoo-in. But no, not our friend, Trackcrap, just ten yards short of the finish and what does he do? He spreads his arms and dives headfirst into the ground. Dumb shit. We all laughed our asses off when we heard about it, naturally, couldn't wait to show him the picture in the newspaper. Truth is, we all respected the shit out Trackcrap in those day. Still do.

Anyway, following right behind is Stonewall. Stonewall's driving his tricked out '32 pickup truck, the one he and his dad built one bolt at a time in the family garage, flathead V-8 with steal-finned headcovers poking out the sides. Lopes like a panther sitting at a stop sign, scary as hell and scary to ride in. Next to Stonewall is Skinny, Mr. Razzle-Dazzle, both heading to Huntington in their cheapy shorts. We all got our towels wrapped around our heads, cooler, Ripple crammed in back, a water-logged surf board riding on top, sand, surf, Huntington Beach Pier just a few miles ahead.

Get there and before we even settle in Wally takes his giant header into the sand and…. Jesus, Wally… you're only fifteen. Whatthehell?

Here goes.

Wally was Goats' friend. Nice kid, always grinning likes he's half stupid. Loved hanging with us older guys, big teeth, hair in his eyes. Followed Goats like a tapeworm.

Unloaded our shit on the beach, towels, surfboard, Ripple. A couple in their twenties was lying in our usual spot so we obnoxiously set up about twenty feet away, banging our shit around, swearing, thinking we might drive them away. But all it got was a dirty look from the bikini gal while the guy stayed flat on his back. Every time the bikini queen turned her head I bent over real big and looked between my legs while giving her the big 'howdy' sign. Boy, did that flip her out. She was so pissed I was sure they would move. All her husband did was lift his head, tilt his sunglasses, and lay down again.

Then Fanch comes running up the beach saying he found a washed-up dog lying near the surf, big one too, deader'n shit, he said.

We all go to take a look. It's true, big, black dog with half its hair missing. Hair's in clots all over, flies crawling around, a crab here and there. One of the dog's eyes was missing, crabs must of got to it, flies swarming in and out. Funny though, didn't smell.

Next thing you know Wally gets sucked into this giant wave, goes crashing head-first into the sand. We all saw it but nobody, not one of us, had a clue how bad it was. And neither did the poor bastard, Wally. Like I said, none of us knew shit in those days.

This was in 58, I think. I was 18 and Wally probably 15.

I didn't see the actual body-slam. Skinny said he did but Skinny lies about everything. Me? All I saw was Skinny dragging Wally by the ankles through the surf, water lapping over the poor kid's head while his lips kept gasping for air. I'm pretty sure Skinny was thinking what I was thinking, that Wally was into our stash of Ripple and, being a few years younger, took a couple swigs and got himself good and drunk.

Next thing I know Skinny is walking back along the shore where the four of us are ganged around the surfboard we hijacked from the top of a car the week before. Skinny gives Wally a big kick in the ass and takes off swimming in our direction. Stonewall took the board home and painted it blue and drew a shark's head on the nose in case somebody might recognize it. We're just outside the waves, Fanch is on top of Stonewall, and Stonewall is on top of me, and me, I'm fighting Goats who is fighting, I don't know, the surfboard I guess. We already drank some Ripple and were having a great time.

Anyway, a few minutes go by. I see Trackcrap. Trackcrap stayed on the beach when Wally took his giant somersault. He sat there for a few minutes then gets up and goes over to where Wally is lying face up in the surf. Wally's still rolling around and getting yanked from side to side by the waves lapping away. I swim over to give Trackcrap a hand. We grab Wally by the ankles and the two of us tow him up the sand where we got our beach towels spread around. We plop him there, his face staring up at us even though that cowpoke smile of his had all but disappeared. He seems okay though, nodded his head like he was. Behind us, Wally's body trail ran right next to the staring gal. She looks at us if we were towing a dead body. Staring gal has such a snotty look that I'm about to give her the finger when I notice how good looking she is and that her bikini top can barely cover the load inside. I figure wait, Buff, wait until she turns around then flip her the bird.

Me and Trackcrap take another look at Wally and see his smile is back and that makes us feel better. I notice boob lady has turned away, so I flip her a giant bird, but her husband sees what I'm doing and looks me square in the face and starts to get up. Guy keeps unfolding and unfolding until he's a good ten feet tall, arm with a snake of some kind curled around it, a skull on the side of his neck. He's coming over. I grab Trackcrap, but Trackcrap shakes his head no, so I go by myself and hightail it back to the water.

Twenty minutes go by. As far as we can tell, Wally is still star-gazing just the way he was when we left. Sure as shit he's been into the wine more than we figured. Soon as I say this, I notice busty gal and her giant friend are walking over to where Wally is. They say something to Trackcrap while Trackcrap looks back like a big dope. And that is when the tattooed guy hightails up the sand to the boardwalk and goes looking for something, talking to people, looking around, pointing, acting nutty.

Two minutes go by and a big crowd starts to gather around Wally, busty gal smack in the middle, naturally. Everybody is yelling up at the boardwalk where three guys in a big white truck drive up. The three guys jump out and run around like they are on fire, waiving at busty-lady, dragging shit, dragging their pants through the sand. Trackcrap is still right in the middle of the crowd, crazy lady giving him a car-load of mouth. Suddenly Trackcrap jumps to his feet and comes splashing and yelling right toward us. "They're taking Wally," he says, "They're taking Wally!"

Okay.

Wally lived across the street from Goats. That's how we knew him. Goats was one of the guys I ran around with back in high school, and if Goats came along, Wally did too. Wally was a little bit younger than the rest of us, fifteen maybe, kind of a cracker, talked real fast and was always trying to fit in by acting like he knew everything when he didn't know shit. We picked on him a lot. We'd pants him at school when the girls were around. We even shaved his pecker one time, shaved it in the locker room and scooted him outside without any clothes. God, that was funny. One time we took him into the hills and made him walk home. Stuff like that. But that was okay, he knew we did it 'cause we liked him and 'cause he didn't have no dad like the rest of us. His mom ran his dad off at the point of a gun when Wally was about nine or ten. The dad was an ex-con.

Nobody had parents in those days. Oh, we had moms and dads like everybody else, but they didn't pay much attention to what we were up to, never checked our grades, didn't know who we ran around with, what time we got home, things like that. The only thing that kept us out of jail was the fact that ever cop in town knew us by name. In those days a guy could steal a gumball machine from in front of Pete's Sporting Goods Store, take it home, drain it of its pennies, put it back, and the next time the cops saw you walking to school they'd yell, "Hey, Pecker-head, Pete loses another gumball machine you're headin' for the slammer." They were our real parents in those days, the cops, not mom and dad, the cops.

Wally's Mom worked as a checker down at Jax Market. She was short like Wally, goofy eyed, always smiling and always happy. She was so slow in the head that she had no idea how bad she had it. As I remember the situation back then, the dad was, like I said, not such a bad guy, he was just screwier than his old lady. He was one of those war vets who hadn't given up his foxhole. The guy was always driving around at night in this canvass-backed pickup truck with a star on the side wearing Douglas Macarthur sunglasses and his arm slung out the window. He'd drive around looking for animals to shoot. He'd shoot dogs and cats and possums mostly, but it didn't matter, he just wanted to shoot something with the gun he brought home from the war. Wally says one night, just before his mom ran him off, he shot up a boxcar full of cows heading for the slaughterhouse. Spent six weeks in the can for it. Says his old man never had a real job, all he did was sit in the backyard regrooving bald tires with a soldering iron. He'd sell 'em for five bucks apiece. Pay maybe a buck fifty for some old worn outs, then sit in the garage and carve wavy grooves in them. He'd shine 'em up and spray paint 'em and sell 'em to the tire store.

And here's something else. Wally told us about how his mom got split in half the day he was born. Said his mom was too tiny for Wally's big head so they slit her in half. Not the belly like you might think, but down where Wally was supposed to come out. That's why she wobbles when she walks, cause the doctor cut her a big smile between her legs, probably the reason Wally's old man was always so damned mean.

Fact is, Wally's mom did wobble a lot, wobbled the way you would if you was holding a melon between your legs, sort of penguin like, like one of those wind-up toys you see at the store. Funny like.

We called her penguin. Wally did too. She was all right though, a little sappy, but all right, always sneaking us kids candy bars when we came around to where she worked, liquorish sticks from this big plastic jar, sodas too, that was when Walt, the owner, wasn't around. I think she was hoping to make Wally popular with guys, like us, hoping he would fit in someplace, anyplace, you know, have a gang to hang with, even if that gang was a bunch of shit-heads, like us.

I hear Wally's mom wound up in the nut house after she heard about Wally, but I don't know. Heard she went to Norwalk after he took that famous tumble down by the pier. Wouldn't doubt it. Sad, 'cause Wally was her whole life.

Anyway, as for what happened after the ambulance went screaming down Highway 39 with Wally tied to a stretcher in back. Us guys hung around for another hour of so talking to a few people who had seen what happened, answering a few questions and dodging a few others. But this married couple who called 911, they were really pissed at us, pissed 'cause we let our friend lie on the beach when we should have been screaming our heads off. Said we were a bunch of creeps and no-goods, that we ought to be thrown in jail for leaving him lying there. What they really wanted was for the police to arrest us. "Drunk as sailors," the buxom wife told the four cops standing around listening to her shouting and pointing at us six dopes. And to prove what she said was true, she kicked one of the empty Ripple bottles we'd been drinking from and sent it sailing across the sand. Cops didn't care, they was too busy looking down her swimsuit.

Truth is, we had been drinking all that morning, that is, all but Trackcrap and Wally, they never drank anything but Cokes and the Kool Aid Mrs. Wally sent along, Trackcrap being such a super-duper track star and Wally a pie-eyed sixteen. Even if Wally wanted to take a drink, which he didn't, us guys wouldn't let him, it'd be like turning a ten-year-old over to a whore, and that didn't seem right somehow. But for the rest of us, the Ripple was pretty much gone by the time we caught our first wave and Wally had taken his tumble and the cops showed up wondering what to do with us kids. I suspect our brains had been dulled to the point where we were a little confused and probably didn't know up from down.

We sat around for the next hour or so, me, Trackcrap, Goats, Sealbold, Fanch and Stonewall, twiddling our feet in the sand with our heads buried between our knees, all of us privately morning over poor Wally and wondering what was going to happen to him and thanking the good lord that it was him screaming down the highway and not one of us. The cops, they didn't know what to do with us; couldn't figure out whether we were grieving over our poor friend or suffering the effects of too much wine. Either way they hung around their police cars for a while, radio squawking signals they couldn't understand, the four of them fighting among themselves for the attention of a blond lady-officer who suddenly become the center of attention. Pretty soon they all drove away. And we did too, right after they did, Wallyless of course, and a waterlogged one-ton surfboard riding on top the car.

I didn't see Wally after that. Goats went to see him in the hospital a few times, but the rest of didn't. His memory sort of faded away.

I got married, completed college, which took the world by surprise, was in the throughs of producing a house-full of children when, one day, as I was driving along the Santa Monica Freeway looking at a few sites our company (Empire Food Supermarkets) was considering for a future location, I happened to notice a sign out of the corner of my eye. It read: Los Angeles County Orthopedic Hospital, Palms Division. I thought… Wally. The name: Palms Division rang a bell. Could it be? I thought… Wally?

It took a few minutes before I decided to see if my memory was correct, to see if Wally was, in fact, where people said he was. He was. The girl at the desk grinned real big and said, "Sure. Mr. Wally is in 214. I'll take you up." She seemed delighted that someone had come to see him.

On his back unable to move, a concertina-type contraption serenading up and down on his chest, Wally looked at me by way of a mirror hanging just above his head, a smile as big as Broadway filling it. "Hey, Buff. Man, I can't believe it. You come to see me." Funny, all these years and all that the poor guy had gone through and I could still see how he deferred to me as an upper-classmate of his. Jesus.

"How you doing?" I asked, trying to sound unaffected by the morbidity of the place, the contraption on his chest see-sawing away. I don't mind telling you, the place gave me the creeps.

"Good. Real good."

"Great. Treating you okay?" How stupid was that?

"Never better."

"How long you been here, Tull?" An even stupider remark.

"Since the accident, nine years now."

"Since the accident. Huh. Really? That long?"

Since the accident, he says. Christ almighty. The poor bastard has been lying there rotting like a carrot for nine years and I've been floating through life like a daisy on a stick.

"So, what's the chance," I asked, stupidly?

"Chance for what?"

"Getting out of this place?"

"Oh, I suppose they'll let me out when I die." And he laughs.

It was like any other Monday morning that Wally took his giant header into the sand and stuck there like a dart in a dart board. His lucky Monday morning. Not the usual Monday morning of ditching chores and hanging around the neighborhood with nothing to do. It was a beach Monday and that was a lucky Monday for a kid like Wally and me and Goats and the rest of us, grab your bathing suit and crowd into the backseat and head for the beach, Monday, rabbit punches and crotch grabbing and Highway 39 all the way to where pier meets sand, Monday. This was a July Monday, a wet and foggy Monday morning, a sand in your face Monday morning, a water breaking over your head, bottom meets the top, shells, rocks, bits of bone, white, lots and lots of white, nothing but white, the world turning white, two-dimensional white kind of Monday morning. That's the kind of Monday I am talking about, a lucky Monday for a kid named Wally.

I went home that night and told my wife about it, told her about our conversation and how I struggled for something meaningful in what I saw at the hospital, about trying to make some truth out of our conversation, how I bobbed and weaved hoping to avoid saying the wrong thing and doing exactly that. I told her about the grim feel of the place and how the bellows rode his chest and pumped air into his lungs and how hot it was and how I couldn't wait to get the hell out of there. She listened. She even wept.

Like me, Jeanie remembered Wally as a kid riding on the fringes of life, never the center, but out there, around, in the background, like a bit player in a play or an extra in a movie, a stick-figure in a color cartoon, an electron buzzing around the nucleus. And as we cried over the kid we both knew growing up, our thoughts turning to Wally for a few precious moments, each of us imagining his awful existence, the silly accident, the destruction of an innocent life, tragic and sordid memories of Wally crowded into a single moment in time. Still it was only for a moment that we did so, one stupid, lousy moment instead of a lifetime of moments, as the poor kid deserved. We didn't caress it or memorialize it or sanctify it the way we should have, the way his screwball mother must have done as she wriggled and wobbled the aisles of the insane-asylum where she ended up after Wally took his header. No, we allowed his memory to fade into the distance as it always had in the past, slowly in the distance yet ebbing like water upon the shore, receding into the whiteness of nothing, horrid, existential, tragic, the memory fading, fading into the whiteness of nothing.

God rolled the dice with Wally that day and it came up craps. Why God in all his wisdom and grace would do such a thing to such a nice kid, or slanting it another way, allow it to happen to such a nice kid, is one reason the guy who writes these words keeps an ax to grind with the man upstairs. My friend Wally had risen higher than he had ever risen before. And God plunged him into the ground like a human projectile. Why? Why should God choose Wally of all people? Why should God choose a kid who lived on the fringe of life when he could have chosen someone like me? Or Skinny? Or Fanch. Or any of the billions of miscreants he stamps out in his eternal search for perfection? But then is it possible to know the mind of the master? Shrill, evocative, meaningless, God, nature, chance, oblivion. How does one go about explaining the randomness surrounding us, the suffering of innocents?

But the memory of Wally is always there, vaguely and fleeting, but there. And it will always be there, hidden of course, but there, always there, always searching for a place to hide inside my brain so it can't be traced or recovered, unless chance requires it to recover, as it has done this day by the slimmest of chance. Cryptic, coded, codified, the memory hides.

It hides

It hides...

LOST AT SEA

"**M**rs. Foxly? Hi. Gel Shakespeare here." The man on the porch pulled a toothpick from between his teeth and tossed it aside. His hand shot through the open doorway. "My secretary called. Clair?"

Seeing the enormity standing in front of her, the woman drew back. Surly this is not the man from the insurance company, she thought to herself. Where is the brown leather briefcase, the blue suit and tie, the Ford Fairlane parked in the drive?

Ignoring the clumsy hand waiving in front of her, the woman studied the man carefully. She examined the broad round shoulders, the enormous oval face, the too-chummy smile, the beefy waist, the smooth white hand trying to link up with hers. After looking him over, she began to take a more balanced assessment of the man on the porch, examining his appearance, the boyish innocence. She cracked the door a bit wider as the avalanche began to melt.

Gathering herself, she rocked her slender body onto her heels and swung the door open wide, reluctantly taking the oafish hand in hers as the man's too-chummy smile grinned with satisfaction. But there was that toothpick resting in her planter.

She straightened her dress and inexplicably found herself standing on her toes.

"My secretary. You remember? About your husband," boldly taking a step forward. The lady pulled her hand free and began to creak the door closed.

The man quickly grabbed inside his shirt pocket and retrieved a business card and thrust it at the lady. "Whoa-hey. Hold on a second."

With the door half closed, the lady took a quick look into the yard where a bright red Ferrari sat with its nose brushing against her favorite azalea plants, its snout poking at the tender young blooms she spent half the morning grooming. Looking more closely she detected what appeared to be a cloud of blue smoke drifting from under its hood.

Taking the card, she dropped to her normal height and opened the door a bit more. "Ah, yes, Clair," she said, somewhat relieved. "Your secretary was very nice when she called."

She relaxed and examined the card. As she scoured the fleshy round face grinning from its great height, she began to reconsider the situation. It was then that she noticed something peculiar about the business card in her hand. There was only a name, Gel Shakespeare, written on it. And a phone number but nothing else. Once again, her eyes examined the human wreckage standing there. Suspicious, intimidating, but there he was. And he was rather handsome, in a brutish sort of way. And she was expecting someone from the insurance company. Still…

"I notice there is no mention of your company…."

The next thing she knew the man was practically shoving his way into the house, brushing her aside like a migrating elephant … not brushing so much as banging her so that she practically fell to the floor, or stumbled, or… but then again she couldn't be sure if she stumbled or was thrown aside but either way she found herself staggering across the room in a daze of confusion, righting and pulling herself together just in time to see that the beast was resting comfortably inside the house.

Her dread turned to panic. What had she done by allowing this Mt. Rushmore person to barge into her home so casually?

She turned and looked at the grinning hulk who appeared to be laughing down her blouse, his fleshy green eyes already man-handling her body. It was then that she caught a glimpse of his clothing, the faded jeans, the frayed hems, knees shiny from use, the Mercedes Benz hood ornament pretending to be a belt buckle, sunglasses dangling from the top of an ordinary T-shirt, Ferrari jacket draped casually over his shoulder, yellow emblems racing up and down the sleeves. She watched as he tossed the jacket over the back of the nearest chair, her sacred 18th century chair that nobody but her had so much as touched.

"Sorry about the time," he said, grabbing her hand and pumping it was if trying to make water rise. "Tried to get here as soon as I could but… Jesus H. Christ, got one speeding ticket already this year." He shrugged and grinned a too-white grin, releasing his grip while staring so uncomfortably close that she felt as if she were sitting in a movie theater.

And that is when it hit her, the loose-flowing mane pulled into ponytail, a rubber band securing it in place. Somehow, she had missed the ponytail. My God, she thought, it's Fabio.

"And where I'm parked…" He glanced through the glass sidelight to his still smoking sports car… "Jesus H….., hope I didn't…"

"No… no, that's cool." Oh God, she didn't. She actually used the word cool. She quickly snapped her eyes at the department store sized face hoping he didn't notice.

"Would you care for some coffee," she asked, trying to sound more adult than she felt at the moment."

"Naaah, don't drink the stuff. Tea's good." He noticed the blank stare. "England. Scotland. Spent some time in both. You and the Mr. travel a bit?"

The mention of her late husband caused her to stiffen. How rude, she thought, opening the subject of her late husband the minute he walks into the house.

"England is one place we have no interest in visiting," she said. And before he could interrupt she changed the subject. "I'll make us some tea."

Mrs. Foxly went into the kitchen and pulled a package from the pantry shelf, taking a teabag and placing it in a cup.

"What are you doing," he asked, standing in the entryway surveying her every move. "Tea comes in these little tins…you…" She wavered. "No… never mind. Didn't want it anyway. I was just being polite."

Mrs. Foxly put the teabag back inside the carton and returned it to the shelf. Shocked by his behavior, she banged the pantry door shut and turned to notice how his eyes were surveying the entire house, jumping from item to item like hailstones on a roof. What was he doing, she wondered, watching him plunder her earthly possessions? Then, to her surprise, the hulk lurched from the entry and into the family room where he stood with his mammoth legs angling apart gazing across the swimming pool to the canyons and hillsides in the distance. "Wow, some place you got here," he bellowed. "And look at that view. That a golf course?"

"Yes… it is," she said, her irritation building. "Coyote Hills. About ten years now." The man brought no briefcase and no notepad, not even the dreaded recording device all the others had insisted on bringing. His uncivilized effrontery caused her wonder if the man was in possession of his senses. Then, just as she was about to suggest they go into the kitchen, he plopped his fanny onto the sofa and spilled his long, powerful legs across the floor, the way her three sons had done when they came home from college. "Please, make yourself comfortable," she said, annoyed.

"Right." Gel placed his hands behind his head and smiled broadly. "Not what you expected, huh?"

"What?"

His hands scanned his body. "You know, blue suit, tie, rental car, briefcase."

Mrs. Foxly blinked. "Well, you are a little younger than…and that car you drove up in…"

Gel interrupted, "Ferrari, 87, Dino. Drips a little oil, that's why I parked it where I did." He looked around. "Say, those your kids?" He jumped to his feet and walked the short distance to the fireplace where a cluster of family photos were neatly arranged along a series of shelves, Mrs. Foxly's history spilled like trophies along the mantle.

"Actually, those are my grandchildren," she said, resenting the way he so easily manhandled them. "The ones above are my children; they're in their thirties now," aware that the older two were well into their forties.

"You don't say." Gel lifted a pewter framed photograph of Mrs. Foxly and what he presumed to be her only daughter, Nancy. He studied the picture too long for her comfort, almost brushing his nose against the glass. When he was done studying the picture he looked up. "This your daughter beside you?" he asked." She nodded. "Real looker. Kind of like her old lady." He smiled and put it back with a clack. "Don't mind telling you Mrs. Foxly, you are not what I expected either."

"That so?"

To annoy her further, Gel practically dove onto the sofa and folded his hands behind his head. "Well, this is nice," he said, snuggling his fanny between a pair of expensive throw pillows. "Been reading your file for about a week now. Sort of get an image of someone when you spend as much time as I have reading their history. Figured you as the Barbara Bush type, Aunt Bea maybe, you know, grandma in a smock. Turned out I was wrong. You're quite a plumb."

Mrs. Foxly stiffened. How was she to respond to such rude behavior, having just arrived and referring to her as a plumb? Still…

"What I am interested in is how a representative of a major insurance company drives a red sports car. And why…."

"Pony tail you mean?" Seeing her annoyance build, he laughed and snuggled deeper into the cushions. "Suppose I sort of misrepresented myself with that phone call, didn't I? Truth of the matter is, I don't work for Bountiful. Used to; not anymore. Use their letterhead sometimes, my way of getting a foot in the door." He grinned a toothy grin, which reminded Mrs. Foxly of the frat boys her daughter used to bring home.

"Truth is, I'm a consultant. Think Magnum P.I. and you'll get the picture. Even got the car. Course…" He paused, "Ah, but that's another story for another time. Don't want to bore you with the details of my job, it's not nearly as exciting as it appears on TV, mostly writing reports and filing them with the big boys up in LA. Gotta have something to back up what they do case the stockholders get all riled up." He was getting to the point. "Anyway," and for the first time since arriving Mr. Shakespeare was beginning to fumble for words, "here's the deal. Big cases like yours… they take special handling. In this case… hey." Gel's eyes had been wondering throughout the house ever since he arrived, a fact that bothered her and made her suspicious of his actions. Now they had taken flight again but this time they had landed on something that brought him out of his chair. He jumped up and sprang to the same group of pictures he had been eying before. "Didn't notice this one. This one of your kids?" he asked, excitedly holding a photograph of Eddie standing next to a purple Porsche 911. In the photograph Eddie is wearing a racer's jumpsuit and holding a helmet against his side.

"Yes, that's our… that's my oldest son, Eddie. He used to race at Riverside."

"That right? Jesus H. Christ, bet I've run into him before. Damn good-looking machine he's got there. Still race?"

"No, motorcycles sometimes. Eddie keeps the Porsche, but he's given up racing." Gel stood admiring the picture then set it down with another whack. Before he turned away he looked at the single photo that caused him to jump from his chair in the first place, the one of Mr. Foxly standing with his arm slung around one of his sons. Next to it was another photo in which Mr. Foxly is seen holding a large fish up to the camera, a trout. Gel observed the two photos knowing from his own experience that the fish was probably a rainbow, the largest he had ever seen. A river was in the background. "Nice shots," he said, referring to both. "This Ed... I mean Ed Senior?"

"Yes. That's Ed and Greg. It was taken on one of his trips to Oregon."

"Oh, that's right, Greg lives in Oregon, doesn't he?" A fact he knew well. "Looks recent."

"Last year."

"Bet you're proud of them, your children that is." He paused then said, "Mmmm... you must have taken this one, referring to the one of her husband and Greg together."

"Why no. I never accompany my husband on his fishing expeditions, even when they included my children."

"Wonder who took it then."

"I don't know, could have been anybody, another fisherman perhaps."

"Yeah, another fisherman... probably." Gel glanced at the woman sitting uncomfortably with her legs positioned just so. "I see why you are so proud of your children. Nice brood."

Yes," she said, ignoring the word brood, "very proud. And so was their father. The last thing my husband would do is give up his family, as I am sure you are aware." Mrs. Foxly glared as she said this. Gel returned to his place on the couch and squished back down, this time almost reclining with a pillow behind his head and the other under his arm. Mrs. Foxly was furious. A few uncomfortable seconds passed before Mrs. Foxly realized she couldn't stand it anymore and let go.

"Just what is it you want to know, Mr. Shakespeare? Certainly, you are not here to fawn over my family? Besides, I've already told everything I know to the others. And would you kindly remove your grimy head from my pillow." Gel complied by yanking it away and slinging it onto a neighboring chair. "It seems to me that you people are intent on harassing me… and why they sent a hired gun to do their dirty work is beyond my comprehension; it's disgusting, especially given the circumstances. And that comment you made…"

"What comment?"

"Calling me a plumb."

"Call 'em as I see 'em."

"Really. Well I don't see how the people at Bountiful can…possibly…"

"You're referring to those bozo's down at the office. Christ almighty, Mrs. Foxly, I don't know where they get those guys. Most of 'em couldn't find their way to the car without a road map. Me… all I do is polish reports a little and that's about it, fill in a few blanks and, 'wham', check's in the mail. Last in line, that's me. Fact is, I'm on your side, Mrs. Foxly," he stopped, "can I call you Jonell?" And without waiting for an answer he zoomed on, "Sooner you get your money, Jonell the better. We're all riding in the same 'boat'." Realizing his reference to a boat and the emphasis he placed on the word, Gel waited for a response. Evidently, she had missed it.

"This is nonsense," she said, her anger building. "The company knows what happened that day and they've known it for months. You've read the file; you know there is only one explanation for what happened. My God, they've turned my house into an amusement park the way they went around digging into my personal life, the Fullerton police, the Newport police, the coast guard, my family, my husband's friends. And you sit there with your stupid ponytail like some biker-dude."

"Hey."

"Presuming to tell me we're on the same side. You've got to be kidding. We're not even on the same side of the street, Mr. Shakespeare. And I am beginning to think we are not even from the same planet. What is wrong with you people, coming into my house torturing me like this? A few months and all you think about is money. Keep your God damned money for all I care." Her language surprised him. "I…I know people like you, you'd drive a woman crazy before you'd shell out a dime."

Gel sat smiling, totally unfazed by the outburst. "Five million is a lot more than a dime, Jonell. And that was a cheap shot about my ponytail….?"

"I don't care if it's five billion. There has to be an end to this interrogation of yours… this…this checking into every cranny you can think of… like

I'm…I'm some kind of common criminal or something. And the money, I don't need your stupid money. I don't need a penny of it."

"Oh, I think you do."

"What?" Mrs. Foxly sat stunned by the insinuation. "Me want your money? How dare you come into my home and suggest something like that… me clamor for your lousy five million. Why… I… I have never asked for anything in my life and you know it. It's you… it's you who keeps investigating… that silly probing you're always doing, asking questions behind my back. Haven't I always cooperated? Have you ever seen me refuse a question? Have I ever brought in an attorney?

"Mr. Stewart knows of our meeting. He approved it. And he advised you to cooperate fully. Isn't that right?" Seeing that he had her, he sat chuckling at his own cleverness, "You bet it is."

Gel Shakespeare. Private insurance investigator. One of the best, at least that is the way *Insurance Weekly* reported it in their January 2002 issue, detailing how Shakespeare and Company had become the *avant-garde* in the rapidly growing investigative industry. Three years at Northwestern University with mountains of praise yet no degree was ever recorded. Gel spent another year at the University of Hamburg, but his restless nature got the best of him and he was soon cascading all over the globe, tramping over Europe and through most of southern Asia before his money ran out and Gel was forced to take a job aboard a cruise ship working as a steward. But it was a bout with malaria that caused Gel to finally settle down so that one day, several years later, he found himself interviewing for a job with Bountiful Life and Casualty. Then, three and a half years later he was lancing on his own and that is when Shakespeare and Company came into being, financed on a shoelace and twenty-five hundred dollars won at the racetrack. Today Gel Shakespeare is a one-thousand-dollar-an-hour private dick with a secretary and an office at Newport Center, California. He owns a cell-phone, a Cessna 414 airplane, and a passion for sports cars and all things fast.

And he is good. The Starling case for example. Gel saved his client a cool three-million when the fire at the paint factory proved arson, just as he had suspected it was. And that drug addicted son who made off with the family jewels, that netted another client, Guarded Life and Casualty, one and a half million.

And now this, another in the chain of curious mysteries given him by a company nearing the end of its rope, one last look at the details of a man's sudden disappearance and apparent demise. They had called because their investigation had burned to an end, and yet smoldering issues remained, certain troubling questions concerning the man's state of mind the day he had disappeared over the side of his boat. Would Gel take a look? So, Gel ran through the folders as his roving eyes widened with interest. He wanted two weeks, that's all it would take. If he couldn't turn something up in two weeks he'd go pro-bono, no fee, no nothing. But if he did, if his probing and sometimes questionable tactics uncovered something of value, if the company were able to prove that it owed the client nothing due to his investigative endeavors, his turning up some small shred of evidence to suggest that the supposed accident was in fact not an accident but a planned affair on the part of the missing client or accomplice, suicide being the most likely, then Gel would receive his standard fee: 30%, or one half a million dollars. All or nothing in other words, he'd either ferret out a plausible suicide or he'd move on.

Edward Foxly. Sixty-three years of age the day he disappeared.

It was the preceding October that Mr. Foxly vanished while fishing alone off the coast of Southern California. He and his wife were reported to be the typical, happily married couple with no prior divorces, no known affairs, no violence and only routine spats reported by certain members of the family, the children in particular. Those members are: four children, the oldest, a daughter, Nancy, and three boys, Ed, Pete and Greg. The missing person had sold his real estate development business ten years before his disappearance, and, as one might expect, his life had slowed considerably since the day he retired. Things appeared normal until a business setback some years later changed Mr. Foxly's outlook on life.

It was during a routine investigation by one of Mr. Foxly's shopping center tenants that toxic chemicals were discovered in their building. The subsequent cleanup and the financial burden suffered by the loss of business came close to bankrupting him.

Passion for the outdoors carried him through however, fishing, biking, solitary rounds of golf. A small office behind Mr. Foxly's house is where he wrote certain fictional accounts of his past, that and assorted philosophical essays, about what exactly, few people know, although one book of short stories was published two years before his disappearance, one that Gel had read and carries with him in his investigation.

It was this narrowing of life, this financial collapse by a successful entrepreneur that brought Gel into the case in the first place. It is why he now sits sprawled on the late man's sofa trying to resolve the puzzling facts surrounding the sudden disappearance of what was believed to be a prosperous and happily married man.

To Gel and from what he read between the covers of those manila folders given him by Bountiful, Mr. Foxly had evidently turned inward since retiring a few years before. In the reports, an investigator by the name of Robert Crookshank had gone so far as to say Mr. Foxly had become a recluse during his retirement and that he spent days holed up in his office behind the house, rarely coming out and rarely talking to anyone but his wife. Accordingly, the man had become introspective and circumspect and spent much of his time writing weird, sordid and extremely depressing stories, some of which reflected curiously upon his personal affairs. What was his state of mind the day he disappeared Gel wanted to know? Accident? Something else? If so, what?

Yes, it was this consistency of theme that bore the man out, at least that is what Gel thought as he poured over the man's file, a certain morbidity of mood, a drift toward seclusion, secretive, reclusive, unsociable, the shift in personality, friends turning bothersome, fishing alone, golfing alone; it all added up, there was something peculiar about this Mr. Foxly character and he wanted to know what it was.

"Just how old are you, Mr. Shakespeare," her mood still combative.

"Thirty-four," he shot back. "And you Jonell, what are you now?" She blinked. "How's sixty-one sound, sixty-two this October? Middle of the month, 11th I believe. Born Los Angeles, 43. Catholic schooling. Graduated Buena Park high, 61. Married at 18. First child at 22. Mother, wife, grandmother.

"Very good, Mr. Shakespeare, I'm impressed."

"Starbuck's, Nordstrom's, chocolate, broccoli, your family, all things you love. Treadmill for an hour each day. Parents dead. No health issues. Irregular heartbeat back in the seventies. Tough cookie."

"Again impressed."

"You should be. Spent the better part of a week learning about you and your husband, a lot of it spilling onto your family, of course. But the more I learn about the man, your husband…"

"Late husband."

"Yes. Late husband. The more I learn about your late husband, the more I can't figure out. And," Gel leaned forward, "that's where you come in, Jonell, I need your help. I want to understand the man you married."

"That's a joke."

"Seriously, What I need you to do is to tell me as objectively as you can, if such a thing is possible," and he laughs, "all you can, especially the last few years. Sort of profile the guy for me."

"Why? To prove that he leaped over the side? That he was depressed? Better yet, crazy? You've got to be kidding."

Gel saw it coming. "To learn the truth."

"The truth is he fell, he didn't jump."

"You've read the stories?"

"Oh, please."

"The one called, *Star Counting*? You've read it. It was in his book, a perfect account of a middle-aged man taking his life at sea. Sitting on the boat's swim-step… just off the coast of Catalina, right? The man putting a gun to his head. Certainly, you've read it."

"No, he told me about it though. Morbid tales don't interest me."

"And another one. *Dark Blue*. Rough seas, a son over the side too exhausted to climb back on board, the drifting boat, the desperate father. And what does the father do as the boy slips under for the last time? He attempts to snag the poor kid with a fishing gaff. I mean, really, what kind of mind writes stuff like that?"

"Trying to prove my husband insane won't work. He wasn't insane. He fell."

"I've put to memory the final lines of a poem of his. Here, I've got it right here in my pocket." Gel rocked forward, reaching into his back pocket pulling out a wallet stuffed with material and bits of paper with writing on them. Currency spewed from the sides and what looked like a credit card dropped to the floor. He quickly found a yellow slip of paper and began reading from it, the credit card still lying on the floor. "What do you make of this little gem?"

A star. A star.

Living as a star, dying as a star, dissolving as a star.

Thereto lies my destiny? My brotherhood? My being?

Jonell only shrugged. "You didn't know my husband, Mr. Shakespeare.

Gel sat quietly while she went through the clumsy process of gathering herself. "You misunderstand me Jonell. I believe you. He fell. He wasn't pushed, didn't jump, didn't run away. He fell. Tragically, he fell. He fell while out fishing. That's what the report in my car is leaning toward anyway. And that is what I am leaning toward too. So how about helping me prove it. Let's you and me get rid of the doubt and…" Gel leaned back and folded his hands behind his head. "You know what this is all about, don't you, Jonell?" her eyes red from rubbing them. "That missing person report? That's what had Bounty all riled up. Missing person it said; not lost at sea the way it should have been. And that is precisely why they called me in at the last minute, to try and figure out what happened that day, at least to ease their mind as to other possibilities. Fact is you need me, Jonell. I'm not the enemy; I'm not one of those stiffs down at the office; it's not my money they're giving away, it's…" Gel rocked forward and grinned, "And no pen, it's all right here," he said, pointing to his head, "like Mr. F's poem, it's all right here."

Mrs. Foxly cocked her head to one side, bewildered and slightly amused at the man's sudden attempt at sincerity, phony though it was. A smile crossed her lips as she contemplated this giant sitting before her, this Shakespeare person, this ponytailed private dick trying his damnedest to steal what was rightfully hers.

They hadn't slept together in years. But he knew all that. In fact, they knew every detail concerning their cohabitation practices, about their tiffs, about Ed spending a night at a hotel, about her spending a night at a hotel. They even insisted on seeing his bedroom. That was the day they came ransacking the house and tearing his garage apart, his office, his files, his computer. My God, you would have thought the man was a murderer.

Yes, right after he retired, if retired is what is what you call it when a man gives up his entire identity, a career built over a lifetime of diligence and hard work. Ten years of not working, that was the result of losing an identity. And that's when it all started, the restlessness, the anxiety, the irritability, the insomnia, the midlife adjustments, the normal effects of a man retiring so early in life. At least that is what she believed.

But it was more than midlife adjustments, and she knew it. There were nights when she would awaken and find her husband roaming the house like a lost soul. One night, in particular, she remembers waking up and there he was staring blankly into her face. Not lying next to her but over her, standing over her, bent over and staring right into her face. It scared her to death. Soon it became the TV, the family room buzzing away at all hours with lights flickering down the hall. And then the nights his car could be heard backing down the drive. She would lie awake for what seemed like hours waiting… waiting, until finally, sometimes it was only minutes but mostly it was hours before she'd see the car headlights gliding somberly across the room and then the garage door swinging open and then the sound of a door being locked and that's when she knew he would eventually find his way back into bed.

But there came a time when she would wake up in morning and he wouldn't be there at all. Instead she'd find him in a chair someplace in the house, or curled up on the coach, or riding atop one of the children's beds with a comforter wrapped over him. Then, after a year or two, he was never there, not even those first few moments when he seemed to be at peace with the world, those moments when he would lie quietly next to her until he knew she was asleep, and it was then, after she was asleep that the terrible something would rise up inside of him and he would slip quietly from between the covers and the nightly prowl would begin.

But he was gone now. Those days were over. It was her footsteps that prowled through the house and not his, her footsteps that silently slipped down the hall to the empty room where his latest book lay on the nightstand beside his bed, the bookmark still peeking from the same location it had the night he didn't come home, the TV with its stupid rabbit-ears flopped exactly the way he liked them, split helter-skelter and sideways, the right one drooping to the floor so he could watch the late night news through the snowstorm that never went away.

"I think we should go into the kitchen," she said. "It's better there. And I'll make something to drink. Not tea," and she laughed. As she turned and walked into the kitchen, Gel quickly got up and walked to where he had seen the pictures on the shelf and plucked one from it. He shoved the picture inside the jacket he left lying on the chair, grinning to himself as he followed her into the kitchen.

It was a late Wednesday afternoon that Mr. Foxly's 34-foot sport fisher *Slam Dunk* was found more than 250 miles south-west of Catalina Island motoring at a speed of eight knots. Earlier that morning he had been reported missing by the Newport Beach Police Department. Within minutes the California Coast Guard had set to work to find the missing person. Almost miraculously, a plane spotted the craft four hours later positioned well into international waters. A coast guard cutter was dispatched to the location.

When the coast guard boarded the vessel about 4:00 pm that evening they found no one on board. The auto-pilot had been set to a heading of 201 degrees and both transmissions were fully engaged. When the crew first climbed aboard the vessel they noted that each of the four fishing rods were still in place and were trolling lures behind the moving boat, except two, the two on the port side which had been stripped of their line. The missing line, they concluded, was the probable result of the lures becoming entangled with a piece of floating kelp or a fish had taken hold of them. The crew shut the two engines down and noticed how only eight gallons of fuel remained in the tanks. It was further reported that the stereo had been set to station 100.7 with the volume barely audible. Most of the bait in the bait-tank was dead and a fillet knife lay bloodied on the tackle center.

Below, in the tiny galley, there was evidence of food having been prepared on the cutting board and the trash container held an empty Diet Coke can, a crumpled Frito bag, a cookie, several bits of tomato and several soiled paper towels, all of which lead the investigators to presume that Mr. Foxly was still aboard when he consumed his lunch. Reversing the 201 heading and calculating a speed of 8 knots, and further estimating the available fuel that would have been carried when the vessel left the dock at about 5:15am the previous morning, a fact witnessed by one other boat preparing to leave the dock at that hour, and confirmed by the manager of the bait barge where Mr. Foxly was reported to have purchased a scoop of live bait at about 5:30AM, the same person who would testify that Mr. Foxly was the only person on board that morning, it was presumed that Mr. Foxly fell overboard at about 11:00 AM on Tuesday, October 16th, and did so in an area just off and near the middle of Catalina Island. The reasons he fell are not noted.

This is the list of possibilities Gel made after completing his review.

1. Accident. Most probable cause of Mr. Foxly's disappearance. The boat was still underway when recovered by the coast guard. All physical evidence supports this theory. Rarely is a body recovered when lost at sea. It is assumed the body was consumed by predators or drifted seaward, therefore recovery unlikely.
2. Suicide. Possible cause of Mr. Foxly disappearance. Deteriorating state of mind supports this view. Note comments made by family and friends in Met report. No predisposition however. No apparent reason other than depressed over recent setbacks. Money a factor? A motive?
3. Foul play. Highly unlikely. While piracy can occur on the open sea, it is rare. Nothing of value was taken.
4. Abduction. No follow through by abductors. Not likely.
5. Fed up. This would presume Mr. Foxly is still alive and his disappearance a ruse. Possible though unlikely. Nothing was taken with him. No money removed from bank accounts, CD's, treasury bills, and misc. bonds. No clothing taken. Automobile parked at dock. How did he get off the moving boat? An accomplice? Who? Unlikely.
6. Lover. Again a ruse. Love presupposes another life, another woman. Again no money had been taken. History shows no past lovers and a stable marriage. Socially unacceptable. Unlikely.
7. Paranoia. No evidence. Unlikely.

8. Timing. Why now? A skeleton about to be revealed? Cancer? Marriage difficulties? Number 2 is the only clue. Questionable.
9. Scheme. To fleece client of five million dollars. Presumes Mr. Foxly is alive. Mrs. Foxly an accomplice? Finances shaky however. No history of larceny. Out of character. Possible but unlikely.

Mrs. Foxly found herself sitting on a kitchen stool chatting over cocoa flavored coffee and ginger snaps. Gel had spotted the ginger snaps in the pantry and had taken them from the shelf without asking. He sat across with his elbows resting on the table, munching and slurping like a teenager. Whether it was done to annoy her or just part of his abrasive manner she couldn't tell.

"Well Mr. Shakespeare, where should I begin?" she said, amused rather than angered about his table manners. She had always enjoyed her children's friends coming over and making themselves at home, eating from the refrigerator, falling asleep on the floor in front of the TV, even dropping by to use the toilet, as Pete's high school friend, Greg Wilber, used to do. "You want to know where he was born, things like that?"

"I understand you met in high school?"

"You want to go all the way back to high school?" He nodded. "Okay. Met in high school. I was a sophomore; he was a senior. Love at first sight, at least that's what he called it. There was the usual dating thing, a couple of years; then came Las Vegas. I was still eighteen, he was just twenty-one... we had no money to speak of, not really, a couple of hundred maybe, I had a job at a savings and loan, and he was," she hesitated, "I think he was still working for Autonetics back then, one of those cold-war aero-space companies over in Anahiem. He lost his job and that's when he decided to go back to college. I got pregnant with Nancy during his last year; she was the first you might recall, and it was then that we inherited a little money from his great uncle. It wasn't much, just enough to hold us over until Ed graduated and got a job."

"And that's what started him in the real estate business, that first job. It was with a supermarket chain called Empire Food. They hired him as a real estate analyst; Empire Food was looking for someone to help locate new sites for them, do the research, that sort of thing. And it was while he was at Empire Food that he met his future partner, the guy I'm sure you know all about, Ron Macalister."

"Yeah, I want to get into that."

"He and Ron were pretty close in the beginning; used to ride motorcycles together…"

Gel's eyes widened. "Hey, that's something I didn't know."

"Oh yeah, raced a little motocross, desert too. They hooked up and started the company that later became Diversified Shopping Centers. Ed had 25% and Ron 75%. It was just the two of them with a secretary and a part time accountant. Our kids have no idea how we lived back then, seven hundred a month, if you can believe it. Even now I wonder how we survived. But Ed did okay and over the years things got better and we got to the point that we could take the kids on vacation, buy some furniture. Then we bought the house we're now sitting in." As she looked over the room with its dented doorways and path worn floors, Gel couldn't help but notice the dampness returning to the corners of her eye. "You wouldn't believe how hard it was those first few years, such a big house, such a big yard and nothing to fill it with except hard work and a piggybank savings account. But we were so excited about moving here, no furniture, no money to buy it with. For years the place looked like a warehouse."

"So how did things turn around, I mean, by the looks of things Ed did all right."

"Took a long time for Diversified to become a player in the business, years; success doesn't just fall from the sky, you know. Have to pay your dues. And Ed paid his. But finally, he and Ron got to the point where they created enough capital to hold onto what they developed and not be forced to sell. And that is when we started making a little money, by actually owning some of what Ed was able to create. By the early 90's he and Ron owned seven shopping centers together."

"And that is when he retired?"

"If that's what you want to call it."

"What do you call it?"

"You've heard the story?"

"Not from you I haven't."

She looked at the cup sitting in front of him. "There must be something I can get you, Mr. Shakespeare, milk, water maybe?"

"Tea would be good," he said, then catching himself he quickly added… "No… no, I'm fine. Go on, what happened with the partner."

"It was about ten years ago. Truthfully, Ed had given early retirement a lot of thought. Fatigue was setting in and he was slowing his pace a little, the stress thing. There was that episode back in his thirties…"

Gel's eyes widened. "What episode?"

"Ulcerated stomach. Lost nine pints of blood in three days, almost died before the doctor decided to go in and look around to see what was going on. He had to do something or Ed was going to bleed to death. It was here at St. Jude that it happened. They opened him up and found a stomach full of blood, like the whole lining just sort of exploded and Ed was bleeding to death. So, they did this procedure, I'm not sure what it's called, Vagotomy or something, it was so long ago, but whatever it was the bleeding stopped and he recovered. But stress had always been a problem for him; the idea of retiring was always on his mind."

"And then…"

"And then one day about ten years ago Ron walks in, just like that, walks in and says he wants to dissolve the partnership."

"Just like that?"

"Just like that.

Why?"

"Big troubles with some hotel up in Reno, needs a lot of capital to pull him through. He knew Ed was slowing down and might roll over to the idea of selling out, so he lines up this REIT to take them out."

"REIT?"

"Real Estate Investment Trust. The big boys. Wall Street. I wanted to do it, sell the whole shebang, get the heck away from Diversified, Ron too. Ed did too. But rather than sell and pay the enormous amount of taxes we decided to trade into one of the centers, Rancho Palos Verdes."

"And the reason I am here."

"Yes. Two years later we lost the center when it was discovered we had a huge asbestos problem and were sued by most every tenant. It caused havoc with the stores and their customers and we lost the center."

"And you think Ed's partner knew."

"Of course, he knew; it's why he got rid of it."

"And Ed didn't."

"No. How should Ed know. Ron managed the centers. His company got all the complaints, so how could Ed possibly know. It was a scam, and being the innocent dopes that we were, we fell for it."

"So, as it stands, you are practically broke?"

"Yes, you might say that."

"And by losing your property and then most of your savings, that's when you sued Mr. Macalister and lost. And the five-million-dollar life policy you hold with Bounty is a godsend, is it not?"

"Don't attempt to frighten me, Mr. Shakespeare, any idiot can see that we… I mean, I need the settlement money. What else do I have? But needing the money proves nothing in your trying to keep it from me, does it? It's mine and you know it and I am going to get it."

They sat with their heads lowered and said nothing. For the first time Gel felt a degree of empathy for the missing man and his comely wife. A royal screwing, that's the way she put it. Course but suitable. And given the circumstances he understood why she was so hardened over it. Whether Macalister knew or didn't know wasn't the issue for him. Still, the stink was there.

"And you've managed on your savings since?"

"We sold the beach house, that helped."

"I knew about that."

"Ed tried selling the boat, but I wouldn't allow it, he was about to go under from feeling so… so… sad or something. He needed the boat to keep from…"

"Going crazy?"

Mrs. Foxly's jaw tightened. She should have known better than to lower her guard. "I think that is enough for today, Mr. Shakespeare. I should have known better than tell you… such personal…" Her face was turning a shade of purple and her jaw clenched even tighter. "I think you should leave. It would be better. So, if you don't mind."

"I've upset you and I am sorry." She calmed herself and resettled back onto her stool. "Last thing we need is get the attorneys involved. We do that the case will drag through the courts for the next ten years. Nobody gets a thing. Besides," he said, "it's getting late and I've kept you too long as it is Gel looked at Jonell. In her eyes he could detect a glimmer he hadn't seen before, as if she too were trying to smile but couldn't. "You know," he said, capturing the mood of conversation and using it to his advantage, "I haven't told you how sorry I am for your loss. You must have loved your husband very much. And I am sure he loved you very much."

The comment took her by surprise. For a moment she didn't know what to say. Finally, she looked up. "Yes. And thank you for saying that. No one from your company has ever said that to me before. And it's true; I did love my husband very much. His not coming home came as such a shock, that… you know… such a terrible shock."

Gel nodded. "I can only imagine how that must have been." He squeaked his chair backward as if he were about to leave. "Must be tough loosing someone you love. From what I've heard, Ed was quite a guy." She looked up and nodded. "Yes, quite a guy," he continued.

"Truth of the matter is… I've always felt he needed something more, something that I couldn't give, that I wasn't enough. I've always felt that way."

Gel, stoic and attentive, suddenly felt his commission getting closer. A marriage in trouble? A fragmented mind? A spiteful wife? Be patient, Gel.

—〰—

He wouldn't be coming home. Not this time anyway, not slam-banging the way he had done for the past thirty-plus years, bellowing her name as if he were calling for his long-lost pal, Bill, the emaciated Labrador he loved more than he loved himself, if that were possible, taking Bill everywhere he went, even on those crazy expeditions he seemed hell-bent on going on, even if it meant leaving her for days and weeks at a time. What did he care; he was too absorbed in his own passions to care about anyone but himself, or anything for that matter, anyone but that God-damned dog and those idiotic trips to who knows where.

And now this, friends and neighbors tramping through the house with their cakes and casseroles pinned under their arms, shapeless, faceless forms floating in and out as if the walls were invisible and doors were missing, dim lit figures drifting like ships at sea, images of things she'd long forgotten, someone, something, a name in the directory cooing softly in her ear, an arm entwined in hers, a daughter, a reassuring son.

'So good of you to come', wasn't that her constant reply those first few days when he didn't come home, over and over and over, words repeated again and again? How many times had she said, 'so good of you to come, it is terrible, isn't it? I am holding up okay.' A wink, a nod, a turn, a shrug, a look of resignation.

Nameless faceless blurs sinking into the horizon, the house empty and still, questions looming in the distance, gathering and collecting like clouds congealing behind a simmering moon, voices murmuring, people gathering in places she doesn't know, dark figures swimming, fading, fading until water covers the room.

Never give up. That was the words they repeated those first few days and nights when his bed remained just as he left it. "You know Pop," they said, smiling with satisfaction at the woman who brought them into the world, the woman who lived for them and would one day die for them, as testament to her lifelong maternal devotion. "Anything is possible when it comes to Pop," they said, "you'll see, he'll come waltzing through the door with some cockamamie story all made up and we'll have a great big laugh about it. You'll see. You'll see."

But that was five days after he had disappeared. And for those five days she believed what they said. Five long days she had believed every word, or at least tried to believe every word. Stayed by the telephone and waited for the call that never came, his voice coming late at night in a dream, a thousand excuses already invented to cover what she feared most, his dying, his leaving, explaining how he'd been holing up a cave somewhere in the Caribbean and not to worry that he was okay and that he'd be on his way as soon as he broke free from the people holding him. Next plane he explained in her fuzzy state of slumber. Then that crazy laugh and everything turning white until she was okay…okay… okay.

Yes, that's the kind of story he'd tell when he called. She dreamed he had been clinging to a scrap of wood in the middle of the Pacific Ocean, or to a piece of kelp, or a huge school of porpoise bobbed him to the surface, or a big freighter scooped him from the sea and… hey, there's an idea, how about flying to Singapore and we can see the sights together. Everything would be okay when he called…okay…okay.

So, she endured. She endured those first five days even though her children's eyes told her what their voices could not. She knew. She knew when the pencil-gnawing detective rolled his eyes every time she suggested the whole thing was some kind of mistake, a misunderstanding, a big whopper, her husband bounding through the door laughing his head off and pointing and jostling the entire room, telling them how stupid they looked.

Yeah, the old Ed would have done something like that, the old Ed who would fake his death just to jump out of the bushes and yell, 'gotcha', the old Ed of twenty years ago, the one who released the squealing pig in John Collins back yard the day of the big birthday bash, the one who lit the Piccolo Pete in Jack Tarr's wastebasket and barred the door so the entire office could enjoy the shrieking sounds he made. Yep, the old Ed would have done something like that, anything for a good old 'gotcha', that's what the old Ed would have done.

But that was the old Ed. The missing Ed would never do something like that. Not the Ed at 63. Not after what happened almost seven years before when someone jumped out of the bushes and yelled 'gotcha' right back. No, her Ed wasn't coming home. Not this time… not this time… not this time.

Her son came those first few days. He never held her or gave hope against hope the way the others might have done. It wasn't like her first son to show sensitivity or compassion in times of need. No, Ed Jr. wasn't like the others in the family. He was more like she and she liked him because he was. Ed came because he was curious. He came because he needed someone to talk to, just as she needed someone to talk to, to discuss the details of what happened to his father and to try to bridge the gap between reality and what could only be called wishful thinking. Ed could do that where the others could not, to push sentimentality aside and look through the tears of anguish and pain.

Besides, there were all those telephone calls to deal with, neighbors and friends dropping in as a means of support, curious support really, offering their tentative condolences in a time of confusion and grief. And the reporters? Demanding interviews. Photographs. Their pushy ways? Ed Jr.'s answers were always the same: NO! A private matter, he yelled through the door, no comment, no pictures. No nothing.

His face was everywhere. She could hardly walk down the street without seeing his face splashed all over the front page of some local newspaper, the same dopey grin she had never quite grown accustomed to, not in her forty years of living had she grown accustomed to his grimy hat pulled down to the eyes, wraparound sunglasses masking years of sun and sea and wind, his ever present floppy towel drooping to his shoulders, a king-size tuna raised to the camera. My God, where did they get those pictures? And the follow-up the next day, and the next, six columns at least, that's when the story really got legs, television crews showing up, cameras peeking out from every bush, the telephone ringing off the hook, friends pulled aside, harassed, interrogated, crumbs about the man she married, loved, the detective from the Fullerton Police Department popping in and flashing his credentials at everybody in the neighborhood, the sky-cam chopping away. What a circus those first few days had been. And that picture. Where did they get that picture, the one of she and Ed standing in front of the casino at Catalina? How do they come up with such things?

They both sat quietly for some time, Jonell ceremoniously dabbing at her eyes while Gel planning what to say next. He rocked back in his chair and pulled a toothpick from out of the air and shoved it into the large gap between his front teeth, wiggling the annoying object with his tongue as if to annoy her. Seemingly at ease, he put his hands behind his head and reclined even further, his enormous weight driving the chair deeper into her pristine wood floor.

"Sort of like sticking it out with the guy upstairs, don't ya think?"

Mrs. Foxly, offended once again, looked up and blinked. Why she continued to tolerate this clumsy oaf she wasn't sure. Intrigued maybe. Or maybe she just needed someone to talk to. "What? I'm not sure I follow you," she said, ready to end the interview.

"Oh, I was just thinking how marriage is a lot like believing your faith. You're catholic, right?" Without waiting for a reply, he continued his rapid fire. "A person is always going to have doubts no matter what they claim to believe. Like taming a horse, you ride it but never completely trust it, damned thing could break your skull whenever it chooses. Faith trumps everything, even when you're given every reason to give up." He rocked back to all fours and pulled the toothpick from between his teeth and jabbed it in her direction. "And that is what you chose to do with Ed. Right?"

She smiled. "Sound like you've been down this road."

"Na. Just me and Clair. Never tied the knot. Never even had more than one date. I'm fickle that way."

"Your secretary?"

"My sis. Dingy as they come."

"And your faith?"

"Just yesterday I was telling Claire how you can't sweeten things by going around smiling all the time. Life's nothing but a fistfight, Jonell. We pretend it's all one big happy family joining hands but it's really you against the world, you and everybody in it. Your husband called it self-interest." Gel shook his head and looked her square in the face. Why he decided to go the existential route rather than play the ace he had been holding he didn't know. Whatever it took to aggravate and ingratiate.

"Me, he said, "I call it chaos. Guy looks around, sees all the stuff under his feet and thinks… wow… all this just for me. Moon, sun, stars, eggs and bacon, waterfalls, rollercoaster, a pair of beautiful legs? That's what he thinks, that's what he believes, the earth and everything in it was put there just for him." Here Gel pauses, snapping the toothpick in half and shoving it into his pant cuff. "You see, Jonell, doesn't matter what you name it, everything grows out of chaos. Chaos. All order comes out of chaos." Having confused her he dabbled on. "Like my father croaking when I was a kid." Mrs. Foxly looked up, startled. She wasn't sure what offended her more, life being a fist-fight, or the word croaked.

"I remember lying in the woods looking up at the trees and imagining the branches and leaves and twigs and limbs all doing their thing, how they'd grow every-which-way as if it didn't matter. But, you know something, Jonell, it did matter, it mattered a lot. Like the tree was following some sort of sacred plan. It wasn't shooting limbs all willy-nilly. It was like a symphony of green, the whole tree in harmony with all the other trees, with nature, with itself. Kid like me lies there long enough he comes to see these random chances being played out in some sort of organized song, like a symphony." Here Gel pauses for effect, hoping to confuse her even further. "Amazing how the whole shebang looks like it's been ordered to grow the way it has when it didn't, all helter-skelter like, coming out looking like a tree. Weird, huh?"

Gel stopped and leaned in, his breath heavy, his eyes alive. "When I was in the woods I could actually feel the symmetry of nature. I could smell it, taste it. Nothing but symmetry, miles and miles of symmetry. To me the trees could talk. Not the way people talk but another way of communicating with the other trees. Animals too. Fish. Plants."

Jonell looked at Gel, confused, almost frightened.

"Kid walks into his back yard and finds his father hanging on a fence with a bullet through his head, it changes things." He shrugged and smiled. "I wouldn't sweat it if I were you, Jonell. It's all chaos out there, decisions you make, choices, ideas, movements, the millions of things you do every moment, every second, forest, limbs, branches, leaves, molecules. You can't screw it up, it's too symmetrical, everything in complete symmetry." Knowing he was pushing the edge of her endurance he gave a polished smile and reached for her hand but quickly thought otherwise. "Ed would get it. Got it from his writings, stuff scattered in his files, bits of paper, notes, articles on chaos theory. No one understands this stuff. Some would think it crazy, don't you agree?"

But she wasn't listening. "You mean you actually found your father dead?"

"What," he said. "Oh, yeah, that." Gel shrugged.

"A gunshot… I mean, what on earth happened? Was it some kind of an accident?"

"More like a something than an accident. People said it was an accident, but sis and I never bought into it. To the cops it looked like he was climbing over a fence. Gun went off. But I don't know. Could have been something else, somebody wanting him dead then making it look like an accident. Who knows?"

Jonell didn't know what to say. Was he exaggerating or making it up, especially the way he so shamelessly and casually threw the matter into the conversation? "Gel, you can't think your father was murdered. I mean, who would do such a thing?"

"Sis thinks it's Uncle Rolly, dad's brother. He was always jealous of dad for having married his high school sweetheart. Never forgave him for it, not after all those years did he forgive him. Dad was always afraid that mom and Rolly might get back together again, Rolly showing up at the wrong time, getting drunk and saying stuff and mom laughing at his jokes, calling him Prince because he got to escort her to her senior prom the year she got chosen queen."

"And where did this take place? Did you say it was at your home?"

"Right out back. Dad was always shooting rabbits down in the woods behind the house, squirrels. A deer once in a while."

"But it was ruled an accident, wasn't it? People just don't go around killing people and getting away with it."

"Yeah, but you don't know what went on in our house. In our house people were always shooting somebody." He shoved back from the table and laughed. "You don't believe me do you, Jonell? Doesn't matter anyway, I shouldn't be telling you this stuff."

"Yes, you shouldn't. It's too ghastly." Jonell searched the large perplexing oval face now staring down into its hands, a face pulled tight by hair pulled into a knot. He had confused her, even terrified her. Now sitting across the small kitchen counter trying to sound unaffected by the events of his life, he was little more than one of the boys her sons brought home from school. "How old were you when they found your father?" she quizzed, wondering if she was being played for a fool. "Or is this some hideous story you are…?"

Gel didn't blink. "Twelve. And it was me that found him."

Jonell gasped. She hadn't expected that. "You? You found him. But how? I mean," she found herself stumbling for words, "that must have been terrible for a boy your age. I can't imagine, your own father and you so young."

A peculiar smile spread across his face as he rocked on his stool. "And that's why I have my doubts."

"Because you found him? Why?"

The rocking steadied as Gel contemplated how much to tell. "It was the shotgun. He never took the shotgun into the woods. He always took a rifle"

Jonell gave a questioning look. When Gel didn't go on she decided to ask. "Why did he have a shotgun and not the other… what you call…?"

"Rifle. ".22 caliber. Sometimes he'd take the 30-30 but mostly it was the .22. I'm not sure why he had the shotgun, but my guess is he was planning to use it on something or somebody. As I said, there was a lot of stuff going on."

Bewildered, Jonell sat and stared. She had no idea what he was talking about. "Gel, I'm a little confused. What stuff? And what exactly happened to your father that you think it wasn't an accident."

Ideas raced through his brain. "When it got hot in the summer I'd take my sleeping bag out to the back porch to sleep. Not every night, just sometimes. And sometimes I'd see some pink fireflies down in the woods. Maybe you've seen 'em, I don't know, but this particular night when I was about ten or so I figured I'd go down in the woods and try and catch one. I had my jar in my hand and was half way there when this firefly lights up, gets real bright, and that's when I knew it wasn't a firefly at all; it was my dad's half-brother, Phil. He was pulling on a cigarette."

"Phil lived over in Moreland, about five or ten minutes from where we lived, so seeing him in our woods in the middle of the night made me think something was up. Then pretty soon I hear this crunching coming down the path, someone from the kitchen heading to the woods. I couldn't tell who exactly, but I was pretty sure. And I was right. It was mom."

Jonell stared in bewilderment. "And what…? You suspect your mom and your dad's half-brother were what, having an affair?"

"That's what I thought at the time cause from what I saw they were either fighting or fucking." Gel noticed her body stiffen. "Pardon the language, but you get my meaning."

So enthralled, Jonell let it pass. "Even if it's true what are you suggesting? That your Uncle Phil wanted to kill your father?"

"I don't know. Could be. Most everybody in my family wanted to kill somebody sometime."

She shook her head and looked away. "This is too… I don't know… weird. I can't talk about it anymore."

Gel scooted his stool closer to the table and placed his two large hands where she could see them. They seemed to be trembling, but his face remained composed. "You're right. I never should have brought it up. It just sort of seemed natural that I… I mean, I've never told anyone about what happened to my dad." Gel dropped his head on the table and smiled into his hands.

"I can see where you…"

"No, you don't see," he almost shouted, jerking upright. "You don't see anything. It's a lot worse than I've been letting on," he said, face now so flush that, Jonell, startled, raised her eyes in disbelief. "You have any idea what a shotgun does, Jonell? You have any idea what I saw when I came home from school and found my dad hanging on the fence. A kid doesn't forget something like that. Only way I knew it was him was by the clothes he had on." Caught up by his own imagination, Gel indulged in more. "Then running into the house and finding mom on the floor, dad's 30:30 resting beside a face blown to bits. Not a good day, Jonell. Not a good day at all. And yeah, life can be a kick in the ass sometimes, but a kid has to move on, has to grow up, has to get over it or he'll end up just like them." His face larger than ever, his two eyes flashing, Gel was on a role.

"And the best part of the story is that it wasn't my mom betraying my father, it was dad going down to the woods that night. You see, he and Phil had been an item since they were kids. She covered for him, Jonell. She took the blame, so I wouldn't find out."

From the moment Gel crashed his way into the house Jonell knew there was something wrong with him. Bit by bit she acclimated to his presence, her fear lessening, her confidence growing until, at last, she found herself no longer afraid. That was before. She now felt like a trapped animal.

Slowly Mrs. Foxly rose from her chair and removed the cups from the table. "It's late, Mr. Shakespeare. Perhaps you should go."

"So, I was wondering, Jonell, what do you think of my story. You think it was dad that did it?" He waited. "No," he said, "Then how about mom? You think maybe it was mom that pulled the trigger, first dad then her? Or maybe they took turns, first dad then mom. Or mom then dad. Had to be one or the other, right? But then again could have been Phil that done them in, after all they were the only people who knew about their swinging in the woods. And him being a Deacon."

Jonell had heard enough. Not only was she confused and angry and very afraid, she wanted him gone. "You are being ridiculous. Don't, don't talk about it anymore. It's crazy. No, you're crazy. No one would believe a word you said, let alone say it. You should leave, take your things and leave."

Gel got up from where he had been sitting and stretched his massive arms, groaning as he swung from side to side. He smiled while she followed his movements. "Then again could have been me." Now terrified, she met his eyes briefly.

"Well," he said, walking to where his jacket lay strewn across the chair… "Oh, I almost forgot, there is one more thing before I go, something I want to show you." He reached into his jacket pocket and pulled out what looked to be a 3X5 card. He began unfolding the card, which turned out to be a grainy black and white photograph. In the photo a group of people can be seen walking up a ramp of some kind. He handed the photo to Mrs. Foxly, who retreated slightly before her curiosity caused her to take it gently in her hand. She studied the photo for a few seconds and looked up.

"What? What am I supposed to do with this?"

Gel pointed to one man in particular, a dark figure in the crowd carrying what looked to be a duffle bag. "This guy. The one with the bag in his hand. Looks like your husband."

Mrs. Foxly raised her eyes in confusion. She then turned back to the photograph. "What? What is this? Who are these people?"

"The Catalina Ferry Company records all embarking passengers when they come aboard. Disembarking too. Morning and afternoon. It's the company's way of keeping count, a safety precaution. This was taken the day your husband fell overboard, the return trip to the mainland that afternoon. We were wondering if…"

"You think… are you presupposing…? What? That he tricked you? That he…" Jonell stood up and looked at the photo again. "You just said… what… I can't believe you really think… no… and that story about your parents… so awful. No, I think you better leave Mr. Shakespeare. I think you better leave this instant…or the police. My brother is on the police force…. And I am calling the insurance company the minute you…."

Gel snatched the photograph and turned away, grabbing his jacket while moving toward the door. "Get the hell away from me. Don't you ever come back… any of you, … you…you son-of-a-bitch." She ran to the other side of the table and swung at his face, her fingernails clipping the side of his cheek. "You have no right to…".

Gel kept walking as fast as he could, Jonell in a rage just behind. "Look, I'm just trying to get at the truth. Thought," he said, continuing to hold the photo where she could see it, "maybe…ahh, it's been nice, Jonell, real nice." And those were the last words she heard as the door slammed behind him.

THE PARTNER

"Hey, jellybean. Been calling for the past hour." It was Gel calling from his cell phone.

"There is something called lunch, you know."

"Yeah, but it's almost 3 O'clock."

Sarcastically, "An hour. I was gone an hour."

"My-my, aren't we snippy. Hey, check out that St. Jude Hospital thing again, okay, have them go back… ahh… thirty years or so and see if this Foxly character has a record for some kind of stomach surgery thing, okay? Twenty-five, thirty-five, check the whole period, okay? And look for follow-ups too, referrals, therapy, that sort of stuff, especially anything psychiatric, got it?"

"Got it. Where are you anyway?"

"On the road. Got a meeting with that Macalister stiff. Then it's off to check out the plane. You sure Martin's got it stuffed? It's over a thousand miles to Eugene, you know."

"I'll call to be sure. Where is Eugene, anyway?"

"Oregon, squat-head. That's where the Foxly kid lives. You made the appointment, dhaaaa!"

"Dhaaa yourself. Tomorrow noon, don't forget. You got the address, right, County Road?"

"How would I forget something like that? It's why I'm flying to the North Pole."

"I hope you run out of gas. Hope you're so deep in the Rockies they never find you."

"Not the Rocky's, Sierra Nevada's. Daaa."

"Nitwit. Really, I hope you crash."

"I love you too. And Mrs. Foxly was lovely. We chatted over gingersnaps."

"Seriously, how'd it go? She say anything?"

"Naa. Shit hit the ceiling when I showed her that photograph."

"What photograph?"

"The one of her husband getting on the boat."

"Oh Gel, you didn't use that stupid picture? Tell me you didn't show it to her."

"Just wanted to see the old broad go berserk. And she did too, scratched the shit out of my face."

"That was really mean Gel. Even Met doesn't believe he was on the boat and you go waving that picture around. God, you do the dumbest things sometimes."

"Ah, who knows? Guy was a wacko, that's for sure, lost his shirt to his good old partner buddy. Think I'll show him the picture too."

"You do that. Maybe he'll sock you."

"Hey, you ought to see my face."

Nine A.M. and Gel was in the lobby of Diversified Shopping Centers. The young, weathered face sitting behind the desk was busy routing phone calls while sorting through what looked like a ten-pound stack of mail. After a few minutes Miss. Pasty-Face looked over and said Gel could go on back. She signaled through a pair of doors and instructed him to turn right and then all the way back, Mr. Macalister would be waiting.

A youngish 65-year-old man with a perfectly manufactured smile stood at the door to his office with his hand extended. They politely shook hands and went inside. Macalister walked behind a neatly arranged mahogany desk and whooshed back into a rich, brown chair, the smell of fresh leather gushing through the room. "So, what's Met investigating me for? Haven't burned a building lately. Haven't shot anybody that I know of."

"It's about your ex-partner, Mr. Foxly. You know of course…"

Macalister waived him off. "I was just playing around; I know why you're here. Companies got a bundle riding on Ed's life and you're here to figure out whether he jumped or not."

"Crudely put, yes, that's true. I was hoping you'd answer a few questions, especially since you're the policy holder and his wife is the beneficiary. I have all the reasons why it was arranged the way it was, but the facts of the matter are a little interesting.

"We've covered all that in detail already. Anything more you'll have to talk to my attorney." Macalister smiled his polished teeth and leaned back in his chair, gushing a leathery aroma about the room. "Now if there are other matters you'd like to discuss I'd be glad to." Again, the synthetic smile.

"How about when you last talked to him, those last few conversations you had. Was he… you know, strange in any way, threatening, unusually upset, things like that."

"Hell yes he was upset. Wouldn't you be upset if your life's work had been yanked from under you? Christ yes, he was upset. He had every reason to be upset." Gel had been there less than a minute and already an opinion had been formed in his mind; he didn't like the guy. Macalister hesitated for a minute as if preparing what to say next. He leaned forward, and as he got closer, Gel could read a certain severity in the smile, the tangle of industry and duplicity spread like limbs in a tree. Then, as if reconsidering what he was going to say, he retreated to his previous position and folded his hands behind his head and smiled the same plastic smile.

"Suppose he'd like to have shot his old partner when he learned how serious that asbestos shit was … and hey, don't take me literally when I say shot, the guy wouldn't shoot anybody, not himself anyway, if that's what you're thinking, I mean he had a right to get pissed, that's all I'm saying. Shit, I would too under the circumstances. But threatening, nah, Ed wasn't the threatening type."

"But you denied him access to your files."

"Wouldn't you? Christ, he could have faked something, you know, planted a letter, bribed a manager. Our attorney told him to get a warrant and that's what he did."

"You've known him as long as anybody, thirty years or so. He the sort of guy who would jump from a boat to collect five million bucks?"

"Don't see it. Ed was as regular as the guy next door. Didn't drink or carouse like a lot of guys in the business do. Went home every night. Hell of an athlete; did you know that? Best racquetball player in the office, could run your ass dry without breaking a sweat. Scratch golfer, or close to it. Last few years we were together he started playing more golf that usual, came in late a lot; you could tell his ass was sagging."

"You suggesting he was… showing signs of depression?"

"Not in the slightest. Nope. More like he didn't love the game the way most of us do, ass kissing, cocktail parties, building balance sheets. He'd rather be fishing or playing golf or coaching one of his kid's little league games than making a ton of dough. Ed's ego didn't run after the dollar the way most people do."

"If it wasn't the dollar, then what did it run after?"

"That's a good question. Don't really know what the game was for Ed. Remember he liked teaching those courses at Cal State. Probably been a lot happier wearing corduroy and smoking a pipe than fighting the war I'm in. The guy was always intellectualizing about shit nobody gave a rat's ass about, like that time me and Ed were at one of those big luncheons the Shopping Center Council was putting on up in Century City, you know, bankers, retailers, brokers. Anyway, we're all sitting around the table bull-shitting about Greenspan and where the indexes are headed, stuff like that, and Ed elbows his way into the conversation and asks the whole fucking table, says, 'Hey, you guys ever notice how the only black face in the room is waiting on our table'. I shit you not, says it so the whole fucking table can hear. And he says it while the black guy is right there, right there pouring our fucking water. Shit you not. Not a lot of liberals at the ICSC. True story though."

"So, he had sort of a liberal bent, that your impression?"

"Hell no. Ed didn't give a shit about black people. Poor neither. He wasn't about making normative judgments about what's foul or what's fair or right and wrong. Didn't think he was any better or any worse than the next guy. Ed wasn't pointing out the unfairness of the system. He wasn't there to remind us that the black guy serving our table was being exploited. He was saying the guy was unlucky, that's all. Born the wrong color. Hard to understand, huh?"

Gel was confused. "Unlucky?"

"Used to say people were no better than a trout, Ed did."

"A trout?" Gel was reeling.

"Yeah. Remember I was married to the guy for almost 20-years, so this is old school for me. It's more like this. Ed made no value judgments about people, distinctions in other words. We are all the same, some lucky, some not so lucky. After all, smart people, rich people, they get leukemia too. And that's the idea, equal importance carried over to the extreme. Everything in nature has the same importance, same value, same purpose. Trout, zebra, worm, microbe, didn't matter, all the same".

Gel remained contemplative wondering how this would sound in court. "You think that's the thinking of a rational mind, this zebra-man thing?"

"More than rational. Too rational if you ask me. I remember the night we were locked in the car together, cold as hell outside. I won't go into why we were there, but we had a lot of time on our hands. So Ed starts rolling on about how absurd things are, meaning life and existence and how we are nothing but a clump of molecules, stuff like that. Not dismal or depressing but more like thinking beyond the ordinary, outside the box, if you know what I mean. Then he said the weirdest thing, and I'll try and get it right because it actually made me stop and think a little. He said, "We exist, then we don't." Something like that. And you know what, that pretty much sums it up, you're here for a while then you're not."

Macalister leaned back and shook his head. "Liked shaking things up. Ask him if he were a liberal or a conservative, or a republican or a democrat he'd say… nope, none of em. He'd say he was a star."

Gel looked confused. "Star? You mean like a rock star?"

Macalister pointed skyward. "That kind." Gel looked confused. "Me neither. We'd just roll our eyes. Exist then die, just like stars."

"Would you be willing express these same stories in court, that is if you were summoned?"

"They ain't stories. It's what he believed. You summon me I'll tell what I know. Truth never hurt anybody."

"Except in this case it could. Ed certainly didn't fit the mold."

"I think it was more that he was old country, not so much intellectual but old school, feet in the mud. He was Buena Park after all. Went to a state college. Not stupid, not smart neither. Nor lazy. Wasn't a businessman, not in the true since of the word. He'd of voted Gene Debs had the guy been running for something. Ed had a knack for the business, that's for sure and people like doing business with him; suppose that's what made him good at his job. Like he always said, "It's the rich that's losing all the sleep."

"His wife thinks you cheated him, that you knowingly peddled a toxic center in your split."

Macalister didn't blink. "Look, I'll go off the record, okay, 'cause I really shouldn't be doing this shit anyway. But far as I'm concerned the whole Rancho matter is nothing but sour grapes." Macalister suddenly jumped forward. "Hey, you ain't recording this I hope. You record any of it and I'll have your ass."

Not intimidated Gel stood up and gently began taking off his jacket. He threw it to the floor.

"Okay-okay, britches are starting to climb up my ass too so let's say you sit down and make yourself comfortable. By the way, saw that car of yours when you drove up. Could use a little valve work by the way it smoked and rattled through the parking lot."

"I'm a poor man, Mr. Macalister."

"Sure, you are. Anyway, where were we? Oh yeah, Rancho. Ed could have had any of the centers he wanted. He's the one that decided on Rancho, not me. Rancho pumped out the most cash and that's why he took it. Rancho was a good deal for Ed. And I'll tell you something else, had I ended up with the problem and not him, I sure the hell wouldn't have gone crying back to my partner. I'd have eaten it the way he should have eaten it and not go whining about getting screwed. Besides, Jonell's not the only one who hates my guts; all the partner's wives hate my guts. I'm the coach who keeps their kid on the bench."

Another half-hour of conversation went by when Gel decided nothing more was going to be gained. He stood up and offered his thanks for Macalister being so direct and informing him about he and Ed's relationship, noticing how Macalister failed to mention the accident or suggest how saddened he was because of it. But in leaving Gel did assure Macalister that everything he said would be held in the strictest confidence and that he didn't record one word of it. But before Gel reached the door he turned and looked Macalister square in the face.

"You see much of Rachel anymore?"

Macalister tried to appear unruffled by the question, but Gel knew the missile had landed. He looked stunned.

"So, how'd you dig that up?"

"We don't miss much at good old Bounty." Indeed, Gel had almost forgotten the name he'd run across while digging through a Met report, a name Jonell had mentioned only casually to the investigators. Ed had talked about the Rachel years as the dark ages for the company, but Gel had little else to go on. It was a hunch and only a hunch, but one Gel thought worth trying.

"Look, that period is over," Macalister said, annoyed. "Besides she has no bearing on our little discussion." He reached for the office door.

Gel took another shot. "Jonell thinks it does."

Macalister studied Gel for a minute. "Jonell thinks it does? What the hell do I care? She only knows what Ed told her and it surprises the shit out of me that Ed told her anything at all."

"Why out of the company account," Gel interrupted.

Macalister, arms folded across his chest, shook his head and smiled. "Sound like revenge to you? Blackmail? Does to me."

THE CHILDREN

It took four hours to reach the Eugene Airport. As Gel's plane touched the runway, the first traces of rain hit the windshield. Gel taxied to the shelter directed him by the tower, and as the engines of the Cessna 414 sputtered to a halt, the drizzle became a downpour. An hour later he was safely in his room at the Valley River Inn making dinner reservations. But before he dialed the restaurant downstairs, he dialed his secretary at home. When she didn't answer he held on, letting it ring and ring until she finally she picked up. Before answering Gel was yelling,

"It's raining trout up here, Claire. Jesus H. Christ, how come you didn't check the weather before sending me all the way to Siberia."

"Darn it, I knew it was you. Why can't you call while I'm on the clock and not at home?"

Gel ignored her. "Hey, you know that Macalister guy? Whooooa. Talk about toxic."

"You think he knew?"

"Hell yes he knew. By the way, there's a girl by the name of Katy Rothwhite I want you to locate. Don't know the spelling, you'll have to experiment a little. First name's probably Katherine or something, not Katy..."

"Daaa."

"Pay attention, this is important. Got a pencil?"

"No. Yeah, got one."

"Okay, here it is. San Diego area. Mira Mesa maybe. About twenty years of age. Check birth registries, adoptions, anything you can find for a Katy Rothwhite… got it, Kathy or Kate Rothwhite, born around 79 or so. Then see what you can dig up for a current Kathy or Kate Rothwhite, same area, address, phone number, anything. If you find something don't make contact, let me do it, okay?"

"About twenty huh? Gel, you need to be dating girls a little older."

"Okay. So, you in that place, Eugene."

"Yeah. Oregon. Part of the United States of America."

Click.

Gel had no trouble finding Mr. Foxly's youngest son's apartment building. It was just off the main road hidden behind a standing grove of moss heavy pines. He parked his rented Explorer and walked the single flight of stairs to the top where he found apartment 202. His watch showed 12 o'clock exactly. He knocked and, as footsteps approached, he noticed two pair of fishing boots resting at his feet. They appeared wet, the rain possibly, although the porch was shielded, and puddles were under both.

"Gel Shakespeare from Bountiful," He said, his hand poking through the open door.

"Yeah, come on in. I'm Greg"

The two men shook hands and went inside. Gel immediately felt the presence of the steaming pot-bellied stove snuggled against the wall separating the kitchen from the living room. A small sofa crouched at one end of the living room, a busy quilt spread over the back and beside the coach a floppy looking chair. Across the room a small television rode atop a table and next to the table a bookcase, paperbacks and hardbacks tumbling to the floor. Several pictures hung along the walls, travel posters and reproductions. At the end of the room a large group of photographs were arranged. 'Intellectuals', Gel thought upon entering.

"Appreciate you seeing me like this," Gel said. "Your Mom told you I was coming, I suppose?"

"Yeah. And your secretary. She called a few minutes ago to remind me you were on your way."

"Good for her. But I was thinking more about your mom. She's a tough read, you know?" Greg said nothing. "Hoping we can finish this thing up, your mom's situation, that is, get it closed so she can go on with her life.

It can be delicate sometimes and I tend to be not so delicate. Guess you may have heard"

"Yeah, I heard." Greg was a gentle, soft-spoken man of about thirty, smaller than Gel, but still tall, six-two maybe, shoulder length blond hair, slim, handsome features. "So, what do you want to talk about?"

"You mind if I take a look at these," Gel said, walking to the photographs at the end of the room.

"Sure, go ahead," Greg replied, still cautious, wondering about his intentions.

Gel surveyed the pictures. Right away he could tell they were local. Forests mostly, a few meandering mountain trails, pristine streams and rivers. At the end of the group and standing slightly apart from the others was another group mounted in matching black lacquered frames. One, the first Gel came to, caught his interest. Looking it over Gel presumed it was taken late in the day because the sun can be seen setting behind a tall group of pine trees. In the picture the trees appeared as black shadows against a bright orange sunset, except the tips, which were a brilliant shade of yellow. The trees appeared to be on fire. In the photo Greg is in the foreground casting his line toward a small outcropping of rocks. His line is curled above his head, and because the sunset captures the line just right, it glows a hot shade of pink against a black lit sky.

"This is nice, really nice," Gel offered, while rudely removing the picture and holding it close to his face. "Like something out of that movie I saw, *A River Runs Through It.*" He placed the picture back on the hook and turned to look at the next one in line. In this, Greg is looking over his shoulder and into the camera. "Beautiful country you have here in Eugene," he said. Gel kept his eyes fixed on the picture then tapped the glass with his finger. "Who took it? Looks like whoever took it was in the river with you."

Greg hesitated. "Oh, that. Mercedes. It was a nice day, so she came along."

"Ahh, Gel said, sliding to the next picture, knowing Mercedes and Greg had been together for more than ten years. Here he paused and studied the photograph of a man standing with his back to the camera. The man is thigh deep in the river. Curiously Gel paused over the picture and studied it for some time. He didn't remove it as he had the first one but looked it over intently, as if there was something familiar about it. "This your father," he said?"

"Yeah, how did you know?"

Gel ignored the question. "What's that on his head? Looks like he's trying to hide?"

"It's a towel. Always had a towel under his cap. Kept it to keep the sun off. He's fished so much he ended up with a ton of sun damage. Kind of a signature of his, the towel thing."

Gel kept his eyes riveted on the photo. "Funny," he said, "my dad used to do the same thing." Greg noticed how Gel seemed to change as he viewed the picture.

In the last of the four photographs Mr. Foxly can be seen wearing the same towel under an Angle's ball cap. In the picture he is holding a large trout up to the camera. Behind him the river appears to be raging rather than running smooth as it appears to be in the others. "Big fish!" Gel said, once again tapping the glass.

Greg looked over his shoulder. "Yeah, five pounds easy, if I remember right."

"When was it taken?"

"Oh, last year some time, can't remember exactly."

Gel studied the picture with the same meticulous intensity of the others. Could be the same photo he had taken from his mother's house, but he wasn't sure. "Mind if I take it with me," he said. "I'll return it in a couple of days."

Greg looked stunned. "No, I'm afraid not."

"Couple of days, that's all."

"No way."

Reaching into his pocket Gel removed a palm-sized camera and adjusted the lens. "You don't mind if I take a quick one, do you?" Before Greg could say a word, Gel was snapping away.

"Your moms got this one a shelf. Saw it yesterday."

"Oh yeah, that's right, sent it to her."

Gel looked at Greg as if he had just sinned. "To her or to them?"

Greg hesitated. "I think I sent it after. I'm…I'm not sure exactly, why?"

"He came up often, didn't he?"

"Two, three times a year. Spend a day or so, fish and fly back. He always said if he had one place to retire to it would be Eugene."

"Really liked it, huh? Ever talk about moving up here permanently?"

"Oh, he'd joke about it a little, but I don't know that he was really serious; he was born in Fullerton and moving at his age would be pretty hard. Besides, I doubt my mom could handle it up here, gets really cold, you know. And then there are the grandkids."

"But they couldn't afford to stay down south, could they, given the reversals?"

"I don't know; he never talked about it. Besides, now that he's gone, what's the difference?"

Gel ignored the question and asked, "Where were these taken?"

"Different spots. This one," Greg pointed to the one of his father in the river, "isn't far from here, few miles up the Willamette, place called Smith's."

"That where the two of you fish when he comes up… I mean used to?"

"Yeah. There and up the McKenzie a-ways. When the water gets too high we go to… used to go to Fry's creek. Fry's is west of here, about 20 minutes, just north of Springfield."

"How about the others, they the same place?"

Greg studied the four pictures. "Yeah, some on the Willamette, some on the McKenzie, different times of the year though."

Gel noticed a large gray cat curled beside the couch but said nothing. Through an open door leading to what looked like the bedroom, Gel spotted a pair of rod cases leaning against the wall. "Wouldn't mind doing a little fly fishing myself," he said, turning from the photographs, the timber in his voice changing slightly. "Raised in Wisconsin. Dad used to take me and Sis on the Chippewa. Madison too, that is, til he died. Made me a nine-foot, split bamboo. Still got it somewhere." When Gel talked, he sometimes got uncomfortably close, as he was at this moment, almost nose to nose close. "Me and Sis still fished some after Dad died, trout, pickerel, pike, few salmon. Fished some when I was in Germany too, that was about ten years ago. Took a float trip down the Puketitire one time, that's in New Zealand. Really miss it." For the first time Gel sounded personal, even likable.

"River's too high," Greg said, interrupting. "Rain'll have 'em up for a least a day or two, otherwise you could go tomorrow." He didn't mean the two of them. He knew he was supposed to cooperate but still he couldn't help resenting the way Gel came swashbuckling into the apartment, ripping the pictures from the wall, scratching them before putting them back, leaving them loose and craning on their hooks. And the way his eyes surveyed the room, studying every nook and cranny as if the apartment were a crime scene.

Greg had talked to his mother just that morning and the advice was the same as before, keep it cool otherwise months of interrogatories and depositions and delays, not to mention mountains of attorney's fees that could drive her to the poorhouse. At least that's what Ed's longtime friend and real estate attorney advised when showed up the day her claim hit the desk.

"Yeah, maybe next time, if there is a next time," Gel laughed, 'that assuming you got a spare rod."

"Got a spinning rod."

"Oh, I thought I saw two in the next room," Gel said, pointing through the door where he had seen the fly fishing tubes leaning against the wall.

"Oh, that. That's Mercedes. She probably wouldn't mind if you used it."

"Ahh. Mercedes. That explains the boots on the front porch."

"Boots?"

"Yeah, on the front porch. Still wet. Must have gone yesterday? Noticed they were the same size."

"Actually they're mine. One's a spare. She uses the old ones when she goes along, takes three pairs of socks to fill 'em up," he said, laughing.

"Ahh.. Used to go through boots like crazy myself, standing in the water all day. And a reader too. Wow."

Gel swiveled to the books stacked against the wall, some tumbling to the floor. "Mostly classics," he said, thumbing through the stack as though he were selecting one for himself, reading the titles and mumbling the author's name out loud. "English major. Didn't graduate though. Went to Germany on one of those study things." He began digging into the back row, "liked it so much I never went back. What's was your major, Greg?"

"Classics. Roman and Greek."

"Your dad a reader?" Gel had taken over, examining every single morsel he could find, his deep green eyes missing nothing, even the few bookmarks. "Saw he had a library. What kind of stuff was he into?"

"You name it. History, science, he liked literature a lot, modern, ancient, didn't matter. Everything from Herodotus to Mailer. He sent Mercedes and I a big box last year, stuff he enjoyed and passed along."

"That right? Like what stuff?"

Just then the front door swung open and Mercedes walked in, tall and sleek, and sashaying like a model, eyes sparkling. "Hey Mercedes," Greg said, feeling relieved that she had returned, "this is the guy from the insurance company, Mr. Shakespeare…"

"Call me Gel," he said, getting up as Mercedes turned and went directly into the kitchen. "Hi there," she said to the wall, opening the refrigerator and rummaging inside it. "Just came by to get something to eat. Have to be back in about 20 minutes."

"Mercedes, what were those books my dad sent last year, you know, that popcorn box full?"

"Oh yeah," she said. "*Anna Karenin* was one… and that book of short stories by… what's that guy's name…Paul Bowles."

"*The Sheltering Sky*, that's it."

Like a fraternity brother, Gel dropped the books and walked to the big chair at the end of the room and plopped hard into it, spilling his thick angular legs across the floor, absorbing half the room. From the kitchen Mercedes stared then looked away. Having just arrived, she was already set to explode.

"Your dad was kind of into that stuff, wasn't he, existentialism, nihilism, the fate-less journey?"

"Fate-less journey?" Greg could hear Mercedes slamming things around, a lid to something rolling across the counter and onto the floor.

"Existence without purpose," Gel said, reclining deeper into the chair, his all-knowing hands folded across his chest, "a world without design, no meaning to anything, just the fate-less journey leading to nowhere. Like something I remember he wrote. Something like… hey, it was to you, in fact," His discovery had him leaning forward in his chair again, "something to do with comparing people and trout."

Greg laughed. "Oh, that. You mean how trout are just as good as people. He loved that."

"Right, what did he mean, exactly, sort of help me out, okay?"

Greg glanced into the kitchen. Mercedes had made a cheese sandwich and was tearing little bits from it and shoving them into her mouth.

Feeling her annoyance, Greg turned back and said, "Hey, we're not here to join your crusade against my dad. What he believed he believed. So what? His philosophy had nothing to do with what happened that day so you're coming here to libel him, you trying to make him into something weird like… I mean this trip of yours…" Greg threw up his hands. "This whole interview crap is a big joke, taking pictures of pictures. What are trying to prove anyway?" Greg could almost hear the cheering from the next room.

And that's when he heard her shout, "Yeah, the trout thing is a philosophic issue. You can't read anything into that. People talk about that kind of stuff all the time, even in church you hear questions about dominion over the land and animals. He thought it was stupid, that's all. You're trying to psychoanalyze a stupid fish and make something weird of it."

Gel didn't blanch. "Then I guess human life wasn't that important to him?"

Greg shot back. "You missed the point. No life is any more important than any other. They carry the same significance, same relevance."

"Same irrelevance, you mean."

"Okay, same irrelevance. But relevance if you put man in his proper context and not against each other, to what exists, in other words," he was starting to ramble but didn't care, "like the universe, matter, the stars and space and the billions of galaxies running around out there, perspective to… as my dad liked to say, his dot in time."

"But you must admit, your father did feel irrelevant. Right? And no matter what context you put it in, galaxies, stars… that thing you call… what was it, his dot in time, well the fact of the matter is… his energy was gone, kaput, spent."

Before either Greg or Mercedes could say anything, Gel added, "If you want the truth then go back to when you were a kid growing up in Fullerton, okay. Look around. What do you see? Where's the fatalism now?

Where's the dot in time now, the pessimism, the nihilism? No, you don't see a man spouting existential phrases and quoting Kant. You see a bundle of energy, you see this electron going a million miles a second, this sorta crazy, middle-aged character down at the arcade playing video games with his kids, pulling practical jokes on his cohorts, being a coach, a family man, a husband, a guy with a zest for life. Now I am asking you both, where'd it go? What happened to the man who thought Nietzsche was some kind of cheese spread and not the late-life role model he later became? Huh? Well I'll tell you where he went. He went where most guys go when their life blows up in their face. Within. Your dad drew within. Hid. Clammed up. Shut away. Loss of self, that's what happened to your father. That's what happens when their identity gets yanked from their skull; they crawl into a hole and wither away. So yeah, my client has some doubts about your dad. And chances are they might want to try and prove it."

Outside a trash truck banged its metal container against the ground. In the distance a woman could be heard calling for her children. Life went on.

"Obviously you know nothing of Plato's four divine madnesses," Greg said, "otherwise you'd know that one cannot lose the self."

"That was just a metaphor."

Greg continued. "Even a kid comes to know that he is alone in the world. That skinned knee, the bee sting, the bruised ego. No one feels your pain but you. Even a doting, loving mother can't take away the pain; can heal. And then we grow older and we come to the second absurd realization of life, that we can never be understood. And again we're alone. The self doesn't leave. It stays. It clings. It hangs. Only love can take the self away, at least that's what Plato tells us. But the fact is it won't leave. We keep it with us because it's too damn precious to give to someone else. That's why we never love as we should."

Mercedes blinked while Gel looked bemused. The lad really believed those books, he considered, blankly. "Okay Lenny, ease up before you kill the mouse."

"What mouse?"

"Steinbeck. English major, remember. Of Mice and Men?" Gel wasn't to be bested. "All I'm saying is the company has to decide what to do and they have to decide that pretty damn quick. Next month in fact. Law gives us one-hundred-eighty days or we have to file a motion for continuance.

We do that the courts can view it as client harassment and that can involve severe penalties. We don't want that to happen, unless, of course, we can show fraud then it doesn't matter, we win. In other words, Greg, is the case worth pushing through the courts or isn't it. Did the man jump or did he fall? We can either say he fell and be done with it. Or we can say he jumped and set out to prove it."

Her cheese sandwich half gone, Mercedes couldn't help herself. She had smelled a rat the minute she walked in the door. "You're the fraud, Shakespeare. There isn't a chance in hell you can prove Greg's dad jumped over the side. What are you going to do, show a video? Who saw it? Nobody. What proof do you have? None. So just leave everybody alone, okay, and quit going around bullying everybody. I heard the way you treated Jonell, that crap about somebody shooting somebody and poor boo-hoo you growing up an orphan. Like who cares?"

Gel remained unperturbed. "Let's say we put Mr. Foxly on the stand, okay. Not literally but figuratively. We tell his story to a jury. I mean the guy practically wrote his farewell in that book he wrote. Then throw in the five million dollars as a motive, after all it was your dad who talked Macalister into making your mom beneficiary of their policy. Then throw in the loss of his beloved property. Then throw in the loss of his income, his life, his job, his career. But wait. There's more, the best thing of all. Throw in a Christian jury and pit it against a godless man like your old man. I mean, come on Greg, even you have to admit, that's a pretty good case."

Mercedes couldn't stand it. Almost shouting, she said, "Godless my rear end. You don't even know what you are talking about."

"Jonell called him an atheist, says in the report…"

Greg interrupted, "You're right, he was godless… godless in a spiritual sense. My dad had no tolerance for what people call religion. What was it he told you when you asked if he believed in God, Mercedes? You remember? What was it?"

She shrugged, "I can't remember, something about a storm?"

"No…, not a storm, the wind. He told Mercedes that most Christians, no… no… most people believe that God made the wind. For my dad God is the wind. That's the difference."

"Oh how sweet," Gel said, grinning. "Bob Dylan would be proud."

Annoyed, Greg gave Gel a look. "You think that's funny? Well he wasn't being simplistic or overly sentimental when he said it. He believed it. There is a difference between God the maker and God the being. It's not a spiritual thing, it's natural, like the way Native Americans believe that all things are connected, linked, one status, same respect, same rights. Even today I look a trout in the eye and watch it struggle in the water, jumping and running around, its eye looking back. That's when I know the connectedness my dad talked about is real. Maybe that's why I let the fish I catch go, cause of the way they look me in the eye."

From the kitchen Mercedes was stuffing something into her purse. "Look, I've got to get out of here." She grabbed her purse and was on the way to the door when Gel reached into his pocket and took out his camera.

"Hey, you guys mind if I get a picture?" he said, taking a few steps in her direction.

Just as she reached the door, Mercedes stopped and turned around, Gel had the camera held to his face. "You've got to be kidding?" She heard a click just as she raised her middle finger and smiled. "Have a nice day." And with that was gone.

CLAIR

It was approaching 10AM when Gel slammed his way into the office, the glass door bouncing twice before it snuggled back into its groove. Claire had been there for over an hour. She had heard the elevator door rattle shut and recognized the heavy goose-step coming up the hall. "Nice shirt," Gel grunted as he passed by her office door. He had no sooner entered his office than he turned and walked back. "No tea. Where's the fringgin tea?"

"We're out. That's what you get for making fun of my shirt."

Gel glanced at the pale blue T-shirt with kittens frolicking across the front. "Jesus H. Christ, Claire. We got coffee and no tea? What kind of operation you running anyway?" Gel walked in and fell into the only chair in the room. "Christ almighty, why can't you keep the god damned place stocked like you're supposed to? Whatdaya do around here anyway?"

"And a good morning to you, sir."

"No kidding, Clair, you know I can't get started without Mr. Grey." Like a spoiled child she watched as he wrestled back and forth in his chair, slightly amused. When he stopped she smiled and sipped her coffee.

"She called," Claire said, mysteriously.

"Who called?"

"Your friend, Mrs. Foxly. Says you stole her picture."

"Oh, that." Gel reached into his jacket and slid the 5X7 framed photograph across her desk. "Take this thing apart, will ya? See if there are any markings on the back, paper number, studio, anything. Film or digital, that too." Then reaching into his other pocket he removed the camera he used the day before and shoved it at her, saying, "And develop these while you're at it, okay, two copies each. And don't slurp your coffee, you're doing it to annoy me."

Clair slurped her coffee. She then pulled herself from her chair, almost stumbling, and hobbled into the small alcove where the copy machine was located. She pulled her car keys from her purse and placed the photograph and camera in a small paper bag. "Bothering you again, huh?" Gel asked, annoyed that his sister seemed to be laboring more than usual.

Claire rattled her keys in his face. "Don't worry your big head, okay? "I can drive just fine." She stopped, "You actually stole this picture from Mrs. Foxly family photos? Phil finds out he's going to blow his stack. He called, by the way. Wants you to call him, pronto."

"Phil ain't going to find out." Gel fell back in his chair and slammed two large feet onto her desk. "You know Clair, this is a shitty business. Real shitty. Sometimes I wonder why the hell we do it. Tell you the truth, if I had it to do over again I'd… I'd… Before you go, tell me you found that Kate person down in San Diego."

"No can do. Came up blank."

"How about the psycho on the Foxly guy? Hospital have anything interesting?"

"He was there in 73. Stomach surgery. That's it. Two days and released. Nothing else, no follow-up, no anything. It's all on your desk."

"Ah… Christ. How stupid were we to take this missing person crap? Told you we should have took the stabbing, or… hey… how about the wrongful termination case, the fag guy, remember, the one who kept coming on to his boss then turned it around, saying the boss was the one that was queer, not him. Jesus H. Christ, we could'a got something on that guy instead of chasing our tail on this man overboard shit. Thought we'd maybe make a killing. Million or so."

Claire picked up the cup from her desk and smiled. She knew that inside that huge exterior lying prone in his chair, feet clumsily plopped at right angles, unshaven, slovenly applied, lay a mercurial heart only she could penetrate. To everyone he came into contact with he was an obnoxious creep. But to her he was her everything, her entire world. "So, things didn't go so well up north, I gather?"

"Ah, the kid's all right. Didn't say nothing. Sort of ring around the rosy the whole time. Pressing the Foxly's to say something… I mean, we can show…" The phone rang and Claire picked it up. She looked at Gel and smiled and handed it to him. "It's Phil, I told you he wanted to talk to you."

Gel grimaced. "Okay, take it in my office. And get some god damned tea while you're out, okay?"

For the next five minutes Gel brought Phil up to date on the investigation, telling him about his meeting with the missing man's wife and the son and the meeting with the ex-partner.

"How much time you need Gel, I want to recommend something to the committee. That means reports gotta be in my hands in what, ten days, two weeks max?"

"I want to talk to the other three kids first, one lives in Colorado, the other two I can get in a few more days. Betty Boop is running through the local shrinks. Oh, and I've still got to have her shake the guy's friends down, so… I don't know, two weeks, yeah, two weeks, I can recommend something in no more than two weeks."

"As it stands now, what do you think? We convince a jury? It'll cost a good seven figures to try this thing, you know."

"To be honest Phil, I think the guy slipped and flopped over the side, I really do. I'm trying like hell to prove he jumped or put a gun to his head. Shit, truth is, I'm hoping the guy blew his brains out. But I don't know. Can we convince a jury that he jumped? Probably not. We're close though, real close. There's enough mental deterioration to get a guys' dick hard, especially over the last couple of years. Losing his property, the way he did, practically handing it back to his partner. Shit, even I would plop a turd or two over that. Deteriorating mental state, five-million motive, that'll go a long way with a jury. And the atheist angle, we can play that till it runs out their ass. Oh, and another thing, the money angle, juries always hang the rich, Phil and this Foxly guy had some bucks, or at least use to. So, we play that up too."

Phil interrupted. "Rob Paul to pay Peter, you mean. Come on Gel, no jury's going to shed a tear when it comes to fleecing a company as big as ours, especially when the grieving widow is claiming her insurance company is trying to rob her."

Gel sighed. "You're right. But I thought it was an angle we could play to our advantage. Still, we're close. All I need is one stupid thing to push us over the edge, tip things in our favor a little. We do that, we can win."

"Like what?"

"Oh, like this Foxly guy said something to somebody about doing himself in, suicide. Wrote it somewhere, thought about it, contemplated it. Even that he just used the word the right way, you know, said something, did something. We'd have him. Couple that with all the circumstantial we got, hey…"

"Only takes a majority, seven out of twelve. I'll leave it up to you to find what you're looking for. And I hope you do. For all of us."

Gel hung up. He spent the next two hours on the computer summarizing his notes of the previous two days before trotting back into Claire's office. She had returned and was holding the phone to her ear. Seeing Gel, she put her hand over the mouthpiece and whispered, "Brea Photo did it," referring to the framed photograph that Gel had taken from Mrs. Foxly's house. "Steve's already examined it. Can't say when it was developed. There's no number on the back either. He's checking to see if the paper quality may say something. Doubts it though."

Gel's eyes widened. "Jesus H. Christ. Brea Photo. That means they developed it down here. The kid said he sent it. Wonder if he meant the negative or… or could have meant the print." He was still contemplating the thought when she hung up.

"Nope, that's it, Brea developed it but there is no way of saying when."

"Can they say whether or not it was from a negative and what kind of negative? How about the camera, can they say what kind?"

"Gel, it's a digital camera, you can tell by looking at it."

"Oh. Then the kid must have sent the chip. Or the camera."

"Or E-mailed it."

"Or he's lying."

Claire looked at the photograph, the one of Mr. Foxly in Oregon holding the fish in his hands. "Now that's a big trout."

"You notice the towel over his head?"

"Yeah, the way dad used to do. The guy even looks a little like dad, got on the Pendleton shirt and the gray vest. Twins almost."

"Remember how Dad always fished downstream in case one of us went under. He had a phobia about our boots filling with water and pulling us under. Looks like the Foxly guy does the same thing."

Claire kept her eyes riveted on the picture. "Weird. Ties his waders over his pants the way dad did." She threw the picture down. "This is too weird," she said, shaking her hands as if she were holding a worm.

Gel grabbed the photo and looked it over. "Hey Claire. You still got the rods dad made for us."

"Of coarse."

"Where they at?"

"Don't worry, I got them. You wouldn't have yours if I hadn't driven up to the university and picked it up. You and that phony 'Study in Europe' program, spending all of Dad's money."

"Ah... that's your version."

"It's the only version."

"Yeah, right. Anyway, so long as you have them."

"Why, you thinking about starting up again?"

"I don't know. Seeing that kid up in Oregon... and those pictures on the wall, especially that one," he said, pointing the one of Mr. Foxly holding the trout... "reminded me of... you know... before he died."

"Oh, Gel. I think you are becoming sentimental. How sweet."

"Told the Foxly lady dad shot himself."

Claire's eyes widened. "You what? Shot himself? You didn't. Come on, Gel, say you didn't. Even you wouldn't say something like that."

"No, I really did. She kept blubbering about how mean her ex was when they first hooked up so it sort of... you know, popped out."

"Gel, what...I mean, you kid around, but you don't kid around about things like that. Not suicide. Why do you have to lie about dad of all people, saying he shot himself?"

"Like I said, I was playing the old sympathy card and it sort of popped out. I wanted to steer the conversation to the suicide angle... you know, see how she reacted."

"And did she?"

"Naa. I was too convincing. She sopped up the story though."

"That's disgusting. Good thing she didn't mention it when she called."

"Which makes me wonder about the kitty cats," he said, pointing to her shirt. "You're thirty years old and you dress like you're in junior high."

'What, you don't like kittens?"

"They grow up to be cats."

"I was raised on a farm…"

Gel scowled and stood up. "Colorado. When am I going to Colorado?"

"You can go tomorrow or Friday. You pick. Either way he'll be there. But, as you said, he won't know when."

"Good, let's do it tomorrow. Man, I can't wait to get this thing over with."

PETE

By the time Gel reached the Rocky Mountains he had caught the tail end of the same storm that had moved through Oregon two days before. He bumped his way onto the Colorado Springs runway and landed in a light mist. The second Foxly son lived in a place north of the city referred to as Black Forrest. An hour after landing Gel found himself situated on a small rise just a few hundred yards outside the forest itself. White siding with black shutters and trim, the Foxly house stood away from the others dotting the horizon. As his car crunched up the gravel path it attracted the attention of a black Labrador. Several other dogs barked in the distance. Gel parked and walked to the front door and rang the bell. Inside tiny feet scrambled like maneuvering troops.

Two kindergarten sized children answered, a boy and a girl both giggling before the girl, in braids, ran away. The boy stayed and stared upward at the giant hovering above. "Hi. My name is Mr. Shakespeare," he said, hoping not to frighten the boy. "Your father home?"

The boy closed the door without saying a word. Gel stood and wondered if the boy understood or whether he was to be left outside to freeze to death. About a minute passed when an attractive and youthful looking woman, who Gel assumed to be Misty, Pete's wife, opened the door. "Sorry, she said." She wore an apron and looked a little frazzled. "Come on in and I'll get Pete. He's in the basement working on one of his cars. PEEETE," she screamed, at the top of a set of stairs that lead somewhere below. "He said you were coming." Gel stood roaming the living room alone. He used the time to memorize everything in the room.

Soon footsteps were heard banging up the stairs. Gel turned to greet the middle son when a man of his own proportions walked toward him wiping his hands on a dozen paper towels. Not as tall or robust as Gel, still the middle son had the look of a Bulgarian weightlifter. The shaved head and the dark eyebrows amplified two glaring blue eyes.

"Hey," the giant grumbled, ignoring Gel's hand. "Grab a seat." Pete motioned to the four chairs around a table where Misty was busy swishing them with a dishcloth. Pete continued wiping his hands on the grimy paper towels and sat down. "So, what goes?"

"Just want to get this insurance thing wrapped up."

Pete shrugged and said, "So, wrap it up."

"Okay. But first I got to talk to each of you kids, sort of fill in the blanks for the company." Pete said nothing. His blue eyes searched Gel's face. "This may prove a little difficult," Gel said, not quite knowing how to begin with a bear sitting at the table, "But your dad... you don't mind if I start right in do you?" Pete said nothing. "My guess is, the two of you haven't been as close since you got married and moved here to Colorado? Is that safe to say?"

"If you say so."

Gel looked up. "I mean, you talk on the phone and stuff like that, right?"

"Yeah."

"How often would you say?"

"Pretty often."

"Your mom says they came to visit a few times."

Pete nodded.

"Like what? When did they come, once a year? More..."

Through a crack in a bedroom door a tiny voice giggled, "*Mr. Shaaaakespeare. I love you Mr. Shaaaakespeare...* followed by the patter of tiny feet and more giggles.

"MISTY, get Austin and Lauren out of here, please."

Gel went on. "I guess what I am getting at Pete is, is... what I am wondering is how well you knew your father, especially these past few years."

"Pretty good."

"*Romeeeoooo. I looove yoooouu Romeeeooo.*"

"MISTY!"

Gel tried to ignore the banging from somewhere down the hall. "In your judgment did you ever think that your dad might be growing a little tired these last few years, like more distant, sullen… you know, angry?" When Pete didn't answer he asked again. "Did he ever threaten to do anything that he had never done before, like run off to a retreat, try and get away, a trip, anything?"

"Nope."

Gel stopped to consider the man glaring across the table. He was screwing it up and he knew it. The minute he saw Pete crash landing at the top of the stairs he knew he would be at a disadvantage, and disadvantage was something he wasn't accustom to. He paused and pretended to become distracted by the noise from the other room. He would get nothing from Pete unless he rearranged his approach. And yet he knew Pete knew what he was doing.

"You're in sales, I hear."

"Right."

"Good too."

"I do okay."

"Can size up a guy pretty quick."

"Suppose so."

"Got me sized up?"

"Sure."

"And what size is that?"

"Peckersize."

Gel laughed. "That's it. Peckersize? Jesus H. Christ, you got me figured as peckersize. And all this time I thought I was bigger than that. Pintsize maybe, but not peckersize." Comfortable now, Gel felt confident his new direction would break Pete down. "I'm as big as you."

Pete almost smiled. "Maybe so, but I can kick your ass."

Again, Gel laughed. "I'm sure you can. But I didn't come all the way to Colorado to get my ass kicked."

"Why'd you come then?"

"To get at the truth."

"Bullshit."

"No? Then why'd I come all this way if it wasn't to clear things up?"

Pete smiled and rocked back in his chair, hands folded behind his head. "For the money, asshole. Never try and bullshit a bullshitter. That's my lesson to you, Romeo. Fact is, that company you prostitute for is paying you a big retainer. Probably more than enough to cover your expenses. Right?" Gel didn't flinch. "And on top of that, they're giving you a percentage of the action. Isn't that right? And since we're talking somewhere in the neighborhood of five mil… your share could send you to Calcutta and back. Denver's a snap." Again, Gel didn't flinch. "So, you flop around the country trying to stir things up, like at my mom's the other day, saying all kind of shit to stir the pot. And you steal. And you make things up. And you bounce up and down on that web you're building hoping something will stick, like little pieces of shit. And sometimes they do. And you take those little pieces of shit and roll them around and roll them around until you got yourself a great big ball of shit. And presto, you've made yourself a turd. Right Romeo, my man, isn't that's what you do for a living? Make turds? Me, I take crumbs from a cake. But you. You make turds for a living."

NANCY & ED

Gel sat with his feet resting on his desk studying the photograph of the older daughter and son, Nancy and Ed junior. Nancy with a cute coquettish smile, Ed lampooning with his tongue wagging and his eyes crossed. Hard not to like this brother and sister act, he thought, studying the picture.

Nancy, the looks of a model, slim, tall, bright green eyes that sparkled like the moonlit lake he remembered somewhere in the mountains above his home in Wisconsin. Even knowing the purpose of his mission, she was nonetheless witty and wisecracking and completely unafraid to say whatever came into mind. And Eddie, the concoction of intellect, avarice and the most bazaar manner of buffoonery Gel had seen since his college days. Eddie's personality was so riddled and so cockamamie that Gel couldn't be sure from one minute to the next who or what he was dealing with. On one occasion Gel asked the two if their father had ever spanked them, hoping the topic would spark a movement toward a dark side of the man, should one exist. When Nancy told Gel, never, Ed popped in with, "Oh yeah, what about the time he tried to chop my head off." At first Gel thought he was kidding, considering the source it seemed probable that he was. But Ed elaborated, even as his sister pounded on his shoulder insisting that her brother was making the whole thing up.

"No, really," he said, shoving Nancy away, laughing, "I was about twelve when it happened. Pop was mad at me about something. I don't remember what it was, but I was feeling bad about it and I remember saying, 'why don't you just chop my head off and get it over with.' So, my dad goes in the garage and gets an ax and tells me to lay my head over this railroad tie he used as a chopping block. The center of the block was all chopped up and kind of concave from years of chopping. It was just a piece of a railroad tie, not the entire tie, about a foot square and about two feet high. So, I did as he said, and I lay my head over the top with my neck lying on the fat part. And while I've got my neck stretched out I remember my dad reaching down and holding my head steady while he raised the ax way up over his head. And that's when I remember seeing the ax glinting in the sun and as I am all stretched out over the block I remember thinking that he is really going to do it."

"That's stupid." Nancy was hitting his shoulder. "Pop didn't try and chop your head off and you know it." She turned to Gel, "He's told that story a million times and no one believes it." Turning back to her brother, "Even if Pop did that, he was just clowning around the way he always did."

Eddie's rolled his eyes in his head. "All I know is I thought I was a goner."

When they were through Gel sat calmly in his chair. After a few seconds he filled the silence. "Do you think you would perjure yourself in court, Ed?"

Ed's eyes widened as he cocked his head. "Perjure myself? You mean lie in court?"

"That's exactly what I mean. If I were to repeat the story you just told me in court would you deny it, or would you confirm it as the truth? You have to admit, it is a little bazaar."

Nancy was furious. "You idiot, "she yelled at her younger brother, "you're making Pop sound like a lunatic." She turned to Gel. Don't listen to him, he makes up that kind of stuff just to get attention." She turned to Ed and hit him so hard he jumped up and found another chair.

What a pair, Gel thought when the meeting was over. They had met at the oldest son's office. Nancy had driven from her home in Temecula and was waiting with her brother when he arrived. An hour into the conversation Gel knew nothing would come of it, other than Eddie's claim of being affected for the rest of his life by his father's threat of chopping his head off. Gel wondered whether or not he could use the story in case he went to trial. Given the son's proclivity to do and say the unexpected, he doubted it. In no event would Nancy say anything unfavorable about her father; she seemed determined to protect his memory at all costs.

He finally sat the picture down and picked up the one of Greg with Mercedes slamming her way through the door. His grin broadened as he looked it over, Greg's long hair and that Platonist oratory, and Mercedes getting all heated up when Gel suggested that he take their picture together. God, people are so easily manipulated, he thought as he sat the picture on his desk with the others. He then picked up the one of Mr. Foxly and the huge trout.

And Pete dieseling through the conversation the way he did, ready to duke it out at the slightest provocation, saying how Gel turned tiny bits of shit into turds. Just thinking about it made Gel laugh. He easily dismissed the thought from his mind and went about studying the photograph in his hands, reminding himself, as he reclined in his upholstered chair, that irritating people was part of his job, rancor, abrasion, irritation, call it what you want, setting them up and whacking them over the head was his way of getting things done. He had been irritating people his entire life. In fact, it had become a way of life.

GEL

A Friday morning, Gel driving by the same office building he had driven by a hundred times before, sunglasses resting on his nose, U-2 blasting in his ears, the car in front diving to the right, breaks slamming, screeching. It all happened so fast his polished Sports car skidded to a halt, Gel surrounded by others, cars jammed together like stacked lumber. He tried maneuvering into a driveway just as a police siren came screaming across his nose, almost hitting him. Gel yanked the headphones from his ears. Sirens filled the air.

He looked around. To his right a small plume of white smoke from an area just in front of the office building. Next to him a car edged forward. A crack appeared. Through the crack he could see the smoke. But it wasn't smoke; it was steam, steam coming from a pile of twisted metal... silver metal... silver Jetta metal... he screamed inside... Oh, God, not Claire... not Sis.

The world changed the moment he saw the tangle on the grass, Claire... inside... steam...smoke.

Gel doesn't remember where he left his car or running through the crowd or fighting the police officer who grabbed him by the jacket and threw him to the ground, pinned, legs twisted, frantic, begging, Sis... his sis, pointing, sobbing...

He remembers the spinning wheel. He remembers the way it kept spinning and spinning as if it had someplace to go. And the silver mass. And the VW insignia. And the smell. The steam. The boiling water, through the grass, over the curb, down the street. The splattered windshield. The explosion. The glistening diamonds spilling onto the ground. The crowd, the gawking, shoving, pushing crowd. The guy in the yellow Laker jacket snapping with his camera. The upside-down window. The gold jacket snapping. Snapping. His screaming. His yelling, his crying, his sobbing. The hand on his arm, struggling, trying.

Handcuffed, hands shackled, shaking with emotion he hadn't felt since the day he and Sis found their mother and father in the bottom of a frozen gully about a mile below the house, the trailer smashed like a soda can, the birthday present horse they had bought for Sis whinnying and baying as it lay dying in the road beside them, he and Claire watching and listening like totem poles dug into the ground.

And again, helpless, the army swarming like insects. The minutes crawling, hours, weeks, eternity, the car holding Sis captive, meters away, entombed, a mummy, water surrounding her, killing her. And what would they find? Alive, scared, suffering…dead. The thought terrified him.

Somehow, miraculously, eventually a frail delicate body emerging through a jagged crevice, face radiant, untouched, perfect, the way he remembered it. A man slicing his way through the silver metal bones, the fire driven saw like anti-aircraft. Her face, Claire.

On it went, Claire's fragile body maneuvered like thread through a needle. Through the crevice, the saw shrieking. Around him the crowd pulsating, throbbing, its pressure building, the gold jacket darting and flitting like a bee in flight. Soon a pale-yellow T-shirt, Garfield grinning, the shirt ripped, a bloody remnant, soiled, hideous, pathetic. Two men inching her body, tenderly, cautiously, lifeless, her arms dragging, bumping, her shirt pulled to her shoulders, her bra undone, the frenzied gold jacket buzzing like an insect. Claire exposed.

Gel lay on the grass crying. The guns had quieted as he watched his little sis being lifted onto a gurney, a mask over her face. The officer relaxed his grip and waived, yelling, "brother", the paramedics turning and nodding. And he was there, next to her, with her, alongside her, his head buried in hers, the tangle of moist sobbing hair rubbed into his face, Claire, white, pallid. They banged the gurney against the ambulance. It happened so fast he couldn't think, her chest exposed, blood everywhere, her shirt shredded, her neck…her poor neck… Without thinking he took the scapula in his hand and yanked it away, bringing it to his lips and kissing it before dropping it to the floor of the ambulance and crushing it with his foot. He quickly climbed in back and took her in his arms and kissed her, his little Sis, the woman he had cared for since Mom and Dad had died, the day he became a man, the day Sis ran into that gully and reached into that passenger seat and found the mangled body and removed the scapula from her mother's neck and placed it around her own, the day he turned fourteen years of age.

And the terror of those next few hours, those next few days. Every minute, every second not knowing, not believing, doubting, sleeping in every chair, pacing every hall, eating miserable yellow food with spotted peas and carrots hugging the corners, the grayish meat beneath a slab of blue gravy, the vending machine coffee, the tea he begged for. Four days and nights he fogged through the haze of not knowing and not believing while his body and soul sagged with doubt, holding the fragile hand beside him, the person he promised to care for and hadn't, stupidly, selfishly abandoning her when he went away. Those two epicurean years trying to find the man inside his soul, flirting with the globe while she waited tables and waited and waited.

She awoke. She would make it. A shattered pelvis, a leg crushed, ribs broken, a concussion. But she would make it. So many contusions, a spleen that would never heal. But she would make it. A wheelchair, crutches, a cane, therapy. But she would make it. Yes, Claire would never gain full strength in that right leg, so cobbled, a brace to keep it steady, riveted, a metal rod, a cane to keep from toppling over. But she would make it.

He paid every cent. When she couldn't feed herself, he fed her. When she couldn't bathe, he bathed her. Even when she cried and cursed because of her nakedness, screaming immodesty and humiliated, he scrubbed anyway. He washed her hair and her back and under her arms. He even washed her panties and her stupid jeans with the holes in them. He washed her bras and stockings and brushed her teeth. He vacuumed and shopped and combed her hair so she would look pretty when her friends came to visit. And in the end, she made it. Claire made it.

And yet he was mean to her. He was mean to the only person who truly mattered, the only person he truly loved. And yet he was mean to her. Still he couldn't help himself when it came to Claire. He had failed to protect her, and she almost died because of it, almost died while he was holding her in his arms. And he was mean to her.

"So, how's the report coming, decide anything?" Claire stood in the doorway spooning peach Yoplait into her mouth.

"Yeah, I guess," Gel replied, looking up from his desk. "Claire, I'm done for. We gotta go with what we got. And that means a month down the drain and no money coming in. Sorry."

Claire shrugged and scraped her plastic spoon along the bottom of the container.

"Truth is… well the truth is, there's not enough too… at least not enough to push through the courts. Circumstantial is okay…and…" he paused, "you remember how the Register played this thing up, front page and all. You'd of thought Foxly was running for governor the way they splashed his picture all over the place, and not some freeking bozo taking a dive over side of the boat. Shit, I thought we'd make it big time if we nailed th son-of-a-bitch. But nahh, press'll clobber us we take the old lady to court; that's not the kind of press we need. Met neither."

Claire licked her spoon and wiped her lips with her fingers. "You saw the pictures from up north?"

Gel picked up one of the several photos she had developed and looked it over. In it Greg was standing waist deep in the river. Behind him the sun glowed a rich, iridescent red. "Not bad," he said, turning to Claire, "like something on a post card."

She hobbled over and took the photograph in her hand, angling a hip over the edge to steady herself. "Great, isn't it? When I first saw it I thought it was the Chocktaw someplace up the west fork; where the canyon gets real wide and has all those trees and things."

"And spiders."

She smiled. "And spiders. You and me and Dad, we'd go up and camp in the summer, remember?"

"Yeah. Dad picking corn and hauling it around the whole day. God, what a dope he was. We'd get to a campsite and dig this great big hole and bury the corn in it… and we'd build a huge fire over the top and… and you and I would roast the fish I caught," Gel looked at her and grinned, "and we'd make some sticks and start digging the corn and… you know Claire, when I think about it there's nothing better than going camping, right? I can still taste the fish and corn and those greasy potatoes he'd make with those onions and peas mixed in." Gel seemed happier than she had seen him in years.

"Makes you want to do it all over again, doesn't it," she said, "simple and nice and easy, me and you and dad and nothing to worry about, not a problem in the world, no past, no future, just the now? Something about being a kid makes everything okay, doesn't it, Gel, I mean the whole world is okay when you are a kid camping in woods. Everything made sense back then, the world, I mean the whole world right there in a little hole in the ground, me and you and dad sitting around that stupid campfire."

"He'd freeze 'em. Remember? The peas. Put 'em in the freezer and take 'em out and dump 'em into his backpack to keep the drinks cold. He always took a beer. Only beer he ever drank."

Claire raised her head. "Yeah, I sorta remember."

"He gave you a swig that time, like this little sip and pretty soon you were acting real stupid, stumbling around and laughing. He said kids weren't supposed to drink beer or they'd get drunk and you were so stupid you believed it."

"You're lying; I don't remember doing that. I remember the Seven-up and root beer and how mom wouldn't let us drink sodas."

Gel leaned forward in his chair. "Shit. We oughta do it." He flopped back and threw his feet up. "God damn, we should do it. Just get up and go."

"Go where?"

"Fishing, you dolt. You got the rods. Ah, screw it, let's pack up and go. I'll finish this Foxly thing then you and I take off."

"Take off? Where? Back home."

"Not home. Oregon. How's Oregon sound. Me and you fly up to Oregon and we'll fish the Willamette. Hey, even better, I'll call the Foxly kid and…"

"Gel, you know I can't go fishing. Imagine me standing in the river… or even making it to the river. I can barely maneuver around the office without my leg killing me. Besides there's Bernie…"

"Ah, screw Bernie. You're not going to marry that twerp…"

"How do you know? He's sweet; he's not like you."

"All right… But we could still do something; go fishing. One last fling before… Besides," Gel handed her the picture of Mr. Foxly and the trout, "you never caught anything this big."

She studied the picture and smiled. "Yeah, it really does sound like fun, doesn't it?" She looked again. "Gel, did you ever look at the hat he's got on?"

"No. Why?"

Claire took another long look before handing it over. "He's wearing an Angels cap."

Gel grabbed it from her, almost tearing it from her hand. "So?" he said, studying the same photo he had seen a hundred times before.

"It looks like a world champion cap. Look here." She leaned in and pointed to the 'A' logo with the wings sprouting from the sides and the words World Champions 2003 scrolled beneath it. "That was October last year, right. And when was it that Mr. Foxly was supposed to have fallen overboard, wasn't that October too?"

Gel held the picture close to his face and studied it as if under a hypnotic spell. He then slowly lowered himself into his chair and sat staring in no particular direction. For another minute he said nothing, just sat staring into space, too stunned so say anything. Finally, after looking at the picture one more time, he said, dryly, "You know what Claire? That son-of-a-bitch is alive. He's… he's… hey." Gel jumped to his feet. "I'll bet that son-of-a-bitch is up there in Oregon with his kid. I'll bet he's up there right now. I'll bet… Claire," Gel was pacing like a mad man, "that son-of-a-bitch is… has… Claire, my God you did it. You…"

Claire grabbed him by the arm and swung him around. "Gel…get a grip, okay. Calm down and think. This cap he's wearing… just look at it. I'm sure those caps came out the minute the World Series was over. And it's possible, just possible he bought it before he went up to Oregon. You know how people run right out and buy the cap the minute their team wins. And the guy had to be an Angle fan; he lived right down the street in Fullerton."

Gel wasn't listening. By now he had turned into a raving maniac, pacing back and forth, his hands pressed to his ears, eyes blazing. "No… no, you listen up." He turned. "Go call the Angels. Okay? Right now.

Do it right now" Pacing and turning he began shuffling through the photographs on his desk like they were dominos. "Find out the day those freeking caps came out, okay, I mean, no, the minute, the second they came out, the... the whatever... whenever a person could buy one? Oh, and the day the old boy took his header, that too... Oh, Jesus H. Christ, Claire, I knew this would happen, I knew I'd find something..." he was practically running in place, "Oh, God, thank you Claire, this was your deal, I'd of never... oh shit, and... Hey, thank you, thank you," kissing her everywhere, her head, her face, her hands and arms, "and... oh, find the exact day the header happened, that too. Did I already say that? It was the 21st, a Monday, no, no, hey, I'm sure, no, yeah, it was a Monday the 21st. Check though, check to be sure."

About twenty minutes passed when Claire came back into his office and sat down. By then Gel had stopped pacing and was glowering at a pair of photographs on his desk. "Gel. Did you know that the Angels had 20,000 caps ready to go the night they won the pennant, I'm talking manufactured weeks before they won the pennant. I had no idea people did things like that. In fact, they went on sale that night, that very night right after the game. Can you believe it? Hey, now that I think about it, I remember the players had them on when they were being interviewed on TV."

With Claire beaming over her discovery Gel seemed to have already forgotten. He was staring at a pair of photographs in his hand. Without looking up, he said, "That was when?"

"The 16th. And you were wrong about the 21st, Mr. Foxly fell overboard on the 27th. You were right about it being a Monday though."

Gel looked up. "Really? Still he'd have ten days to buy a cap, put it on, fly up, or even drive up to Eugene and go fishing with his son." He sat back and looked at his sister. "Doable, wouldn't you say?"

"Yes, it's doable. It's interesting but it's definitely, as you call it, doable."

Gel pondered the situation while gazing across the room where his sister sat with her arms resting in her lap, one leg beneath the chair, the other slung awkwardly forward, something she never did in the presence of others. Sweatpants had become her preference after returning to work nine months before, the springy cotton fabric hiding her metal supports. He would rather be dead than see her flawed the way she was. Better her than he, he thought, admiring the way she patiently coped with the severity of her life. So much to deal with. How does she do it, he wondered, recognizing the weakness within himself.

Gel got up and handed the two photographs to her and smiled. "Notice anything, Miss. Smartypants? Claire took the two pictures and studied them. "Come on, look hard, you're the brains in this outfit, not me." She kept studying the pictures but saw nothing, nothing that jumped out anyway, Mr. Foxly holding the fish and the other of Greg casting in the river.

"No, same pictures I've been looking at for days. Why, what do you see?"

Gel's smile broadened into a sly, sinister smirk. "The sun. Look at the sun, Cumquat." Clair looked closer. In one she noticed the sun creeping behind the trees, the other the sun high overhead.

"Okay, what's your point?"

"The position, dummy. First, they're taken on two different days, you can tell by the sky, clear in one, cloudy in the other. And even though it's two different days, they're taken from the same location. Right?" She nodded. "This one," Gel pointed to the one of Greg standing in the river, "look at the position of the sun. Now look at the other one, it's way over here, way more to the east."

Claire compared the two. "Yeah, meaning?

"Meaning? Meaning?" Gel snatched the pictures from her hand and glared. "No wonder I make ten times the money. You don't see anything that matters. Look," he said, shoving the pictures in her face, "this one was taken in the summer. Had to be summer, sun's almost straight up, or am I going too fast for you?" Grabbing the other he said, "This one it's a whole lot later, winter maybe, sun's way to the east." He looked at her. "Jesus H. Christ, Claire, look what the guy's wearing," Gel's hands were shaking. He pointed to Mr. Foxly in the photo, 'big flannel shirt, thick vest. It's winter Claire, it's fucking winter. I get cold just looking at it."

Claire turned and glared. She hated him when he got like this. "Okay. Okay. Freaking winter, not fucking winter. But Jesus H. Christ, Claire, you're such a prude at times, what am I supposed to do. But this is big, really big. This one picture right here is going to turn this whole case around."

Claire stayed calm. "I think you're reading way too much into this Gel. I see what you mean; it is a lot later, maybe even winter, but there is no way you can tell how much later or what time of year it is just by looking at these stupid pictures."

"Want to bet?" His eyes were dancing, and the big broad smile returned. "Go home and get those rods ready, Miss Priss, cause you and I are going fishing. I'll call Martin and have the plane ready. Oh, and bring some warm clothes and some boots, if you got any, that is. Oh, another thing, fix some coffee and tea for us… and don't forget to bring some kind of snacks, not those cookies you always bring, those fig whatchamacallits. God, I hate those things. You know they give me the runs. Anyway, I'll call you tonight and let you know what time, probably first thing, seven or eight."

Claire was almost laughing. "What's got into you? Fishing?"

"Right. And were going to do it right here." Gel was pointing to the photographs spread across the table. "Me and you, my lovely sister, are going all the way up north to go fishing, and while the two of us are jack-poling our way to riches, we are going to check the position of the sun." He grinned and grabbed her cheek, pinching it the way he did when they were children. "And then my sweet, you and me, are going to run over to that university and find some hotshot professor of meteorology or climatology or whatever the hell they call it, and we're going to have this professor guy plot the exact position of the sun right on this freaking photograph. And we'll have him do it for every freaking day of the year if we have to." Gel grinned. "If this picture was taken anytime after… what did you say, the 27th," Claire nodded, "then we got 'em. We got 'em big."

MR. FOXLY

By noon of the next day Gel and Claire had rented a white Ford Explorer from Hertz and Claire was sitting in the passenger seat guiding Gel from her rent-a-car map. As soon as they touched down Gel ran through the Yellow Pages and found a fly-fishing shop just off the route to the McKenzie River. He wanted to pick up some fishing leader and a few trout flies. While there he would try and get one of the local fishermen to identify the exact location in the two photographs. Luckily, they found the man they were looking for. He was clad in overalls, his name, Ernest Medford. Ernest was the owner of the shop and, as it turned out, Ernest was a direct descendent of the early Medford family who settled much of the Willamette Valley.

Handing him the photographs, Earnest immediately poked the picture and identified the location. Grover's Corner. "Took the name from that play some famous guy wrote a long time ago, *Our Town*, I think it's called." He smiled a nicotine smile and said, "Here's what you do. You and the little woman drive up 62 a-ways, go till you come to Cook's. Big sign. Follow Cook's along the river to the bridge, cross over the bridge and then… oh maybe… naaa, you cross the bridge and scoot on down another mile or so till you come to a turnout. Don't park there though, that's where the school bus does its turn-around, no you go on up a-ways till you get to a big rail fence. You can park right alongside the fence and then take the trail down to the river. Good path. Easy casting place, wide and good wading. Some nice Brownie's this time of year. Rainbows too, mostly small though."

Gel followed the man's instructions and penciled them onto his map, telling him thanks. He turned to Claire and pulled her close. "Me and the little woman," he bounced her, "would appreciate you picking some flies for us, dozen or so, hoping to get some of those brownies you were talking about. And some leader too, 3-4 pound, whatever you got."

Earnest led them to a case where the flies were located. He picked out a few, pinching them between his fingers and placing them in a small plastic container. They seemed like miniatures to Gel, much smaller than what he and Claire were used to back in Wisconsin. Gel laughed, reaching in a pulling out a photograph. "Me and the wife were hoping to catch something big, like the one in the picture," he said, referring to Mr. Foxly and his huge trout.

"Ain't no trout. That's a steelie. Have to wait a few months to get one though."

Claire was the first to pick up the scent. "You mean," she interrupted, "that's not a trout in the picture?"

Gel grabbed the photo from Earnest's hand and looked it over. "What did you call it? A Steelie? Looks like a trout to me."

"Ain't no trout. Steelhead. That there's a winter Steelhead. You can tell cause it's got no color. All silver. Winter steelhead's a cold-water fish, comes from the Pacific every winter. Summer steelhead got more color in 'em, they's a warm water fish, got spots round their gills like a rainbow does."

Gel and Claire looked at each other. Gel's eyes widened. "You telling me that this fish is a winter steelhead?"

"That's what I'm telling you. Any fool can see that."

"What's the season for these winter steelhead, I mean when exactly can you catch one, what months?"

"Too late now, been gone for a good sixty days."

"I know, but when can you catch one, like ahhh…," he looked at Claire and noticed her expression, "that is if me and the wife here want to come back next year?"

"Startin' November I expect. Then they run into, oh I don't know, early February, maybe. Depends on the snow pack and the water. Gets high sometimes."

"Then you're saying a fish like the one in the picture had to be caught after November last year."

"Oh, I don't know about that, could have been caught any year, I suppose."

"No, I'm saying, if it were caught this past season then it had to be after November 1st, that what you're saying.'

"Oh, last year they didn't start till more like the fifteenth; they was later than they normally was. First fish showed up round… I don't know exactly, but they was late." Claire and Gel looked at each other. "I'd say you need to go up to maybe six-pound test on that leader, four's too light for the McKenzie."

"Would you be willing to say that in court, testify that this is a winter steelhead in the picture and that in your professional opinion the picture I'm showing you in my hand was taken at a place just up the road at a place called," he looked at Clair.

"Grover's Corner."

"Right, Grover's Corner, and that the fish in the picture is a what you call a winter steelhead? Oh, and that the run last year didn't begin until around the 15th of November?"

Ernest looked bewildered. "Well can't say I'm no professional but that's what it is, Grover's and a steelhead. Like I said, any fool can see that."

The trip to Grover's took almost an hour. Afternoon fog and drizzle had settled over the valley and Gel not only missed the bridge but had taken them for a ride so far removed from their real destination that they had climbed in elevation and broken through the clouds. He backtracked down the mountain and into the gloom until the bridge was sighted. There he turned and found the road to Grover's. They parked along the rail fence, just as Ernest had told them to, and noticed a white Toyota pickup parked among the trees in the distance. As they emerged from the car the chilling cold hit them.

"Picked a swell day, didn't I," he said, his hat already dripping around the brim down onto his shoulders. He glanced at the trail leading to the river and noticed the wet foliage running all along its border. Ahead, through the fog, the river was barely visible. Somewhere in the distance, the sound of rapids roared in his ear. He grabbed the rods and stuffed the fishing tackle into his vest, along with his cell phone and camera. Claire was buttoning up her vest and checking the trail.

"What do you think," he said, jabbing a rod tip at her butt?"

"The top looks okay," she said. "If it doesn't get too steep at the bottom I'm sure I can make it."

"Here, you go first, and I'll follow you."

"No way. Knowing you, you'll fall down and take me with you. Just go ahead. Besides, you got the equipment. I'll poke along on my own." She sounded annoyed and a little afraid. "Besides, I don't like you babying me.

"Jesus H. Christ, have it your way. I'll go on down and when I get to the bottom I'll listen for crashing noises, maybe some blood curdling screams."

It wasn't bad going down and Gel was sure Claire could make it without too much trouble. When he got to the bottom he saw the river open up, mist so thick that he could barely make out the other side. He was about to step onto the river's embankment when he noticed a figure about thirty yards ahead, a fisherman standing knee deep in the water, with his back turned. The man was expertly casting upstream where a series of riffles were cascading through a series of rocks and boulders. Gel watched as the man allowed his line to drift with the current, patiently keeping the slack at a minimum until it was well below then he would flip it back again. From his place behind a small outcropping of trees and ferns, Gel remained hidden from view. He watched as the man continued his series of casts. After a few minutes Gel was sure. The man he was looking at was Greg Foxly.

His first thought was to walk into the opening and give out a big "Howdy". But waiting for Claire seemed better, staying where he was and watching. What luck, he thought as he crouched behind the rocks while steadying himself against the slope. The photographs in the car, the incriminating evidence, the Angels cap, Ernest at the tackle shop. He almost laughed at the comedy about to be played out. He turned and listened for Claire but heard nothing. It had only been a few minutes but still… he couldn't help but worry. She was so god damned independent. Damn her anyway. And the damnable weather too, he saw no way of positioning the sun with it being so overcast.

Just then Gel noticed Greg raising the tip of his rod and holding it skyward. The line jerked taunt and a small fish went skipping across the surface. Then, just as suddenly, the line sagged, and he saw Greg shrug and throw his hands in the air and wave downstream in apparent disgust. Gel steadied himself against the rock and looked on, perplexed. Who? Who could he be signaling to? He glanced down river to where Greg had gestured but there was nothing, nothing but the black churning river gushing into a dark, dank hole.

Then suddenly, as if a curtain were being raised, the fog seemed to suck skyward and sunlight filled the canyon. Out of nowhere a shimmering halo swooped from the sky. And that is when he saw it, a second figure about fifty yards down river. On its head was a cap. And beneath the cap, a shaggy cloth drooping to its shoulders. A dark green vest covered its chest. The figure appeared to be gesturing to the one above, a salute perhaps, a tribute. Then, just as the figure appeared, it suddenly disappeared, fading into the fog and rain so that it became nothing, an apparition, a vision.

"Dad?" The word came from somewhere deep within Gel's subconscious, as if waiting a lifetime to be heard, to speak.

He was sure. It was no vision. What he had seen was a man. They had signaled to each other, Greg upstream, his two hands together, the other raising the rod, signaling. He had seen it. He was sure. It was him!

Something bumped his leg and he turned. Claire had scooted the last few feet on her fanny and was looking directly at him. "Dad?" she said with a curious look on her face.

"What?"

"You said Dad."

"No, I didn't."

"Yes, you did. And who's that," she said, pointing to the figure in the river."

Gel was trembling. He knew they couldn't be heard. The roar of the river was too great. "Claire," he said, "you ain't going to believe this, but do you know who that is," nodding to where she was pointing."

"Who?"

"The Foxly kid, the one we came up to see." And that's not the best part, Claire. Guess who I just saw standing down river. You'll never guess in a million years."

Claire scrunched her face and shrugged. "I donno. Dad maybe? You're acting like a complete idiot, you know."

Gel reached into his vest and yanked out his cell phone and began punching numbers. "I'm calling Phil. He ain't gunna believe this either. Jesus H. Christ, how lucky can one man be."

"What are you doing. You're not going to…"?

"Shut up, … I'm… Oh hi, Claudia, it's Gel Shakespeare. Is the bald eagle in, I got something to tell him." Gel was practically dancing. Then, "Yeah, same to you too Claudia. Nice talking to you too. Now let me speak to… Okay, I'll hold." Then quickly, "Hey, Phil. You'll never guess where I am. No… no, I'm looking at the McKenzie River. That's right, the McKenzie River. Up in Oregon. That's right, Phil. Now, why am I calling. That's what you want to know, right? Okay. You'll never guess who's standing right in front of me. The Foxly kid. That's right, the Foxly kid. I can practically reach out and touch his little fanny. And Phil, this is the really interesting part. Guess what I saw standing about fifty yards down the river. That's right, about fifty yards from where I am right now…"

Just then Claire, who had been clutching his leg to keep from sliding down the path, began to slip away. As she moved she clutched her brother's leg but couldn't hold on. Gel dropped the phone and grabbed for her, luckily seizing her by the neck of her parka and holding her there until she could take hold of his arm. Slowly he pulled her back up the slope. The path was most steep where they were and the fall to the bottom was no more than ten feet. Still Claire held him as if the fall would have killed her. As she clung to his shoulder he could feel the desperation in her grip and see the fear in her eyes. She was terrified.

Once he knew she was okay Gel pulled her chin up and looked into her face. God, how much he loved this woman. Clair nodded, smiled weakly. "You still there, Phil?" he said, picking up the phone, shaking the mud away. "No, just Claire taking her daily tumble. Yeah, she's okay, dorky as ever." He smiled but he could see that she was still shaken. "Anyway…" Claire was crying. "Downriver… that's right. About fifty yards I'd say." Claire and Gel remained huddled like lovers in a thicket, Claire holding onto her brother while he held onto her. "Yeah, in the fog, still saw it clear as day though." Claire looked up, her face covered in mist, her rain-soaked jeans pulled to where he could see the metal rod pushing into her boot.

Suddenly he felt ashamed. So eager to prove himself that he had forgotten and left her on the path alone. Her stupid determination did this, always having to measuring up, to keep up. And that stupid promise he made to himself to always take care of her. Then failing-failing-failing. Such an ass-hole.

Something in her face caught him and he couldn't speak. Tears were streaming down her face, rain down her hair. "You're not going to say… it wasn't dad, Gel."

"No, it wasn't dad." He brushed the tears away.

"You're always telling stories, making things up."

"It wasn't dad Claire, I promise.

"What then?"

Using them, Mom, Dad, Claire, whatever it took. He smiled. "A bird, Claire. I saw this big bird, a heron or something. You should have seen it…" The phone was back in his ear. "That's right, a heron, Phil. Big as day. Standing still as can be. Right in the middle of the river waiting for a fish to come along. No, I'm not crazy. You'd had to have seen it. Me? Came up to do some fishing. Wanted to tell you the report will be in your hands like I promised. That's right, still the same. You want to go ahead, be my guest. I'm recommending you don't though. That's right… that's right… you're breaking up Phil….call you later." He flipped the phone closed and looked at Claire. "Let's get the hell out of here, too crowded."

"What about…"

He put the phone away and picked up the rods. "And give me your hand before you break your stupid neck."

"Just help me stand up, okay?"

"No, give me your hand or I'll break your stupid neck for you. Jesus H. Christ, Claire, you don't know the first thing about hiking, do you? I remember how dad and I would have to carry you across every little puddle…"

"Oh, come on Gel, you're the one…" He helped her to her feet and as she struggled to right herself he took his arm and put it around her waist and pulled her close. "You cold? You're shivering."

"Yes, I'm cold."

"Good, cause I want to try another spot before it gets dark" He laughed. He then shoved her ahead. "And don't go sliding into me, okay? You might break the rods."

FISHING WITH SOPHOCLES

*"A man growing old
becomes a child again".*
Sophocles

Nearing the leeward side of the island, the wind has dropped considerably from what it was during the crossing. The sea has become so calm that it looks as if a large gray liquid canvass has fallen over it, sky and sea joining at the distant horizon, so they come to look as one. My sense relief of having made in across in the dark is hard to describe. Even with the radar glowing it's warning signs at me and the direction finder plotting my course, navigating in the dark is like walking through a pitch-black cave, you're never sure what's in front of you, a floating log perhaps or buoy set adrift. But with the sun finally sneaking its way into the sky and the sea lying so flat if feel as if I am slicing through it with a knife, the unease of before is gone so I can sit at the helm and watch the clean clear curls of water peel from the bow like clouds racing through the sky. A man can lose his bearings at a time like this, alone at sea, the horizon endlessly spreading before you, hypnotic, infinite, limitless, the constant lapping of the sea, that he becomes temporarily loses his bearings even his mind.

Just ahead is the island. God, how lucky to be where I am at this exact moment in my life, in the middle of nowhere and as far away as I can put myself without disappearing completely. But then maybe that is what I am trying to do when I pulled my sagging carcass from my bed in the middle of the night and drove to the marina alone, climbing aboard the boat that would take me the 20 miles into the open ocean to do what, to disappear, to become a name rather than a person you know. You don't know me.

No one knows me. Even those who think they know me, they don't know me. I've been invisible since the day I was born, a coat hanging in the closet, a man with a name, a body taking up space, talking and listening and hearing and not giving a shit. Life spins and people jabber nonsensical noises trying to be heard or thinking that they matter. You don't know me.

The sun, thankfully, the sun is there, my old friend. God, look at it, so high from the horizon I can see wisps of fog rising from the ocean's surface. Shreds really, vapor or misty particles that build during the night until they stretch some hundred feet into the air. On mornings such as this it seems as if the sun can dip its hands into the ocean and scatter particles high into the sky, bending them and stretching them and morphing them into strands of vapor dancing like ballerinas along the water's edge. Some have human features. Most do not. Some have arms and legs that look as though they are literally dancing to the motion of the sea.

Crazy? Maybe. But I've been doing this for a very long time and I've only seen this event twice before, once early in the game when I was still exploring the depths of the ocean, and again last year when I was fishing for Albacore just north of the Mexican border. And each time I've seen these mystical figures rising from the ocean's depth I've come away doubting what I have seen. A mirage? A hallucination? Tricks of the mind? The ocean in all its grandeur and majesty can do that to a man, cause him to lose his bearings, maybe some portion of his rational brain. Who knows? State of mind? State of being?

So here are the hard facts you will come to know, and possibly doubt, as you read along. As far as I know, other than the man who writes these words, no one has seen the misty creatures but me. To the few people I've mentioned it to, including my friend, Joe Rankin, who runs a daily six-pack out of Newport, and a person I would trust to know, he and the others seem to either ignore me, or as in the case of Joe, roll their eyes and walk away laughing to themselves. But I know what I see, and I know they are real. Just as I am real.

Presently I am looking at one. I see it as easily as I see the sun. And others too. It's only on particular days such as this that I see them rise out of the ocean and do their silly dance, days when a mild Santa Ana kicks in and the sea goes as smooth as a freshly polished floor. The sun appears, the misty strings lifting into the air, rising and turning a brilliant shade of pink. It's kind of scary the first time you see it, rising out of the water, swaying and lifting and getting pinker and pinker as they drift higher and higher. And just as the mist begins to glow a hot shade of pink, the whole thing disappears. Just snaps and vanishes. Not evaporate, but actually pops. And what makes it even crazier, and this may sound as though I am inventing the whole thing just to make the story interesting, but when these things disappear they really do make a popping noise, like a loud pop or a snap.

Crazy?. A Ulysses moment? And as I say this, the last of the dancing clouds has just snapped about two hundred yards off the starboard side. In all my years of traveling on the water it's never been like it is today, so vivid and loud and so outright unnerving that I am actually doubting my sanity. These things are hypnotic, whatever they are. And disbelieving. The only question is: are they real? Or am I out of sorts and imagining the whole thing? Who knows?

Anyway, I am nearing the island now and the sea is a dead calm. I love it when it is like this, like gliding through the air, content and excited, the dread of in the dark all but gone. I know without knowing that it can take but an instant and the dread can return, or should I say, will return, because pleasure is nothing but a thin layer of ice protecting the frozen lake inside us all, momentary at best, transient, fleeting, thawing, cracking, breaking and melting. And when it breaks there is nothing but the gaping cavern deep down inside.

But I am good now, so I decide to work my way up the backside toward the west end of the island. It's my usual routine. I will do this for an hour or so and then, depending on water temperature and sea conditions, make adjustment accordingly. Ahead I can see a group of birds moving aimlessly in the sky, fifty of so, both hawks and gulls spiraling high above the water, ducking occasionally as if something beneath the surface has caught their attention. Their movements are so casual that I ignore them and keep to my destination ahead, up the backside and along the ridge where the cool upwelling brings deep nutrients to the surface, and with it, what I am looking for.

Slanting at an angle just above my left shoulder, the sun's rays' glance off the ocean making it hard to see what is below. Still I can see a small blue shark swim lazily off to the side. Feeling my wake, the shark dives well beneath the surface and snakes downward until I lose track of it. Gliding effortlessly along the baron Catalina landscape, I notice the breeze slackening even more so that the boat slices effortlessly through the clear deep water, like slipping through a cloud or gliding through the air. In the distance, and to my left, perhaps twenty miles or so, San Clemente Island stands tall and blue, like a drugstore postcard, its sunlit peaks shimmering beneath halos of orange and pink and purple clouds. Behind me I can see the lures dancing their melodic song. From where I am in the tower I notice how each lure is perfectly placed, all three skipping cleanly through my silent wake. They pop to the surface every few seconds then submerge before coming up and popping again. Nothing to do now but watch and wait and wonder. Wonder. Wondering what has become my life's idle conspirator, that certain milieu that keeps me company.

By 9:30 I am halfway up the backside of Catalina and have seen nothing of interest, a few kelp stingers, which I avoid to keep from tangling the lures in them, a seal or two lying on their sides with flippers in the air, the kind of thing that always makes my heart jump because the flippers can be mistaken for a marlin fin, or even better, a sword fish. From the stereo below, I hear Rod Stewart rasping out one of his heartbreaking songs, something about a *straight-faced woman* who cheats and lies and does so with the face of a cocker spaniel. It's a song I love, although I can live without Rod Stewart. But he distracts me from a certain hollowness that is trying to take me in its grasp, so with Rod blasting in my ears I grab my first Diet Coke of the day and feel the caffeine rocking through my system. In minutes I feel juiced and ready for a fight.

It's just me and Rod now, me in the lead, of course, screaming out the words from my place on the bridge because no one within a thousand miles can hear how stupid I sound. And it is then, while screeching like a fool, that I grab for a bag of microwave popcorn and slurp my Diet Coke and for the moment feel right with the world.

The temperature gauge on the dash worries me though, the water has cooled from 69 degrees, where I started my troll, to a cool 66.5, too cold for marlin, I think. So, I consider another heading, another direction where the water will warm up and my confidence with it. On the horizon and in the direction of San Clemente Island I notice the outline of another boat. It's the only one I have seen since leaving the mainland about an hour before daybreak. The tiny dot is a long way off, miles to the west and yet, gazing at the tiny dot, I have a hunch the boat may be onto something. Excitedly, I turn the wheel in that direction and begin to motor toward it, knowing that I am a good hour away. I have moved only a few meters when a loud 'bang' startles me out of my chair and I notice that the port-side rigger has gone off.

4:21am Monday

I'd be lying if I didn't say the thought of doing this doesn't carry a certain degree uncertainty with it, like the way the early morning mist hangs so heavy you can feel it bearing down on you, my slip-ons slithering along the greasy gangway, ropes groaning, watery noises slapping, boats yawning, air so thick I feel as though I have never left my bed. It's unnerving to be here the way I am at this ungodly hour of day, or night, or something in between.

But it's what I do. And God knows I've done it so many times I'm beginning to question the sanity of it all, the alarm driving me from my bed so that even before I am alert enough to navigate my way through the front door I find myself sailing down an empty freeway to a place that scares the bejeebers out of me. I should be more of a man when it comes to the flights of fancy that invade my soul every time I do this, drag my aging wreck to the water's edge with my crazy imagination planting all sorts of wicked things in my brain, creepy figures waving wispy arms in the air, snatching at my legs and feet so that I find myself scampering along the dock hoping not to awaken the werewolves lurking in the shadows below them. I've done this with friends and I've done this alone and no matter how many times I've drug my belongings down this long wooden plank to the water's edge it's always with the same trepidation that I do so, apprehension and dread. And I'll bet you a million to one that any man that, no matter his bravery or his age, if he has done what I now set out to do, he will know exactly what I am talking about.

Like every other morning, this one is no different than the others except that the month is November and it is late in the season, so late in fact that I move with a sense of preconceived failure over the expectations of the day, doomed in spite of the warmth dripping down my face and along the brim of my cap. A certain clumsiness is in the air and I feel stupid and out of sorts as I waiver toward my objective, slip C-17, the place where she awaits my return.

As is my custom, I scan through the morning haze looking for her tall, sleek figure swaying in the distance. Seeing her, I suddenly feel better, more secure. I quickly make my way to the swim-step and notice the groan deep inside as I climb aboard and begin the task of putting things where they belong, so many things that I suddenly regret the excess I go to when planning such adventures of the soul. But soon everything is in place, so I quickly climb onto the bridge and plop myself into the captain's chair. The feeling is like falling into the cockpit of a 747. Even so a certain degree of security radiates in all that technology in front of me. Anxiously, I turn the key in the ignition and stare motionless as countless lights flash across the dash and above my head, buttons whirring, numbers scrolling, radio crackling. And for the moment I am transported back in time to the tiny arcade where my children and I used play our games of Packman and Pole Position, Eddie and Nancy, Pete and Greg living out their childhoods with an infantile man purporting to be a father, ten-twelve-fourteen, I can't recall their ages, so very long ago this all took place, me the youngest of the bunch. Quickly I shake the thought away.

Starboard is to my right. I allow my finger to touch the silver button marked starboard and like magic the sound of diesel breaks the silence. I reach for the port button and another roar barks in the dark. All is ready, engines, systems, switches, running lights, shore power, dock lines.

As I look around the helm the thought strikes me: What would my father say if he could see me now? What would this three-pack-a-day man say if I were able to somehow transport him to the present time and he could see me readying for my late November expedition into the far reaches of the ocean, to places that he and I could only dream about when I was a boy and he was doing his best to raise a son? I suppose every boy wants his father to be proud of him; I know I do even though I am anything but a boy inside. As long as I didn't end up in prison or interned at the Betty Ford Clinic or wind up spending my nights sleeping in some deserted alley, he'd be happy.

The familiar smell of exhaust fills the air. The diesels begin their rumble, levers pivot forward, teeth crash, transmissions engage, propellers churn. I can feel the throbbing engines pulling me from the dock. She is alive. And for the moment I am alive. And the day of days begins.

4:55 am

The boat creeps along the black narrow passage where her sisters sleep in their births, creepy, solemn images swaying like canyon walls beside the river I navigate, our wake nudging against velvety sides. The gentle slapping sooths the anxiety I felt when I left home more than an hour ago and the unexplained trepidation that always invades my soul. I am reassured, more confident that all will be well. Between the moon and I a pelican lifts softly into the morning air. Everywhere slender threads of green and gold shimmer across the water, phosphorous waves magnifying the solitude of the moment. My last trip, I think to myself as I maneuver cautiously among the dim silhouettes surrounding me. Last chance before winter sets in.

Cautiously I reach the main channel. I pull the starboard lever toward me, keeping the port side in its forward position, then slowly smooth the boat from west to south. Reaching the bearing that will take me to channel's end I return the starboard lever to its forward position and relax for the 20 minute ride. I am now completely alone.

I love the mix of living a life of adventure. And I love the feeling of self-worth, of knowing that I did the best I was capable of, even though that best wasn't always enough, or was misunderstood by someone who mattered, or was misdirected. Like most people, I sometimes pandered to dreams of fancy and challenged myself with thoughts of adventure and clumsy turpitude. The ship of good intentions is, for the most part, captained by fools and I was a fool when I was young, a good intentioned one but nonetheless, a fool. *There is no accuser so powerful than the conscience that dwells within*, according to my companion and good friend, Sophocles, the person who accompanies me on all my solo fishing adventures, like the one I am embarking on today. And yet, thankfully and proudly, I have never disgraced myself or my loved ones by betraying them.

Still I sail with a sense of pride and comfort having few regrets for my many commissions and omissions in life, leaving few debts or obligations in my wake. Nothing sways me or jars me into the negative except that at times I find myself venturing into places I try to stay away from, places that I rarely go. So curious and divergent are they that I don't understand what it means to go there. It's a feeling I get sometimes, a feeling that something is missing in my life, my existence fading into evening shadows, never to understand exactly what it is, something always missing. Clique I know, but there are occasions when I find myself living in a cave with Plato's shadows as the only beings to keep me company. I have been born blind or deaf or without the sense of touch and I grope in the dark for what I don't' know. I feel nothing except the rhythmic heartbeat in my chest. That is what it feels like. A folly I have, a failure. Reaching out and not being able to touch. To be misunderstood. To never understand. That is my failure, everyone's failure, to never be understood. No, I am not alone when it comes to the part that matters most, the milieu that floods my mind with sorrow.

Lights from the Balboa Fun Zone trickle across the water. To the right, across the way, the ferry sleeps in its birth. Except for a few restless souls readying for the office no one is awake at this hour of morning. To my left a man sits in a darkened house with a kitchen light blazing above his head. He reads the morning paper, the business section no doubt because he is undoubtedly a man of great wealth, as all men living at water's edge are of great wealth. Eventually he will leave his paper, shower and shave and dress himself. He'll grab something to eat, kiss his wife goodbye and leave in a grand automobile. He will spend his day in pursuit of personal gain. Which makes me wonder why it is he drives himself to such an end, why the kitchen table at 4:30 in the morning rather than in bed next to his third flaxen bride? For pride does he do this? For profit? For a house with an ocean view? For a car in a wallpapered garage? For a wife with smothering kisses and dubious intentions? Or is it vanity that yanks a man from his bed at the devil's hour? The way I am yanked from mine.

November. An autumn sun sinking into a sunburned sea. A last chance too... to do... something... anything. But what is it that I am I supposed to do?

On my right I notice the Chevron fuel dock coming awake. I see Gary inside tallying yesterday's receipts. I like Gary. He runs a good operation. Like me, Gary's ailing father died of cancer a few years back. When he died Gary took control of things. And like me, Gary misses his father, yet memories of a former time are enough to get us through our days. Soon the Chevron badge will come to life and the pumps will be put to work and the covey of blurry-eyed kids in blue and white tee shirts will hose the dock to make it habitable. Beside Gary's, I notice Davy's Locker swarming with fisherman, blurry eyed men stumbling with fishing rods and rolled up gunnysacks under their arms, tackle boxes in one hand, thermos in the other, a dopey, sanguine, scruffy look on their face suggesting that this will be the day.

Like a kid holding a tin can, I take the mike in my hand and dial the radio to 72.

"Bait barge-bait barge, you read? Slam Dunk. You there, John?"

A certain lingo exists among the occult of fisherman awake at this ungodly hour of morning, a fractured, esoteric nomenclature to let people know that we are a special breed of men, fishwives and Barbary thieves and gypsies. John is one and I am one.

"Gotcha Ed," John says, sounding drugged from a night wrapped in a bundle of soured clothes and mildewed rags.

"Morning John. Just making my turn. What's in the bin?"

"Chovies. Some big deen's," meaning anchovies and sardines.

"Roger. Be there in ten."

"Yeah, got your lights. See ya."

Looking in the distance I see John's solitary light swaying atop a slender radio antenna held in place by a simple guy wire. The hut he calls home is anchored near the entrance to the harbor. As I make my way up the channel and into the morning breeze, I see the rest of the lights come alive. Magically the harbor-end is set aglow. I imagine John beginning his day. He'll be wearing rubber boots to his waist, a cap blackened with fish parts and bird tailings, hands seasoned and cracked, a youthful smile sagging from days of fatigue.

John is a live-aboard, a 24 four-hour day, six days a week pontooned prisoner. His job is to man the bait barge from June through November and after November, the unemployment line. His soul contact with the outside world is a cell phone and the few fishermen like me to clue him in on what we think of as real. His sole companion during his exile is a mutt he calls Briscoe. From the radio I hear the Mona Lisa's chatter in the background, Lee, the bait-boat skipper bragging of his success during the night just ended, saying, 'Come to me', meaning his place just outside the harbor entrance. During the month of August when things heat up and fishing is at its best, a dozen or so boats, some as small as aluminum dinghies, some as big as Las Vegas hotels, crowd against the tiny shack John calls home, rubbing against old tires laced along the sides, positioning and repositioning their crafts hoping to be next in line. Not today though. Today I am his only customer. It is mid-November.

For now, I ignore Lee's offer to come to him and come alongside the barge instead. John throws me a line and says howdy. Thirty, he looks younger, blond hair, surfer tan, scruffy, fit, arms like Tootsie Rolls. We chat while Briscoe, John's snaggle-toothed semi-Labrador, runs helter-skelter around the barge, barking and making a fool of himself, all while he tries his luck at one of the hundreds of seagulls taunting him with their squawking yells, which he never does.

I throw a dock line and John pulls me alongside and secures the boat to a cleat. Before I can say a word, John is bringing me current on he and Meg, his live-in girlfriend who he shacks with when he's not on the barge. They have been a couple since Meg graduated from high school. Since that day she has worked her way through college and is now teaching at an elementary school somewhere nearby, Corona Del Mar, I think. They plan on getting married someday, but John keeps confounding the situation by finding one excuse after another, prevaricating and hesitating like a kid with a menu in his hand. He'll lose her someday, he tells me, shrugging, reaching down and dipping his long-handled net into the sardine infested well and handing it out to me, 'unless I get off this f...ing shit-house barge,' he says, grinning. 'We argue all the time,' and he laughs, 'then she starts calling me bait-boy and that really pisses me off'. And he's right. No self-respecting woman wants a man who swills fish guts and bird droppings for a living. But John will never leave. I've been waiting ten years for John to settle like the rest of us, compromise, make do, sediment filtering to the bottom of the tank. But it's the same thing every year, pitiful stories, broom in hand, lived-in clothes.

I think it's a way of life for guys like John, simple, manly, plenty of spitting and cursing and staying stupid. My guess is John will go through life ignoring the trappings of conventionality, as few of us have the guts to do, skirting responsibility, dodging manhood, throwing away the love of a good woman. And for what? The ocean? The unfettered life. The overwhelming desire for an unrestrained existence? Is that what we call vanity?

As I pull away from the tiny bouncing raft with its lights streaming across the bay, I see John and his friend Briscoe silhouetted beneath, Briscoe leaping into the bay and John pushing the dip-net handle after him. It's a routine they have rehearsed over and over a thousand times. I see the dog tiring and I see him take the handle between his snaggle-toothed mouth while John tugs him back onto the deck. Faintly I see what appears to be Briscoe's image dripping and running alongside his master, the two friends going about their task of cleaning up the dock, John scrubbing the nightly trimmings into the bay and Briscoe happily licks at what John leaves behind.

John. What kind of man is John? And even as I draw the question to mind, I already know the answer. And I understand the answer. Not only do I understand, but part of me honors his way of life, the part inside that lives as a boy, the part living with Pack Man and Pole Position, the part screaming to be free, the part untenable, unafraid, unconquerable, the unbearable part, the part of every man who nurtures the simple, unencumbered, shallow, existence of people like John. The part that wants to run away.

5:38am.

A faint pink glow begins to show in the eastern sky and I feel the sway of a gentle breeze coming from the north. I know it is my imagination that sees the glow, but I see it nonetheless, to the east, the sky still black as Hades but I still see it. Trying to catch a few good-sized mackerel before heading out to sea, I move just outside the harbor entrance a few meters off the east end of the jetty and shut the engines down, keeping down-breeze of the rocks so I don't have to worry about drifting into them. Like the previous one, this season has been a bust, not only for me but for every marlin fisherman along the Southern California coast. From San Diego to Oxnard a total of thirty have been recorded this year, thirty marlin for the thousands in search of them, not t mention the millions spent in their pursuit. Stupid I suppose but it is what we do. Luckily Newport has the most at a total of seventeen, so that runs in my favor. Most years, if I work hard, I'll get maybe one, two in a good year, three being my high. But this has been my worst season to date. And being mid-November and with the water cooling the way it has, today may be my last chance, if I have a chance at all.

With deck lights blazing and the engines off, I grab my mackerel rod and drop it over the side. I shove the rod into the rod holder and take a can of canned mackerel from the cupboard, open it, and scoop chucks over the side, chumming the cannibalizing mackerel to come to me. Within seconds the rod heaves toward the water and line zips from the real. Hastily I drop the can and take the rod in my hand, raising it high then dropping four shiny mackerel into the large oval tank resting in the center of the deck. I repeat the process again and again, dropping the gang of hooks over the side and raising it back over the rail. With the deck lights shining above I can see mackerel by the hundreds, by the thousands slashing through the water as they compete among themselves for the bits of food I have thrown to them.

Soon the tank is full, several marlin size baits swimming nicely in the tank and several smaller ones in case a dorado of a yellowtail happens to come along.

Loaded, I shut the deck lights off and climb onto the bridge. Using my GPS I plug in the east end of Catalina Island and check my bearing. 221 degrees reads. Next I set the autopilot to the same heading and start the engines. With the transmissions engaged, the boat automatically turns and adjusts toward my destination: Catalina. Above, the sky is starting to fade from night to morning, black to grey to a deep shade of purple, with whispers of pink shimmering on the mountains tops to the east. Moving away I now adjust the throttles to a modest ten knots, and with the boat held in the autopilot position, I can navigate while I go below and make my breakfast.

I've been navigating this way for years and it doesn't bother me the way it used to. Those first few trips to Catalina in the dark were troubling. In time my fears abated and I found I could run in the dark without much trepidation.

So I travel blind now, at least the first hour or so until the sun rises enough to see what lies ahead or what is around me, and that's when I punch the throttles for the island, engines singing and the breakfast dishes put away and the day with its many adventures and unknown consequences lying somewhere beyond the bow. Unless something crazy happens, like a partially submerged object or that oil tanker that I fail to notice, I can run safely for as long as I want. Still I know from the many close calls that I have had over the years, a false sense of security can turn a man into a complete idiot.

An hour later I am six miles off what is called the slide, or the east end of Catalina Island. It is where an abandon mining operation has scarred the land and the tailings of that mine still spill down the sides of the cliff and into the sea. A mild chop ruffles the water so that I worry about the morning being too sunny. Morning clouds lessen the westerly afternoon winds common to this part of the ocean, the sea stays lazy and more fishable that way, the way every fisherman likes it. But this is not summer, but mid-November, and with a good early morning breeze blowing out of the north-east rather than the traditional south-west, I suspect a mild Santa Ana in the offing and that delights me. If I am right about the Santa Ana, things should settle down by mid-morning and by noon the ocean should be as flat as a pond at dusk. At least that is my hope.

Lures out at last, one from each of the two riggers and another dancing from the middle of the stern. It's the way I traditionally fish when I fish alone. I use the lures to bring marlin to the surface, teasing them with the slippery imitations I make at home during the off season. Snagging a marlin using a lure is an iffy proposition at best, although I have done it many times. Teasing a marlin excites the fish so that it chases behind the boat hoping to take hold of the homegrown decoy I'm dragging. Sometimes they stick but usually not, the fish slashing the plastic lure like crazy but giving up when it fails to kill it. The best hope of actually snagging a marlin is, using a separate rod, you drop a live mackerel over the side and allow it to fall back to the streaking fish. All excited they often race to the bait and swallow it, hook and all. It happens. Sometimes it happens. But usually not. Takes years sometimes. I know guys who have been marlin fishing for years and never even seen on.

With the lures knifing through the boats wake I take my bait-rod in hand and snag a lively mackerel from the bait tank and slide the large, stainless steel hook into and just behind the fish's dorsal fin. After the mackerel is hooked, I carefully place him back in the tank so he can swim in circles with his friends. He swims as before and I am excited as the bait seems not to notice the large metal hook running through his back. Nor is he aware that there is a good chance he will become a meal for a hungry marlin, at least that is my hope. Having completed my routine, I return the rod into its holder and climb the tower to have a look around.

8:10 am

The bang causes me to panic. I always panic when a rigger pops loose. It is so sudden that the mind goes blank for a second or two. Frozen, not knowing what to do or exactly what happened, I quickly look up and see that the rigger is standing erect and not flexing from the pressure of the lure. Then I notice the rod, whose line the rigger was clipped to, is pulling naturally, as if nothing has taken hold. What happened, I wonder to myself? Why did the rigger go off? A piece of kelp snagging the hook? A large swell pulling it from the clip?

Confused, I hurriedly gather my thoughts and think what to do. The drop-back I tell myself, it could have been a marlin snatching at the lure and not a something else. Don't wait, drop the bait behind the boat. But I do nothing, doubting, confused, probably a piece of kelp snagging the hook and breaking the clip from the outrigger. Looking at the wake behind me, I see nothing. No sign of anything. No tail. No marlin slashing at the surface, no fin darting back and forth, no wild pursuit, nothing, just three lures slipping effortlessly through a quiet aqua-blue ocean. Still I stand frozen with my eyes suffocating the ocean.

After a minute or so I decide to make a large circle of the area just in case. One line is still working from the back, another loose from its clip but zipping nicely along the port side, the third snug in its clip, bouncing along the starboard side.

Within seconds the starboard rigger goes off. And like an idiot I hesitate again. The bang has sent a shock through my system so that I cannot move. Instead I stand frozen as a stop sign. But only for a second, for in that second I see the starboard rod doubled over and line is screaming from the real.

'Marlin', I silently scream at my feet as they ignore the four steps leading to the deck and hit it with a thud. I quickly wrestle the bending rod from its holder and feel the line peeling in gulps. With the rod safely in my hands I struggle with the force at the other end. But before I can steady myself against the rail the rod goes limp, the slack causing me to stumble backward so that I smash into the tackle center, hurting my back in the process.

"God damn it", I scream as loud as I can, lifting the rod and taking a few limp passes of the crank just to be sure.

"God damn-damn-damn", I curse again. With the fish gone I throw the rod back into its holder and reach for the one with the mackerel pinned to it and drop the live bait over the transom. With the boat still running at trolling speed, I see the bait wash aimlessly behind the boat, sliding further and further back until it approaches what I think to be the proper distance and there I thumb the spool to a stop.

Then suddenly the ocean explodes with marlin. Beaks and tails and fins are everywhere. I see baitfish peeling in waves. Birds appear out of nowhere. Gulls are beating the water into a crisp, white froth. Hawks dive like bombers straight into the frenzy beneath, their black and white bodies driving the poor, terrorized bait deeper and deeper into the slaughter below.

It is at this moment that the rod beside me goes off, the port rod, the same one that was hit just seconds earlier. The next thing I know a marlin is jumping about fifty yards from the boat. It is racing like a rocket to my right. Then in a blink of an eye it turns and moves directly at me, jumping wildly in the air, its purplish-blue stripes glowing feverishly as I stand watching like kid at the circus. Again he jumps. And it is then that I notice a peculiar object flailing in corner of its mouth, the green and black hand-crafted lure I made in my workshop the previous winter. I had rigged it the night before and there it is blazing like the Fourth of July, the plastic skirt made from an old seat cover shaking in the fishes' mouth like strands of spaghetti.

The rod continues to scream, line peeling in gulps as the fish continues to jump in my direction. But instead of picking up the rod that the fish is attached to, I stupidly keep the bait-rigged rod in my hand. Surly, I think in my frazzled state of mind, something will take the bait behind the boat; it rests smack in the middle of a giant feeding frenzy. There are so many fish I lose count. "Grab it," I scream, "grab it!"

With the one rod solidly hooked and line peeling off to my right, it seems crazy not to pick it up. But I know that a lure-hooked fish is more likely to come undone than one hooked in the gut. But how long do I wait?

Then I realize that the boat is still moving forward. Holding the bait rod in my hand, I run the two paces to where the throttles are on the tackle center and pull the levers back and shut the engines down. The reel to my right is still losing line, which causes me to lose patience, so I finally turn toward it in an effort to exchange the one in my had. But before I can take a single step the line under my thumb jumps and starts spinning from the real, spinning with such force that I can smell my skin burning from the pressure I apply.

"Oh my God," I think, still panicked at my predicament, "he's got it." The line spins even faster... "He's running for the border." I begin my count to ten, just as my friend Hamner taught me to, knowing that it takes a good ten seconds for a marlin to swallow a ten-inch mackerel. "Two-three-four," I yell in rapid succession. But I can't wait any longer. The line is sizzling my thumb raw. The rod next to me is going berserk and there are a million or so marlin waging war behind the boat, beaks and tails still slashing like sabers at war. I can't wait. I've got to do it now.

So I shove the reel in gear, too soon I worry for I had only reached the count of four, and instantly the line begins to hiss through the water. The rod heaves in my hand. It is at this exact moment that the water explodes in a shower of blue and silver and violet and the most glorious sight I have ever seen goes leaping into the blue Catalina sky, a fluorescent marlin lit up like a neon light.

Never have I experienced anything so powerful as what I see taking place right in front of me. Marlin everywhere, all slashing like bullets through crystal glass, one hooked to a lure far off to my right, another dancing wildly off to my left. But then I think to myself, what is my strategy? Stay with one? Try for both? But how? The rod with the lure is pulsating like a water-witch, surging and yielding, surging and yielding with the fish at the other end at least 400 yards from the boat and heading in any number of directions.

The fish I am dealing with in my hand has taken several more jumps and is heading south. I should restart the boat, begin a backward crawl, try to keep pace. But no, backing up would cause me to run over the other line. So I play it dead in the water and trust the fish to tire before the line breaks.

At this point, and with about 2/3 of the line gone, I can feel the line start to slacken. I suspect the fish is turning and running toward me. Quickly, I retrieve line as fast as I can, praying that the marlin at the other end won't come undone. Ten, twenty, thirty seconds go by while my right arm cramps with fatigue. Then I feel him, closer and down slightly. He is pulling hard and the line is coming off faster than it went on. Suddenly the line begins to lift, rising to the surface so rapidly that I can't keep up. The fish jumps headfirst and rattles its head trying to shake the hook from somewhere deep within his throat. Again he jumps with the same force and the same shake of the head.

Next to me I notice the other rod is tugging only occasionally, not steady as before; the other fish still hooked but so few wraps left on the spool that I know I will lose the fish.

It's been a good ten or twelve minutes and I am beginning to think that if I am skillful and very, very lucky, I have a chance of landing both fish. All I need is to get the one in my hand close enough to where I can reach the leader and cut him loose (leadering is considered a catch by the standards of the Balboa Angling Club) and then I can concentrate on the other. And if I have the presence of mind I'll snap a quick picture with the disposable camera I keep in my vest pocket. The camera is there to keep doubters at bay.

For the second time the fish turns and runs deep and directly at the boat. I begin another manic effort to retrieve line as fast as I can, spinning the crank so that my knuckles crack against the side of the reel, bloodying them to the point that red dots form across the front of my shirt. I do my best to keep up, but the fish moves faster than I can reel.

All of a sudden the marlin is almost in my lap. It is fifty yards, forty yards and closing. He is dancing on his tail and coming directly at the boat. He dives but is up again, again on his tail and closer than before, so close that I can see the hook glinting precariously in the corner of his mouth and not in the gut as I had hoped. Thoughts of counting to four and not to ten come to mind. Being almost on top of me, I feign to my left ready to dive to the deck in case he crashes into the boat. It is then, just as I think the fish is about to dive under the boat that he is practically in my lap, his black tapered spike pointing at my head while his body flexes and his eyeball looks directly into mine. Startled, I duck just as the marlin bangs hard against the swim step. The boat shutters from the blow. Thoughts of injury to the fish both sadden and sicken me and my mind imagines the swim step being ripped from its mount.

Instantly I jump to my feet and swing the rod over the back, shoving the tip as deep into the water as I can, praying that the fish hasn't come undone. Thank God, he hasn't. Handfuls of line zip from the reel as I lean further and further over the edge of the boat. While dangling over the back of the boat, I catch a glimpse of something jumping on the other side. It's the fish at the other end. He's going like a locomotive and there is nothing I can do about it. Line sizzles along the bottom of the boat so I reach the rod tip even further into the water hoping against hope that somehow it doesn't break.

Then a pop is heard and the rod snaps free. I realize the line has touched a propeller and the fish is gone.

"God damn it", I curse out loud. "Son of a…" But there is no time for swearing, so without attempting to find a holder, I throw the rod to the deck and pick up the other one. I retrieve line as furiously as I can, cranking so hard that my hand keeps slipping from the knob and my clumsy actions make me feel like a rookie. Twenty cranks, twenty-five and nothing. I look at the reel and quickly realize that the spool is empty.

"God damn it," I scream, only this time it's not merely frustration, this time I want to kill somebody.

Calming myself and regaining control of my temper, knowing that in all probability all is lost and the season over, I set the rod in its holder and regain the one I had thrown to the deck a moment before. I place it in another holder and run to the bait tank, forgetting momentarily that the line on my bait rod has snapped in two and needs to be re-rigged. Within minutes I have another mackerel in the water hoping that my opportunity has not vanished. But when I look behind the boat I see nothing at all. The water stands as peaceful as a morning sunrise. Above I notice a few birds gliding effortlessly in the sky and the ocean maintains is deep blue presence. My instinct tells me my chance has come and gone.

Thirty minutes of wishful thinking go by and I give up the game. I reset the lures as before and climb the tower.

But I feel like shit. Never have I seen so many marlin ganged together in one spot. A man sees maybe one or two a season, sometimes more, sometimes none at all. Some guys fish their entire life and never see one. But that many? And three lures going down in a matter of seconds, another running off with the bait? How many chances does a guy get? I am disappointed and disgusted with myself.

There'll be no call to the angling club this day, no Ed Bach listed on the board, no call to the nightly fish report saying how Slam Dunk released a marlin six miles up the backside of Catalina, no credit given, no award or recognition at the dock, no blue and white flag flying from the rigger, no glory, no dockside parade, nothing, just a lot of smack about the one that got away. My ego has been trammeled and my vanity sapped. And I wonder if this is what it all comes down to, why I do what I do. Is it self-glorification? Is that what this is all about, boasting and bragging and finger pointing, the alpha monkey thing, super ego, recognition, status, a pin, a trophy? And yes, I think to myself, that is precisely why I do it. We men… we love our medals. Vanity drives is, pride, recognition, celebrity. Again I am disgusted with myself.

And yet I know deep inside that this is not why I do it. I am disappointed, yes. I am competitive and egoistic and just as vain as the next guy. And yet this is not why I do what I do, not to flaunt a medal on my chest. I do it because I can. I do it because of what took place just moments ago, man and beast in a rhythmic rhapsody of nature, natural and personal and completely raw.

Yes, that is why I do it. And yet I know that is not the reason I spend the countless hours at sea seeking the raw adventure of ocean and sky while combating all the discomforts nature can deliver. The reason I do it is to distract myself from the forever gloom that rides in the backseat of my brain, the unrest of a unsettled mind.

10:56 am

I discarded my friends a few years back, or should I say my friends discarded me, however you to look at it, they are gone. Age does that to a man, sends him into the sunset when people quit paying attention. The only thing people notice at the age I am today is the slow deliberate meeting of nose and chin, that and the fact that my ears now sprout what looks to be stalks of corn and my mating spear has lost its spirit. Sharing my adventures was the kind of thing I looked forward to when I was young and hard and full of surprise, me and the boys at the 24-hour coffee shop hitched and ready to go, back-slapping from sunup to sundown, ball caps and beer and laughing til my nose started to run.

Yeah, those were the good old days. But I'm Hemingway now and the kind of stuff I used to kill for only irritates me and makes me mad in the face. It's the winter of my discontent, the beginning of my 63rd year. (67th as I rewrite the words I first penned four years back and am reading and changing once again.). Friendships and pals and slaps on the back are a remembrance of a bully-bully past. But life is what interest this old man now, what's left of it anyway, its currents and variant streams, the intrinsically native existence of a seasoned old soul. This feeling of solitude I have is something one cannot share or pass along or barter away. It deserves more. It deserves better. It is the search for the missing part, the link to that mind-numbing milieu that haunts my very soul.

Beginning a move to the outside I see the other boat still hanging in the far distance. Maybe he's on to something, I think to myself. I turn in that direction and set my heading and my speed to eight knots and I reflect back on the opportunity missed earlier in the day. Still there is no regret. Sure, I wanted the fish, but catching is not the prize I am after. The angling club, bragging, a snap-shot, the blue and white flag, all important, all ego thumping, but not the reason. I was there. I had seen what I had seen. I had been a part of it. That's the reason. That is the reason I suffer the night.

Moving directly toward San Clemente and in the direction of the boat still miles on the horizon, I settle in the tower to begin my survey of the glassy surface spread as far as the eye can see. Never have I seen the ocean as flat as it is today, like floating on top of a cloud. I wish my sons had been there to see the swarm behind the boat. My daughter too. And Joan. They would have marveled at what they saw, marveled and become frightened and a little sad by the spectacle nature endures. But it wouldn't be the same with Nancy and Joan as it would be with the boys, they wouldn't treasure it the way a man does, or a boy, or me, absorbing the gift and feeling it burn deep inside my bones.

I wish my father could have experienced the day with me, although he would be in his eighties by now and probably too feeble to travel the ocean, even on a day such as this. We fished a lot, he and I, back when I was a kid and he was still alive and healthy and free from cancer, the day-boats we use to take from the San Clemente Pier, how the boats would pull beneath the pier and my dad and I would waggle down the wobbly steps to where the ocean surged beneath our feet, the two of us struggling aboard and grabbing our place among the mob of fisherman heading out to god knows where. There was the barge, and Newport bay, the Huntington Beach Pier, surf fishing, a rental skiff rowed around the bay.

I think of our trips to the Newport jetty and how we carried our crummy bamboo rods and our bucket full of dead anchovies and our lunch-filled gunny sacks, dragging them atop the huge granite boulders that guarded the entrance to the bay, hopping from rock to rock all the way to the end where we would plop our fannies on a rag and sit there with our warped wooden rods and cheap Jig Master Reels wedged between a pair of rocks. We'd sit there for hours hoping against hope that a big halibut or white sea bass or even a sand bass would come along and add substance to our day. And on those few occasions when we were lucky enough to catch something considered worthy of our efforts we would drag it to our car and carry it home and proudly display our success to those who mattered to us. And when all was done and the fish cleaned and cooked and eaten I would notice the pleasure on my father's face and the reassurance it gave him to know that he was a man of considerable worth

To my left and a few hundred yards distance, I make out what looks like a truck size kelp paddy floating silently on the surface, the largest I've seen all day. I click off the auto-pilot and just before reaching the paddy I ready my light tackle rod by hooking on a sardine and leaving it to swim free in the bait tank. Once back in the tower I pull within a few yards of the paddy and shut the engines down. With my polarized glasses focused on what lies below, I look deep into the water. The sun's rays penetrate so deep that it seems as though I can see the bottom, which, of course, is impossible. But the ocean is a lake and the sun is at its zenith and whatever happens to be lurking just below should become obvious. But I see nothing, only blue turning into black.

Almost giving up, but thinking better of it, I scale the ladder back to the deck and dip a net full of wriggling sardines from the bait tank and throw them over the side. Even before I can take the rod in my hand, my peripheral vision catches a white flash just to my right, then a boil, then another, further out but definitely a boil. My bait hits the water and in an instant the rod in my hands bends in two as the fish runs directly toward the kelp paddy. It is then that I realize I had pulled too close to the paddy and the yellowtail is doing what his natural instinct tells it to do, hightail it for safety. I tighten the drag but that does nothing. He's moving at the speed of light. Frantically, I thumb the line and that too fails except that the spinning spool removes another layer of skin from my already blistered thumb. In a matter of seconds, the yellowtail has attached my line to the world's largest kelp paddy and I am doing all I can to get it free. I free-line the reel for a minute (slacken it) but that does nothing, I am snagged tight. Five minutes go by and I decide the only thing to do is pop him free. I put the reel in gear and point the rod-tip at the piece of floating kelp and give it all I got. I hear the line pop and I go about re-rigging for another cast.

Ten minutes later I am back in the tower moving as I was before, in the direction of the other boat. My presence had contaminated the water and spooked the fish into a sort of hibernation.

Moving as I am, the water lapping so gently against the hull it's as if the boat is no little more than a silken thread cutting through a gentle breeze. At times like this I want to lie down and sleep in her lap, but I know that mother nature in all her majesty has a mortal sin in her soul. She hides her a savagery at times like this, her ravenous beauty lulling us to sleep. But at her core hides the marlin frenzy of before, thousands of anchovies mutilated by a team of ravenous fish, gulls and pelicans and hawks feeding on the spoils, an oil slick a thousand feet across. It is hard to detect this cruelty in its purest form because, we humans with our social morality looking the other way, as a subconscious subterfuge to camouflage the inherent cruelty within nature's system. But it is there, nature in its rawest form, the ocean erupting in a private yet very cruel system of kill and be killed, a system almost completely invisible to the human eye and mind.

12:21 am

Now I notice the other boat moving in my direction. The boat is still a mile or so away, but even at that distance, I can make out the long, slender bow-sprit snorkeling over the front of the bow. This tells me it is a plank-boat, a sword-fisher. And a small one too, probably an independent working out of San Diego or San Pedro. My guess is the person running the boat is a free-range gun-slinger who prowls the channel looking for the biggest and richest game in town. How these guys eke out a living by harpooning the toughest son-of-a-bitch in the sea I'll never know.

Soon the distance between us narrows to the point where the plank-boat is only a few hundred yards off my bow. Thinking he doesn't see me or more likely that the captain is challenging me to give way rather than him changing course I begin angling a few degrees to the starboard, thinking that I'd give some sort of salute as we passed along side, a sort of scornful nod in deference to his superior ranking among deep ocean anglers. Like it or not, a natural animosity exists between harpooners and sports fishermen, something along the lines of cattlemen and sheep herders. We sport-fisher types are little more than piss-ant rich kids who take their toys to the beach to play in the water where harpooners make their living in the water. Naturally a certain hostility exists. So as I move about ten degrees to the right knowing he probably resents my being in the same ocean, he shifts the same way, closing the gap between us rather than widening it as I expected. We move closer and closer until there are only about a hundred yards separating the two of us. And it is then that I notice his speed has slowed and the skipper is signaling for me to come along side, not waving exactly but holding his arm to the side as if signaling for a left turn. I follow his direction and crawl close enough that we angle next to each other and steady our boats side by side. He shuts his engine down and I do the same, the two of us almost eye to eye, our towers almost touching, the ocean so serene and so calm that we are like two people pulling up a chair for a little chat.

"How ya doing?" he says, relaxing, a somber grayish grin sneaking beneath a grim-filled cap. The cap has browned with age but the word Caterpillar seeps through. "See anything? I'm Nick."

Nick wears a long sleeve shirt and a five day beard. Side-curtains angle beneath the moldy cap and run from eyeball to eyeball completely around his head. Sunglasses fill the gap between. Beneath nothing but a black void with white zinc lips and nose. I look pretty much the same except my cap holds a large terry towel that droops to my shoulders and I don't use zinc.

In a flurry of words I tell Nick about the huge patch of marlin I ran across earlier in the day. He chuckles as though he'd experienced the same thing a million times but willing to allow me a sacred moment. He talks of the day and how quite it's been for him except for the one little peek he had around nine o'clock that morning, "Fish went deep before I could get on it," he says, laughing rather than chuckle, laughing so effortlessly that a pang of envy runs through my system. "Spook easy now… this time of year anyway…. water getting cold the way it's done. Fish know when I'm there… know even before I do," he says, a big white laugh showing beneath his cap. "Week ago… no more like a month ago, they'd lay on top and wait all day…til you was ready anyway… then cozy up…take aim… zip."

We talk for several minutes, Nick reclining in his weather beaten tower the way a businessman does in a chair, feet splayed across a makeshift instrument panel while the two of us jaw about the ups and downs of fishing. We joke back and forth like two old friends. And while we are there I can't help but marvel at the picture we must make as we drift side by side in the middle of nowhere, a plank-boat skipper with his make shift boat trying to earn a living in an internet savvy world, and me, the retired old geezer sitting atop his spotless, teak and stainless-steel sport-fisher dicking his life away.

How different we are. I'm surprised he doesn't hate my guts. And yet here we are, two very distinct and different individuals sitting in the middle of the Pacific Ocean on a picture perfect Monday with nothing better to do but yak and trade stories and enjoy the magic of moment.

I suppose the ocean can do that to a person, make brothers of people the way a foxhole brothers up men in uniform, bonding them to a common enemy, or as the case may be, to a common God. Calm and clear and as quiet as the earth can make itself, the only sound the gentle lap of the sea against the hull of the two boats, it is definitely a Godlike moment.

We talk and I begin to I wonder how it is that Nick can harpoon a moving swordfish while operating the boat at the same time. Then, as if to answer my thoughts, a girl with yellow pigtails jutting horizontally from her head and looks to be no more than sixteen, pokes a sleepy face from the tiny cabin, stumbles and waves in my direction. She pulls on Nicks leg and says something and goes back inside. "Bout time," he says, throwing what looks to be an empty plastic water bottle after her. Okay, I think, that answers my question, at least one part of the question. But seeing the freckled sun-burnt face and the pigtails brings to mind another question. Which of the two throws the spear, he or the girl? "Amy steers," he says, "I stick the fish," he tells me, evidently reading my mind. "She's two weeks late already. School," he says, shaking his head, the merriment of before turning more somber and more reflective. "Man, her mom's going to kill me when we get back." Which makes me wonder what school he's talking about, grammar school?

I want to ask but can't. The question would come off as judgmental, mainlandish, condemning. So I stay on subject. "You use a plane?" I ask, trying to sound in the know.

"Nah. Spotter's too spensive. Grand a day. For the big boys. Not me. Sometimes the fish showing real good, I split with three, four guys. Mostly don't. Me and Amy spent a few days at Clemente, got a ton of Albies in the bin. Heading back to Pedro. Got to get Amy home. Thinking maybe a swordie on the way. Flat enough."

Amy. Ton of albies. A deck littered with barrels and ropes and buoys and enough junk to sink a merchant ship, not to mention a galley that smells of pork rind and cheap beer. It's the place Amy calls home, the place where she cooks and washes and sleeps and who knows what else, two crazy, non-conforming, poles apart, vagabonds wandering the ocean looking for a place to land. Christ almighty, where have I been?

We start our engines, my twin turbo diesels roaring to life while his single four-banger sputters like it's coming down with the flu. Then I hear his engine catch and clutch and begin churning for all its worth. We wave. No sign of Amy. I watch as his mostly used up boat slowly creeps away to the west while I push the throttles to the east, to San Clemente Island and in the opposite direction from where I began the day.

It's nearing two o'clock now, late if I want to make it back before dark. And I don't want to wind up on the other side of the world before heading back either. If I don't turn back soon, it'll be dark before I reach the harbor. But I do want to make San Clemente for a quick run along the front side, and I've gone this far so I might as well go for it. Besides, Clemente is more likely to hold the marlin I am looking for.

As most fishermen do, I lament having left Catalina and that big pod of marlin. Probably a huge mistake knowing fish were there and I am somewhere else. But I'm committed and there is no turning back. Besides, it's not every day the ocean squats the way it does today, allowing a guy in a 34 footer to fish this late. And with just a few hours left, this is undoubtedly my last shot at a marlin this year.

At my 8 knot trolling speed I figure I'll be close by around 3:00 or so then give it a couple of hours along the inside ridge where the best upwelling is, maybe till sunset then when dusk settles in I'll start hightailing it for home. What the hell, I think to myself, three hours in the dark at 22 knots, knowing my impatience will cause me to cook the engines and not limp on in as most sane people tend do. Scary and nutty dark. Crazy dark. 22 knots dark. But the ocean is as flat as a cookie sheet and if I die, what the hell, it's a good way to go. Sanity is nothing but conformity anyway. And being no believer in fate or destiny or any of that predestination baloney, I'll cook it on in and that'll put me at the dock around 9:00 o'clock, and that'll get me home by 10:30ish. She'll give me hell for being late, but we'll eat a late dinner and I'll tell her about the marlin and Nick, and she'll shake her head perplexed as always. Conformity has its virtues.

Maybe Zane Grey said it best when he contemplated why he fished. "*I cannot help but marvel at the strange, imbecilic pursuits of mankind, fishing being just one.*" And Hemingway, "*And while you wait, man has time to think. They can put a man in jail for what he thinks, mostly it's nobody's business. But it's mostly about the fish that he thinks.*"

3:12 pm

I am a couple of miles off the island and so far nothing, nothing to get excited about anyway. A few birds working here and there, the water still so flat that it looks like a roller-rink, a little cold at 67.5 degrees, but warm enough to know that what I am looking for could still be around. Doable in other words. And I notice plenty of red streaks on the Fathometer, meaning small bait-balls popping beneath the boat. And the closer I get to the island the larger red clots get, all good signs. Over my shoulder, the sun's rays feel crisp and cool against my clothing, chilling me and warming me at the same time.

I am alone in the world and glad of it. Nothing hinders me. Nothing distracts from the moment, the perfect, peaceful, alone moment that I long for. It is mine. A million years will pass with eternity rocketing at the speed of light, and still nothing will recapture the feeling of this moment. For the moment is perfect. And I feel happy not to have to share the moment with anyone, to feel the rattling sensation of someone's presence against my back. I am alone and that is all that matters, for I believe that being alone in the world is when man is truly free, free of obligation to anyone but himself and all that surrounds him; nature. Perhaps that is the emptiness I feel, the completeness of being alone.

The sun burns the sky the color of dark amber and I squint into the sinking sun for signs of life. A gentle rise and fall of the boat tells me that all is well, and I slice through the oncoming swell like a knife cutting through a cake, cleanly and skillfully so the water peals from the hull in layers of silent relief. Never have I felt more alive than at this moment. The sea is as serene and as loving as a woman on her wedding night, her hands tender and caressing, and me the nervous groom trembling with anticipation. What fury this woman can bring when she raises her voice in anger, her screams building into a mountain of rage, her arms a torrent of disaster. I have experienced this rage many times in my life and I have done so with great trepidation, like a sailor in a storm, fervently, cautiously, wary. Perhaps this is the reason I worship her the way I do, because I tempt the fates so foolishly, so recklessly, fouling her impetuous pride like an inebriated sea captain. And yet, today, she slumbers before me like a sea of dreams, and I know all is well between us. And it is days like today that

I love her more than I have ever loved her before, this mercurial, fickle, impetuous woman I call the sea.

Clear blue water continues to fill my binoculars with miles and miles of ocean. About a hundred yards to my left a big hammerhead shows itself. I troll to where it swims like a lazy snake just beneath the surface, his huge dorsal rising like a tree in a swamp. I give little thought to the shark, other that to admire his size and his enduring hulk, shuttering momentarily when I shut the engines down and climb into the cockpit to take a better look. His enormity stuns me and I watch from my place at the rail as the hammerhead turns in my direction, his head and frog-sized eyes zigzagging back and forth until this man-eater is directly beneath the swim step. No matter where a guy stands in relation to an eight-foot hammerhead, he is scalded with fear, and I jerk away as if being yanked from behind. I have no thought of tossing the big fellow a bait, no rod in the world is up to the task for this giant. Even if I did make a try, Mr. Hammerhead would chomp the leader into threads.

I restart the boat and follow the big fish, keeping after him for a few hundred yards before he gets tired of me breathing down his neck and makes a run for the bottom.

A few kelp paddies in the distance prove empty, a huge sunfish basking on the surface beside one, but no sign of a tail or a fin or a group of feeders as I had hoped.

It is nearing 4 o'clock when, through the binoculars, I notice something in the far distance. A wisp of something white. A wisp of something white and soft… feathers dancing on the horizon. Whatever it is I am seeing, tiny, wispy feathers, they appear like tiny flecks, appearing and then just as soon disappearing. I keep the binoculars trained in that direction and with the boat running smoothly I can keep focused on a very small patch of ocean. Then another wisp shows. Then another. My hope is building. I can tell from the pattern that it isn't a jumper. These are no acrobatic marlin in the distance. The wisps I see are irregular and tighter. And there are many of them, more and more as I keep a trained eye.

So I wait and watch. More wisps. And more wisps. They are as I expect, porpoise, a lot of porpoise, a huge school about 2 miles directly upstream. And with porpoise are yellow fin. And November means big yellow fin, Clemente is known for them.

Excited, I pull in the lures, jump to the bridge, zip closed the curtains, and gas it. Twenty seven knots, wide open I make my run, good old Slam Dunk skipping like Uncle Greg in the Addictor. I am heading west toward the setting sun, a million porpoise racing for the moon.

Ten minutes and I am alongside, me and my bone-shattered corpse rattling inside. What looks like a hurricane tearing at the ocean is really a countless school of porpoise on the move. They are scattered as far as the eye can see, several thousand yards across and maybe a thousand yards deep, all hightailing toward the setting sun, and doing it at a clip I can barely keep up with. They are jumping and diving and breaching, some hurtling their glistening, sun-bronzed bodies more than twenty feet into the air, twisting and somersaulting like an acrobat at the circus. It is beautiful. And as strange as it seems, I can't help thinking that their performance is for me and me alone.

With throttles wide open and careful to keep well to one side, lest I spook the school and send the entire herd swerving in another direction, I dash for a position at the head and to a place where I am in front with the porpoise coming directly at me. They are formed like an enormous V, migrating birds or a squadron of f-16s, only bigger, much, much bigger. I am so excited that I almost break my leg jumping from the bridge onto the cockpit. I pull the throttles back and grab my 30-pound rod and pin on a small mackerel, 7 inches or so, one snagged that morning off the north jetty, the same jetty my father and I fished so many years in the past. With the boat gliding forward, I drop the mackerel over the back the way I do when dropping back to a marlin, and allow the bait to glide maybe 50 feet or so before shutting the engines down.

The school is shooting along both sides of me now, the ocean alive with large silver bodies breaching and rolling and jumping like children with a new bike. I am awed by what I see, so many fish so close to the boat, so close that I fear one of my outriggers will get hit. A mother and her pup streak beside me. They dart and weave in perfect symmetry, which makes me wonder at the magic that guides them, what sort of mysterious telepathy is at work in their brains that allow them to navigate the way they do, changing directions and accelerating in such perfect unison, as if bonded by some mysterious tether. The scene I witness is both glorious and magnificent, and terrifying too. There are so many fish that I feel as though I am under attack, at the very least, an intruder.

Suddenly the reel jerks in my hand and the line sizzles under my already swollen thumb. Numbed be the ferocity of the strike, I give it 2 counts, no more, and shove the reel in gear. The rod doubles over. The reel literally screams as line disappears so fast I can hardly believe it. I have caught hundreds of yellow fin in my life, most between 10 and 20 pounds, but the one at the other end feels twice that size, larger maybe. With line disappearing in chunks I have no choice but to go after the fish, it's either that or run out of line. While holding the rod in one hand, I restart the engines with the other. I spin the boat so that the bow is pointing directly toward the disappearing line and begin the chase.

Ten minutes later I have gained most of the line back. But the fish, which, to my surprise, is so strong that I think it could be a marlin after all. But then again whatever it is, he seems to be doing all he can to keep up with his friends who are still jumping all around me.

But we are falling behind, and I suspect it is for that reason that the fish begins to change tactics. He now feels as if he is going deep rather than keeping up. No longer is he running and because the change is so swift I almost run over the line. He's straight down now, a hundred, two hundred feet or so and holding firm. It's a tug of war and I realize I have a tuna on the line and not a marlin, a big-eye maybe, but most likely a big, big yellow fin.

I shut the engines down again and start the old heave ho, that is, pump up and down as hard as it can. But for every few inches of line on the reel the fish takes more. It's a loosing cause. Ten more minutes of bending and weaving and I know I am in for the fight of my life. I've come to realize that this is a big, powerful fish wrestling at the other end, 50 pounds at least, maybe more, certainly larger than any tuna I've ever caught, or have ever seen. And that makes me wonder if I am up to the task. Dark gathers in chunks and I can feel my 60-year-old bones weakening from the long day and the sleepless night of before. He has only been on a short time, maybe 30 minutes, and already I feel like yesterday's gruel. In the distance I see porpoise blasting into the sunset, small flecks of white against a purple and gold sky. The sun is hovering majestically above Catalina with smoky cirrus clouds filtering the fading light across the sea. Remarkable.

With the fish still down and holding steady, I do something I have never done before. I raise the rod and set it in the rod holder and go inside the cabin and flop onto the bunk. Spent, I want to lie in this spot forever. Crazy as it seems, I even contemplate turning the TV on to distract me from the rod bending and heaving just outside the cabin door. I am that delirious. From my place on the bunk I watch the rod bend mightily toward the water, almost to the breaking point before I see it flex upward before bending down again. I watch the dance for several minutes, lying on my back ashamed and disgusted with myself. This is truly one of those times I am glad to be alone. Here I am lying like a wimp while the poor bastard fish is fighting for his god damned life.

Shamed, I get up and glug a few gulps of water from the fridge and race to the deck. There I struggle to take the rod from the holder and begin the fight once again. But it's not the same as before. I know I cheated and that I deserted my station when I cowardly ran from the field. This sudden loss of manhood makes me doubt who I am. What would I have done had I been lying in a rice paddy in Nam, or a foxhole in Korea, or behind a tank during the Battle of the Bulge? God, what kind of man am I?

My guilt makes me redouble my efforts and I dig in even harder. Tightening the drag to the breaking point, I give it all I got, lifting the rod a few gulps then lowering it, then raising it again, then lowering it. I do this for a good ten minutes, the sweat leaping from my brow, my shirt soaked from neck to waist, my efforts redoubled when I realize that I have gained nothing, the line slipping as fast as it goes on.

Desperate, the sun lower now, I tighten the drag even more. From my foxhole I crank the handle like a maniac. Finally the line begins to build on the spool. Another ten minutes of lifting and lowering and I am ready to burst from fatigue. My arms are on fire and my right hand has lost all sense of coordination. It is dusk with the sun falling behind Catalina. Still enough time.

It comes in clumps now, green monofilament gathering bite after bite until suddenly there he is, the fish, my fish circling some twenty feet below, silver and blue flickers swimming in a large deep circle. From experience I know he is in his death spiral, swimming counter clock wise on his side as all tuna tend to do at the end. Around and around he goes, pitifully around in a giant loop of death, under and away, under and away, all the while thrusting his powerful tail in a desperate attempt to break free.

But he comes. Closer now and I feel revived, elated at his size, ecstatic at the enormity swimming below my feet. I try and ignore those moments spent in the cabin and my cowardly retreat, thinking instead of my strategy and the best way to land the giant fish without killing myself in the process. With the rod in my right hand, I wedge the butt against my thigh and take the transom-door clasp in my left hand and open it. It swings to the side where I quickly lock it in place. With the door open it is just a matter of standing on the swim step and gaffing the fish then lifting him onto the cockpit. I also realize that this is not so simple samatter considering his size and the frenzy he will make once on board.

Sixty, I think, sixty pounds, at least, the largest tuna I have ever caught, and that includes my trip to Mexico when Eddie was only twelve years old. In my mind I see myself making the call to the angling club. I'll report the large school of tuna roaming the far end of San Clemente, I'll give longitude and latitude, the size of the fish, and oh yes, the sixty pounder I just put on board, that too. Yes, bragging without the appearance of doing just that is what it is all about, like scoring the winning TD and then tossing the ball back to the ref. No big deal.

He swims recklessly now, his life all but wrenched from his exhausted body. I stand above him with gaff in hand. His large eye locked onto mine. He's finished. He is giving himself up. He circles to a certain death.

Knowing the strength it will take to pull 60 pounds of writhing fish through the transom door, I decide to do as before. I set the rod in the rod holder and take the gaff in both hands. The fish apparently takes no notice of what I am about to do, focusing instead on the gaff being lowered into the water where he circles helplessly on his side. He moves slower than before, away and then turning in my direction, methodically and rhythmically moving away and then back, his giant body turning as if offering himself to me, all the while a giant eye focused on mine. I can almost taste his meaty flesh sizzling on the bar-b-que.

Regardless of the reciprocity I feel for the creature struggling below my bare feet and the way his magnificent eye beseeches mine for explanation, I am ready. This is the moment I have fought for and longed for, the gaff with its pointed shaft ready to slide into the fish's solid flesh. He slips directly over the point and that is the moment when I take my knife and cut him free.

With the fish darting into the dark faster than my eye can follow I collapse onto the deck and think of what I have done.

It is over.

6:11pm

Off to my right the yellow sun hides deep within the western sky. Catalina sleeps now and I see it drip rich and yellow and orange with mountains so purple the clouds shimmer above like a silver crown. To the east San Clemente explodes like fireworks in the sky, the sunset coloring it red and yellow and gold, like a painter's pallet spilling its contents. Through the fight with the tuna the sea has become a golden mirror so I take what the moment allows and set myself down on the swim step and dangle my feet in the clean water below. It is as though I were sitting on the edge of a swimming pool.

All is steady and calm and I remain like a placid monk watching the remnants of the day fade into the thickening night. I think of the many marlin earlier in the day, an entire school of them slashing through the torrid water. I think of swooping gulls. I think of the water alive, of panic, of rods and reels and Chinese alarms. And I think of me, the man on fire. I think of the yellowtail and the yellowtails flight for freedom. I think of the plank boat and our eye-level conversation miles at sea, of John and Briscoe and a pig-tailed girl called Amy. And I think of the circus act of a million porpoise flying like geese through a pale evening sky. And I think of a tuna looking me in the eye.

And I think of Sophocles and how 'One must live till sundown to see how splendid the day has become'.

And splendid it has become. Splendid indeed. I contemplate my life and my numbered days and it occurs to me that no matter how long I live and no matter how long my body occupies this place on earth, it will never be better than it is at this very moment, this perfect peaceful moment, a Monday in the middle of the sea, sunset, tranquil, glorious, perfect, a tiny fabric of this thing called nature, a miniscule member of the planet earth, a lowly particle of what we can never see and will never know. I sit cradled in the lap of the one I love and feel lucky to be alive. It will never be better than this. Nothing can ever be better than this. This moment. My moment in time.

CHOKING ON SUCCESS

My name is Zero. I am seventy-three years old. I have lived a long life, including most of the previous century and a good chunk of the next. During my seventy-plus years, I have come to certain conclusions about the future of my three children, One, Two and Three. I fear that our world is becoming so fragmented by the inclusionary passions of good intentions that we cannot possibly survive as a people.

Personally, I am okay with the decay I see surrounding me. All one has to do is look at the colossal forces set in motion by the human lava flow that goes ripping through every crevice of our planet to see that this can't go on forever. How long? How long before this erupting volcano sweeps our precious civilization to its righteous and deserved end?

As I sit in my office writing these words, the numbers are climbing into the billions, all those so-called reverent causes legitimizing our superior position in the world, the division among races, culture, beliefs. A tidal wave of humanity is what we have become, a populated crest racing toward the shore, a mountainous whitecap gaining such speed that nothing can survive its plunge onto earth, every fiber and mortal thread vanishing like light into dark, heaven into hell.

For me, an ordinary human creature alive and struggling to make sense of what his fellow human-beings are doing to each other, life has become too hideous to make any attempt to preserve it, let alone try and save it. Screw it, I say to myself as I ponder the actions of my idiot counterparts. Perhaps when our unrecorded history has erased all memory of our existence another life form will come along and undo the damage we have done to the earth and all its living matter, the same matter we plunder and take as our righteous possession. Until that day comes I will do nothing but sit in my office and spin in my chair for time is of no consequence anymore, not at this point in my fading existence it doesn't, for the ignorant have the upper hand in the world, you see, not us. They know only to survive. We know only to think.

Last week my middle son, Two, pulled a message from a fortune cookie and sent it to me. Regretfully, Two is one of those individuals who spends too much thinking rather than reacting, as was the habit of those who linked our family chain a million years ago. Like me, his father, Two has yet to learn what a dangerous undercurrent serious thinking can be; thinking in the abstract that is, something he does far too often, especially when serious thinking is misapplied, as it usually is by members of our considered superior species. Misapplied thinking can only lead to despair, for absurdity is the logical conclusion when indulged to the degree that my son tends to do. Serious contemplation should be left to people like me, not the pure of heart, like Two.

Not to engage in the pursuit of ideas is to live like ants instead of like men. That was the message hidden inside the fortune cookie. Alas Two, what are we to draw from this sentiment you sent to your aged father? That ants do not think? That ants have no ideas? Only men? Are we to assume conclusively from your thought-sent missive that man is the only animal which can summon in the abstract, the only creature which can build within a landscaped of ideas a fast and hard reality, that ants build for necessity where man builds for amusement?

Ah yes, the truth of the matter is this: pleasure is the engine that drives all human action, the raw, crisp pursuit of satiating the higher senses of man, pleasure, amusement, adventure, comfort. And I say this assuming man's higher senses are in the abstract and not in the real, for when we are void of pleasure, as only man can be, he will seek what pleasure is at hand, even if that means taking pleasure from those in possession of it.

Land is what comes to mind in this monstrous world we live in, the possession of land, the struggle for it, the limbic need for it, the warrior intent to control all space within our limited venue, that territory we rightfully define as ours, given us, granted us, ordained us by a superior sky-god. Land. Yes, the pursuit of precious land.

And with land comes culture. And with culture comes race. And with race comes civilization, followed by the foolish notion that sacred covenants are meant to govern our habits and ideas and thoughts. And when land is taken, as is the habit of civilized man, all is lost, including the right to be free. History bares me out in this.

As my second son aptly points out, ants are incapable of thinking in the abstract. Ants are digits, not a whole. They are component parts of a living organism. They think as fingers think, they reflex to the command of a higher authority, the mind, or as with the case of all social insects, including the ant, the colony from which it is a part. And yet the colony has survived earth's cataclysms for hundreds of millions of years whereas man has survived but a paltry million or two. Which brings to mind whether the pursuit of ideas are, indeed, a noble cause? Or can the earth spin merrily onward without our will to guide it in its path?

Objectively, and without sentiment, the earth was a better place before we thinking animals took possession of it, certainly before civilization took root and man selfishly burrowed his way into the earth's noble crust. We humans think, and because we think we recognize our thinking as a purposeful craft. And yet our craft has smothered the planet with success, cruelty being our specialty. Should we disappear tomorrow not one living organism would miss us: body louse and bacterium being the only exceptions that come to mind.

And yet the earth depends upon the poor miserable, non-thinking ant beneath our feet. Without the ant to cultivate our soil the entire landscape would slowly harden into a barren concrete skull and all living matter, including the ultimate of all living matter, that being humankind, of course, would slowly wither away leaving nothing it its wake but dust.

Any day now I expect the earth to be blown to smithereens. Certainly, smithereens are where we are headed if we keep thinking the way we do, patriotism and religion heading the list of causes to die for. And kill for. Rarely do I walk into the catacombs of modern shopping mall that I do not think of a suitcase bomb quietly nesting beside a luxury department store, or near the marble front of a sexy lady's apparel boutique, or along one of the many jewel encrusted shops lining the royal main court. And rarely do I walk inside the same mall that I do not marvel at the comparison to a perceived colony of ants, the same robotic rituals being played out, the same rhythmic motions, the same purposeful activities for the same instinctive reasons. Thinking can do that to a man, plant a suitcase bomb and blow the place to smithereens. And thinking can allow us to imagine our own triviality, as is the case with me.

And yet civilization is man's greatest idea, his willingness to abide by a set of rules to prevent his natural murderous intent, which, of course, is his civilized want. Thinking alone has done this to him, advancing his lowly-status to a point where man places himself above his non-civilized counterparts, elevating him to where mass extinction is not only possible, but inevitable. I shudder to think of the bright pink cloud that will one day rise outside my office window melting the flesh from my skull while the atomic boom quiets all that lives. Ideas will one day strip the bloom from the rose, not the boom that follows. Yes, the earth will go quiet one day and I can't help but marvel at the prospect.

It is not Two alone who thinks more than he should. Sadly, my first son, One, suffers this proclivity too. Lately he has become so enraptured with his work that he no longer suffers the hallucinatory effects that too much thinking can cause. Work is the great distillery of ideas, you see, filtering them to the bottom of the lake the way sediment settles in a pond. Several thousand years ago Egypt elevated work as the measure of civilized man. And we humans stupidly followed its command, all of us, each and every civilized soul marching to the beat of a ritual so prescribed and so axiomatic that we no longer give thought to our place in the world. Instead we march to the beat like blinded soldiers advancing to the front, bayonets in place, blood in our eye. Unremitting.

It was several years ago while my number one son and I were hunkering over a glittering rail at the same supermall I mentioned above that he happened to mention the possibility of space travel. As our eyes followed the many shoppers busy mining gold from the jewel festooned shops just below our feet, women mostly, my wife and his among the pack of thieves, and with nothing better to occupy our time or fill our vapid minds, we began to shoot ideas back and forth, me noting how most galaxies are so very distant from our own, billions of light years as it turns out, that time alone would prevent anyone from making contact with us, should they try to do so. Naturally this caused my oldest son to laugh at my ignorance. "You forget space-time dilation," he said, "voyagers do not age when traveling at the speed of light." And, of course, he was right, erudite as always.

And speaking of wives, it is said that women have a civilizing effect on men; that were it not for a women's superior influence over her inferior companion, men would strip the world of all its living matter, including each other, I presume. I prefer to think of it as something else and not the civilizing effect women have on men that have tamed her companion into leaving his perch for a place in the nest. I prefer to think of it as something more deadly and insidious than the taming of a frog or teaching a dog a new trick, something more invasive, like a virus invading a cell. I think of it as something silent and deadly, the kind of thing that slips into your flesh when you least expect it. I think of it as stupidity and not the effect women have on men that have lobotomized her earthly counterpart into his present-day stupor. If not stupidity then let us call it as it is: man's submissive dependence on woman's occasional favors, man's unremitting passion for reproduction that burdens his existence and saps his strength and dulls his resistance to the point of submission. Woman has done this with their insidious cleverness. They have coaxed and coddled man into complete submissiveness, surrender man of his limbic ways. She has seductively created a tamer, a controllable domesticated partner, his manliness thrown into the wind, his sense of responsibility a thing of the past, his tomahawk slung to the heavens. In this modern world where man has pledged his entire existence to a single source of favor and finds himself deservedly, or otherwise, out of favor, then it is safe to say that he has thrown in the towel. He has become one of them.

One has only to visit any Sunday service or watch any sitcom on TV to become reassured that my thinking is correct on this. Civilization rests on a platform of mass conformity and conformity is little more than sanity run amuck. In this regard man finds himself sanely riding in the trunk of the car.

To my wicked mind, civilized thinking is little more than the art of assembling a broken lawnmower or removing a damaged spleen from a car-wreck patient. Civilization is voting, and caring, and utensils resting aside a fancy plate. Ask the man next door the year Elvis slipped into his here-after and he'll jump from his chair with his hand waving in the air. Ask the same man to name the nearest star and he'll stare blankly into space, having no understanding that the nearest star is our very own sun. Civilized man has no concept of his place in the world, nor does he contemplate a reason for his existence, nor the meaning of his existence, presupposing there is a meaning to his existence, not to mention that stars are, indeed, suns.

Today's man sees no stars, only the piddling few that shine through the hazy neon civilization he has ignorantly created for himself. Today's man witness's no human death, excepting his own of course, and that innocence of our final disposition predisposes him to the ignorance of his own death. Today's man kills nothing but that which occupies his plate or his land. And today's man knows nothing of what lies beneath his feet, having shoes to blind them from where they tread.

Stars may be suns, but people are ants. They follow the same pheromone trail that ants follow, a trail of simple axiomatic responses to social stimuli, survival in a social context, if you will. What truly separates man from his lowly counterpart is not thinking or ideas, but his sense of wonder, going beyond the real and into the abstract, into what can only be called the 'what if' and not the 'what is'. The DMV is crawling with 'what is', as does our nightly sitcoms on Fox TV.

Sadly, my third son, Three, the one who lives in the great north-west, may be the most afflicted child of the bunch. Like his two brothers, he too thinks more than is healthy for a man of his age, as I write this he is 44-years-old. Whenever I challenge Three with some well-reasoned argument, he'll fight back by saying how reasoned thought is no more than redundant conventional wisdom run amok, that today's science is little more than tomorrow's dogma. And he laughs out load as he goes about demolishing my primitive thinking, as well he should.

At a dinner party given by one of my old business partners the other night (my partner's way of showing off his newly remodeled multi-million-dollar beach-front home, the most impressive abode I have ever set foot in) our discussion climaxed when someone at the table brought up the topic of stem cell research and with it the hope-filled prospect of finding a cure for cancer. Naturally our reasoned intellect caused our heads to nod approvingly at such a notion as a cure for cancer, the thought of stem cells extending our lives beyond what nature intended was very intriguing to a table of 60-year-olds. And yet my sense of wonderment wanted to cry out, "Don't you know," the words sticking in my throat, "don't you know what we have done? Our species is doomed to extinction. Look at us. We are murdering the earth. Others obey. Why shouldn't we?" That is what I wanted to yell, but couldn't, for I am civilized man and civilized man atones for his limbic misdeeds by conforming to the standards of civilization.

And while I like to think of myself as being exempt from the civilizing effect of wine and friends and an ocean view, and of course my wife who has spent the better part of her life trying to civilize the orangutan she married more than 40 years ago, I am not exempt. Selfish we are and selfish we will be and selfish has served us well in our dot in time. We prosper. We conform. We have dinner parties with the sea crashing in, but reason will kill us in the end.

Stem cells are no different than every other idea man has ever curled atop his brain stem. Stem cells are just another step in the wrong direction my son, Three, would have thundered to the table of friends had he been there that night the ocean came crashing in. Like so many others, ideas will one day lead to our immutable destruction. So will kindness. So will crop rotation. So will foreign aid. So will our insane government policy of redistributing income from the rich to the poor thereby aggravating the growing genepool of unfit and ugly and deformed and maimed and diseased people who live among us. That, and every other well-intentioned deed civilized man has crudely ploughed into the earth's crust will one day kill us all. We large brained creatures must find a way to look beyond our well-intentioned kindness because, fail as we will, this crushing title wave of empathy currently sweeping across our shores will benignly and triumphantly trample us all into extinction.

I can't wait.

INSTRUCTIONS FOR WHEN I DIE

At my funeral, everyone is to be miserable. No faking. No teary-eyed smiles or maudlin handshakes then see people running off to the buffet. Here is what I expect when I am dead.

I expect everyone to be wailing and blubbering. That's right. I want people heaving their body onto my open casket. I want them fighting for space like college kids crowding into a packed VW. I want tear-soaked shoes and sobbing sessions that last for weeks. I want episodes of spontaneous weeping from people who know me only by name. Fainting will be permitted at my funeral, as well as catatonic lapses and periods of gravity defying tumbles to the ground. Should anyone be unable to, or unwilling to comply with this request, my oldest son has been instructed to remove them from the premises.

People today celebrate just about everything, even the poor stiff lying in the box in front of you. Sixth graders celebrate their passing grades by riding in a limousine. Proms are staged on aircraft carriers. High school graduation necessitates a passport to Paris. Wedding budgets exceed the GDP of most countries. And a funeral, well, a funeral should include a Broadway production starring the Radio City Dancers performing eye-high leg kicks atop wedding cake.

Over my dead body will this happen at my funeral. Here are a few handy instructions I give to my loved ones about what I expect the day I say adios to the world.

Music: None. Nada. No Neil Diamond. No Cat Stevens. Elton John can beg if he wants, but no "Candle in the wind." No Elvis impersonators. No organ music. And nothing remotely akin a church hymn. God help me! Anyone caught even humming a few lines of "Ave' Maria" will be cut from my will. (And this extends to graveside visits as well.)

Food: No food. No snack or beverages of any kind. Gum chewing is also forbidden. As for diabetics and the elderly, don't come.

Pharmacology*:* None. Check all your meds at the door. My will instructs my eldest son to monitor people's pockets. Should you be on Prozac, Xanax, whatever, stop a week ahead. I want everyone in the crowd free of mood-stabilizers ready to howl their heart-felt lamentations to the heavens. You want to snort Comet when you go home, be my guest.

Floral. This should be obvious. No Plants. Nothing green. Nothing living except the weeping attendees. All windows should be drawn to reveal nothing living outside.

Dress: Black only. Including underwear. Except men. White shirt under a black jacket permitted. Otherwise the place will resemble something out of a God Father movie. Stripes and patterns, even in shades of black are forbidden.

Location: Obviously indoors. Preferable an obscure location, possibly a log cabin or in the home of a Shaker. Sterile with no adornments. Unless the adornment is a single photograph of the deceased. A cramped hall or an auditorium would do nicely, one with a low ceiling and buzzing fluorescent lights.

Eulogy: Short and bleak with no reference to God. Anyone mentioning God will be shot. Here are some other no-no's when speaking about the deceased.

Words to avoid: "passed away" "gone" "pine condo" "shipped out" "dearly departed" "dead Ed" "Dead as a doornail" "Stone dead". Any attempt to be flippant or comedic or casual is expressly forbidden. Euphemisms are okay so long as they are maudlin and spoken in Latin.

Subjects to be avoided: Poignant jokes and wisecracks while faking a tenderhearted sob. References to special moments and remembrances are out as well. So are amusing stories of my so-called idiosyncrasies, those are out, things like my proclivities to exaggerate, or embellish, or brag, or cheat, even when told with humor, even if they are true, they are out. I will tolerate laughter by the insane. That is okay. Going insane over my passing, even temporarily insane, is encouraged.

Narcissism: Don't fake it. I'll know. Like how sad you are at my passing when it's me that's dead and not you. Admit it, you're happy. Just don't show it or you're out.

How I died: No mention of how I died. I'm dead, so be it. Undoubtedly slow and painful. Mentioning how I died could translate to late-life cowardice. Unless, in the unlikely event my dying was in some way heroic, then it is not only permissible, but to be rewarded.

Burial: So far, all talk and no action. Nothing will bring the misery I intend like having attendees dig my grave. Everyone in attendance will be handed a shovel with instructions to dig a hole-six-feet deep, no, make that ten feet deep with plenty of room for my body. No casket, just my loved ones dropping me in and filling the hole with dirt. Anyone found not pulling his or her weight will be asked to leave and, if appropriate, be summarily disinherited. Hey, who put me there in the first place?

Printed in the United States
By Bookmasters